Praise for
eMortal

"Schafer writes brilliantly clean prose with natural dialogue, gifting the central protagonists—and the strangely appealing Breck—deep emotion and depth. The characters are sharply defined and likable, each undergoing meaningful transformations during the novel. Liv is a strong central lead, able to drive the plot forward, but Breck also becomes a surprising development as the book progresses, more complex than any of the main characters originally thought possible. The worldbuilding is organic and flows smoothly, but what sets this novel apart is the shocking ending—and the humanity gifted to the story's sentient AI lead. Score: 10/10."

—BookLife Prize review by *Publishers Weekly*

"The characters are so well developed... A well-constructed coming-of-age novel that stands out in a crowded field of AI-focused literature."

—*Kirkus Reviews*

"A gripping YA sci-fi akin to *Ready Player One* and *The Lunar Chronicles*. Liv must save her sentient AI from digital oblivion, leading to a thrilling exploration of consciousness and identity."

—NewInBooks

"*eMortal* is a clever, fun-filled novel full of twists, turns, and heartfelt moments between friends. It's unputdownable."
—Kim Turrisi, Emmy-winning writer and YA author of *Just a Normal Tuesday* and *Carmilla*

"With nuanced contemplations on existence and a compelling, compulsively readable narrative structure, *eMortal* is simply stunning. Liv and Breck will stay with me for a long time."
—Jared Reck, author of *A Short History of the Girl Next Door* and *Donuts and Other Proclamations of Love*

"*eMortal* is a mind-bending exploration of AI and humanity that will leave you questioning the very nature of reality. Steve Schafer has crafted a thrilling, thought-provoking tale that hooks you from the first page and refuses to let go. An absolute must-read."
—Joshua Fagan, author of *Misdial*

"Relevant, unexpected, thoughtful, and engaging. *eMortal* is a timely, technological take on the age-old, deeply profound question: What is real?"
—William B. Miller, author of *The Gospel According to Sam*, *The Beer Drinker's Guide to God*, and *The Last Howlelujah*

"If ever there was a book that made me question whether life imitated art or if art imitated life, *eMortal* would be the one. With a prescience not found in most coming-of-age stories, it forced me to question the ideas of existence, sentience, and reality, all while captivating me with Liv's genuinely relatable struggles. Much like how George Orwell's *1984* brought Big Brother to life, *eMortal* will no doubt play a similar role for the next generation of young readers while they navigate their own future amid AI and the numerous ethical implications surrounding it. 'Am I simply a collection of data that I'm unable to see because I exist within it?' I'd sure like to know that too."

—Shaila Patel, author of *Soulmated*

"Steve Schafer has penned a story worthy of biological beings and sentient AI alike. Make room in your cerebellum or internal hard drive for this AI hot-topic presentation on new ways to look at our own existence. You'll be thinking about this book long after you finish reading it."

—Mark L. Berry, author of
13,760 Feet: My Personal Hole in the Sky

"In a world where creation blurs the lines of reality, the essence of existence is confronted. With time running out and forces unseen closing in, *eMortal* showcases a thrilling exploration of consciousness, identity, and the meaning of 'real.' Schafer takes readers on an electrifying journey."

—Emily H. Keefer, author of *The Stars on Vita Felice Court*

"I enjoyed every moment of this thrilling, thought-provoking page-turner that kept me pondering long after the final chapter. With his relatable and unique approach, Schafer introduces young adults to existential thinking, sparking deep reflections on life, identity, and purpose. An absolute must-read!"

—Natacha Belair, award-winning author of
A Stellar Purpose trilogy

"*eMortal* captivates with its heartfelt narrative and complex character development in a gripping exploration of technology and humanity. Schafer takes readers on an exhilarating journey through the realm of AI, revealing the depths we'll go to protect those we cherish. This compelling story challenges our perceptions of life, prompting us to question what it truly means to be alive. This must-read will keep you on the edge of your seat—prepare for unexpected twists and turns!"

—Todd Hugie, author of *House Down Dirt Lane*

"*eMortal* is a compelling journey into the essence of consciousness and the moving intersections of human and artificial life. This thrilling book challenges us to consider what truly matters in our lives as we witness Liv's transformative path from creation to crisis. An essential read for anyone captivated by the challenges and opportunities of navigating our ever-evolving world."

—Ana Parra Vivas, multi-award-winning author of *I Trust My Inner Voice*

"*eMortal* is an engrossing young-adult novel about AI, the ethics surrounding it, and how it could change the world for the better or worse."

—Gerardo Delgadillo, author of *Summerlypse*, *Fractalistic*, *Bacon Pie*, and *Avocado Bliss*

"*eMortal* is the epitome of perfection in the fiction genre. The book's remarkable storytelling, unique plot, and well-crafted characters make it a captivating read. Schafer's ability to intertwine suspense and science fiction with emotional depth ensures that this book is an engaging novel that will leave readers eagerly anticipating what comes next."

—Literary Titan

eMortal
by Steve Schafer

© Copyright 2024 Steve Schafer

ISBN 979-8-88824-578-1

All rights reserved. No part of this publication may be reproduced, stored in a retrieval system, or transmitted in any form or by any means—electronic, mechanical, photocopy, recording, or any other—except for brief quotations in printed reviews, without the prior written permission of the author.

This is a work of fiction. All the characters in this book are fictitious, and any resemblance to actual persons, living or dead, is purely coincidental. The names, incidents, dialogue, and opinions expressed are products of the author's imagination and are not to be construed as real.

Published by

3705 Shore Drive
Virginia Beach, VA 23455
800-435-4811
www.koehlerbooks.com

eMortal

STEVE SCHAFER

VIRGINIA BEACH
CAPE CHARLES

For Vicky

An amazing mom

BRECK: SIMULATION #34

This room will explode in eight minutes. The clock on the wall reads 9:52 p.m. At 10 p.m., time is up.

The door is still locked.

The knob still won't turn.

Seven minutes.

The keys are still missing.

Six minutes.

The window still won't open.

Five minutes.

The glass on the window still won't break.

Four minutes.

There is only one other person in this room. He is also trying to escape. He has also checked everything many times today.

What else is there to do?

Two minutes.

The door is still locked.

The keys are still missing.

One minute.

All is still. The space is silent. The clock ticks down.

Three . . . two . . . one.

OLIVIA (LIV): SPRING BREAK 1.0

I bite off the corner of a cold grilled-cheese sandwich as I watch the explosion. *What am I missing?*

"I've tweaked every bit of your code, and yet—" I wag a finger at Breck, who is technically no longer there, having just been eviscerated.

I reach for the sandwich once more but pause as my fingertips bump against the firm crust. *Was this from yesterday?*

I grab my phone instead.

"Boom?" Lana asks.

"How did you guess?" I ask.

"It's just past ten. And I watched it."

I turn to peer out my second-floor window and there she is, across the twenty feet of my driveway, in her own room, waving. She might as well be holding a tub of popcorn.

Lana is my neighbor, best friend, and coding consultant. Actually, calling her my best friend involves some fuzzy math. She is my *only* friend, well below the ideal threshold for most, but not me. One is the perfect number of friends. Everything in one place. It's efficient and awesome, like frozen orange juice in a can—friend concentrate.

"Any progress?" she asks.

"Nope, but I still have—" I sneak a glance at a wall calendar with dates I've Sharpied over with my own numbers. "Six days left."

"I think he's getting better." A bedroom lamp silhouettes stray locks of Lana's hyper-curly hair.

I wish she were right, but fact is fact. He's not getting better. "Your feelings are noted and appreciated."

"Want to take a walk and talk about it?"

"Who are you and what have you done with my best friend?" I ask, rolling my desk chair toward her and propping my feet on the empty windowsill.

"We can't stay inside all spring break."

"It's only Saturday. We've barely tried," I say.

As if on cue, several drops of heavy Houston rain ricochet in plump streaks across the window. My grin widens.

"Talk about timing. Whose world are you controlling, dork?" She mutters, her frown as pronounced as my grin.

This isn't an insult. It's a bond. We are both self-proclaimed giant dorks. To get more technical, I'm more of a geek. I code like the wind. I challenge you to find a statement that invites less social interaction than that one.

And Lana is more of a nerd. She's literary, annoyingly knowledgeable, and socially awkward in her enthusiasm to share her perspective about anything—especially if that anything is written.

It would be more accurate to say that we are dorkily proud of our geeky and nerdy interests. But that's a mouthful. Dork suits us fine.

Together, we are outcasts, asteroids who tumble throughout the social cosmos, inviting fear from anyone nearby that we might enter their gravitational orbit and make an uncomfortable impact.

I tidy one of the brown curtain wings, which is close to falling loose. "Now, can we skip to the part where we try to fix this?"

Halfway through my question, Lana's father appears in the doorway behind her in his usual crisp khakis and buttoned shirt.

"Hi Doctor O," I say, waving through the window in my sweatpants and the stained T-shirt I've been wearing for far too long.

Lana thrusts her phone in his direction, as though he's officially invited to respond on our speakerphone conversation.

Doctor Owens waves back. "Hey, Liv. I'm just bringing a book back to Lana. What are you two fixing?"

Lana continues her role as mediator, glancing back at me to respond.

"A programming contest thing," I answer.

"Okay. I'll bite. To do what?" He moves closer to the window. "And by the way, I can't believe I'm actually talking across houses like you two do. You're nuts. You know, we have doors."

"And windows," Lana chirps.

He shakes his head. "Your contest?" He turns back to me.

"The official goal is to code an entity capable of developing broad autonomy across a range of semi-cognitive functions," I say, editing out the most technical words as best I can.

Lana pipes, "English, dude."

"No, I think I got it," Doctor O interrupts. "You're trying to code a character that can think and learn for itself."

I smirk and Lana rolls her eyes. Doctor O is a psychology professor at Rice, so I figured he'd get it.

"It's this big annual competition held by the government—the DoRC," Lana adds.

"Dork?"

Lana gestures in my direction.

"Department of Recreational Computation."

He laughs with the same tiny snort of surprise that runs strong in his family's DNA. "That's funny," he adds.

"Yup. It's supposed to be ironic," Lana takes over, as is her custom. "Think of the contest like a video game with no controller. DoRC programmed the world, they set up challenges that get harder as you go, and the character has to figure it out, solo." Lana adds, "Liv's grand creation, XNR908, better known as Breck, is stuck on the first challenge. He can't find his way out of a box. Literally." She looks in my direction, "Sorry, Liv. You're welcome to take over."

"Technically, it's a room—not a box. And yes, he's stuck."

Lana continues. "So, this room explodes every night at ten, and then resets the next morning, unless Breck finds his way out. He's been there for thirty-four days now, and the contest ends in less than a week."

"Well, actually," I interrupt, "Breck and another character named Sam, a mandatory control variable."

Lana turns to her dad, who's quick to speak. "Standard character, no special coding?"

"You got it," I answer.

"Anyway," Lana adds, "Sam is supposed to contrast Breck, but right now, they both do the same stupid shi . . . stuff all day."

"Has anyone's character made it out of the room?"

"We don't know." Lana raises her arms high for emphasis. "All characters are in their own separate version of this world, so we can't see what they're doing or how they're doing."

"And the winner gets?"

"The coveted DoRC summer internship in DC with Jessica Anders," Lana chimes.

"Sounds cool. So, why aren't you doing it?" He asks his daughter.

"Dad, coding is Liv's thing. She literally has trophies for it."

"Trophy," I correct, glancing behind me at a small golden figure with hands frozen in typing pose. I won it years ago at a computer camp with Lana. The lonely figure rests along a narrow wooden shelf, an arms-length long, designed to accommodate other trophies, because this is what a disappointed mother buys when she won't acknowledge that coding achievements are not trophied in the same turnstile manner as little league soccer.

It's an ironic display, which Lana is now trying to celebrate unironically—I think. Lana constantly corrects me on how I use *irony*.

Lana's dad takes a moment to absorb this. Lana loses patience and continues. "Besides, I've got too many books to read."

Doctor O raises the thick blue paperback in his hand, signaling a change in subject. "Speaking of, here's the third book," he says, softly tossing the novel onto her bed.

"Finally!" Lana says.

"You're still on the second book. I can see your bookmark."

"I'm pacing myself."

"Whatever," he smirks with a faux teen accent. "But you're not going to believe it when—"

"No spoilers!" Lana slams her palms flush to her ears and chants, "*La la la*, I'm not listening. *La la la*."

Doctor O smiles and wishes me luck, then closes the door on his way out.

Lana approaches the window, now fully streaked with rain.

"Is Hot Toddy there?" she asks. "I could come over if he is." Todd is my mom's boyfriend of four years, a mechanic whose wardrobe consists of mostly jeans, medium V-neck T-shirts, and biceps. My mom isn't the only one who finds him attractive.

"He's here. In fact, I can hear my mom yelling at him right now." I answer, then hold the phone out, inviting the distant sounds of my house to enter Lana's.

I'm not sure if she can actually hear it, but regardless, she returns an expression of both sympathy and her desire to stay put. I pull the phone back to my body. She waits for more, but I don't have anything else to say. It's just another night I'm grateful to be immersed in code.

After a long pause with a stare that I think is supposed to make me fess up some feelings about the Hot Toddy situation, Lana softens. "So, what changes did you make today?"

Finally.

For the thirty-fourth night in a row, I share my screen online and we open the hood to tinker. I explain exactly what I did, and Lana asks for my reasoning, peppering me with questions:

"Is that modulated in biphase?"

"What's your bool rate?"

"Why not receive in one string and translate to the other by looking at the change in transitions rather than the received bitcode?"

Several hours and multiple tweaks later, our brains are squeezed dry of fresh ideas. Curtains close, and once again, it's a waiting game to see what tomorrow will bring.

◆ ⁂ ◆

I'm in my recurring dream—me, in Breck's world. I'm lying on the couch in his room, watching him watch me. Submerged in his world, the pixilated distance between us evaporates.

From this view within, the room feels far more expansive. The round dining table anchoring the center of the room, the slender kitchen galley with cabinets that meet the ceiling, the half-open paneled door to the tiny bathroom, the orange morning glow from the lone window above my head. All tempt exploration in my periphery, as though each could be examined in as much detail as I were willing to give it.

But my focus remains fixed on Breck. Each strand of his cedar-brown hair twists in its own direction, his gently arched nose is no longer a perfect curve but contoured and lightly spotted with the imperfections of textured skin, and he seems taller and leaner than the athletic Disney prince build he has on my screen. We stare into each other, as if each of us is searching for something more. He opens his mouth, primed to ask me the deepest of life's questions. I ready myself. Then he turns and tries to open the window for the umpteenth time.

"Stop!" I hold my stare, pushing my will toward him beyond my words alone. "Think."

He doesn't hear me—or doesn't acknowledge me. Breck and Sam motor through the room like ants, tapping objects with their arms like giant antennae, bumbling around for information.

Then Sam opens one of the cabinets. *The* cabinet.

My body tenses.

A light by the door illuminates. Breck turns to look at it, but where I'm hoping to see a twinkle of curiosity, there is none. Sam closes the cabinet. The light goes off and both move on. Like always.

"Try to connect some of this," I beg.

They continue as if I were on mute.

"Fine. Don't listen."

Behind the unguarded curtain of sleep, something within me snaps in a way that seldom happens when awake. In my dreamworld, I vault from couch to feet with a deftness I don't have outside of this realm.

"Why the hell am I the one lying down here? You might as well be. Here. Take a nap." I swing my arms toward the couch. "It wouldn't matter. You could sleep all day and you'd still be in this stupid room!"

Breck stops mid-step and he turns to face me.

We lock stares.

"I do not know how to sleep," he says.

I'm suddenly awake inside of a dream. It's exhilarating. Epiphany surges through me.

Breck doesn't sleep.

Breck doesn't dream.

I am trying to create someone who thinks like a human but hasn't experienced a huge chunk of what it is to be human. Homo sapiens spend a third of our time in sleep. Resting. Reflecting. Drifting among nonsensical thoughts. Being creative.

I once read that Keith Richards woke one morning to find an acapella chorus of "Satisfaction" on a tape recorder next to his bed. He had created and recorded it while in this miraculous other dimension that Breck does not know.

How could I be so foolish to overlook this? We even studied sleep in biology class this semester. It's what restores us, clears toxins, files away memories, allows neurons to communicate. It's a daily reboot that allows us to clean, organize, and process. If we didn't sleep, we'd be walking and talking Brecks.

He needs to sleep.

Breck breaks his gaze and diverts his eyes to the wall, with a gentle toss of his head, suggesting that I too should look that way.

I turn. It might as well be 10 p.m. in this room because I nearly explode on the inside.

Behind me is a digital wall filled with code. Gorgeous clusters of brackets, dots, parenthesis, underscores, commas, backslashes, functions, commands, sprawl from corner to corner.

"I want to sleep," Breck says.

I stretch a hesitant hand to the wall. The text beneath my fingers moves. It's a touchscreen. I begin sliding pieces of code, slowly at first, exploring, until chaos starts to resemble order. My momentum builds to a nearly possessed pace, splitting, joining, carving flow and order among the disparate elements. It's as if I'm staring at pieces of a puzzle to which I intuitively know the solution. Until at last, I slip the last bit in place.

Breck's eyes close.

Mine spring open. It's 3:45 a.m.

I leap from pillow to computer so violently I nearly jam my thumb. First graders pretending to type do not slap at the keyboard with this intensity.

I close my eyes and I can still see it, as if I had stared at the sunrise and burned the divine image through my retina.

Hours whip by like minutes. Somewhere in between, the sun rises, and a new day begins.

FROM: JESSICA ANDERS
TO: DoRC LEADERSHIP TEAM
SUBJECT: Interesting Programming Adjustment (XNR908)

    I'm writing to inform you of a new development in the competition. A programming adjustment was made to character XNR908 that incorporates sleep. This is a novel approach that has not yet been used in any other characters that I'm aware of. I'm flagging this as something to keep an eye on. Early signs suggest this could have a significant impact on development, but this is still speculative. I will continue to provide updates as necessary.

~ J

BRECK: SIMULATION #35

Moments ago, the clock struck 10 p.m.
There was light.
There was heat.

Then here. Back in the same room as before. The clock is again back at 8 a.m.

The other person in the room is seated nearby. It is the same person as yesterday.

"Is it time to start?" This person asks for the thirty-fifth time.

"Yes."

First, a survey of the room. There is nothing different. The twelve cabinets of the kitchen area are all closed. So is the refrigerator, which is next to the cabinets. All food on the counter has been replaced from what was eaten yesterday.

The bathroom door is slightly open and light from inside is visible. The other person enters and closes this door, the same as always.

There are four chairs at the only table.

A long brown couch rests against one of the walls, below the only window. The sun rises outside.

Further scans show that nothing has changed. *One day, something will change. Progress toward the goal will happen.*

A new exploration begins—flipping switches, moving furniture, examining walls. Then it is time for breakfast. Energy levels are low.

"Oatmeal?" the other person asks.

"Yes."

He boils the water and opens the cabinet to retrieve the oatmeal. A light turns on by the main door in the room.

This has happened before. There is something different about it now.

"Has the door been checked today?"

"No."

LIV: SPRING BREAK 2.0

I watch Sam on my computer screen open *the* cabinet. The light turns on. Breck looks toward the door. It's nearly a replay of what I saw it in my dream.

Anxious fingers dig into my palms. *This is it. This is the breakthrough.*

Breck walks a quiet handful of steps to the door.

My pulse feels audible.

Sam places his palm flush against the cabinet.

Breck pauses, staring inquisitively at the illuminated door. I watch him as though I can see through him, as the puzzle pieces slowly rotate into connection.

Do it!

Breck then reaches for the knob, just as Sam returns the oatmeal to the shelf and sweeps his hand across the handle of the cabinet.

The cabinet shuts fractions of a second before Breck twists the now unilluminated knob.

"It is still locked," Breck says.

I could scream.

My eyes fall on the Jessica Anders picture on the wall between my desk and bed. Lana gave it to me last year, both as a gift and as a suggestion to decorate. Jessica is the closest thing I have to an idol, though I'm far from her only fan. Besides heading DoRC, she's a programming legend. You'd be hard pressed to find anyone more admired. Below the portrait is a quote:

"Success is a destination. Failure is the only path to get there."

I've failed for thirty-five days in a row. I'm not the most emotional critter in the house, or maybe even the neighborhood. But that much consistent sucking can take its toll. I linger on Jessica's words, giving them a chance to settle in.

Eventually they do. And my growling stomach forces me to take a helpful break from the screen.

As I step out of my room into the clutter of the hallway, I'm greeted by a charred whiff of something burning.

"Again?!" My mom yells downstairs.

I consider returning, but my stomach grumbles once more. I start down the upstairs hallway, dark and Tetrised with boxes, bags, and assorted things that don't fit well into either boxes or bags. I step around an ironing board and over a humidifier where my bare foot finds the end of its plug, digging one prong into my arch. I silently curse.

If you want to see the difference between me and my mom, a great place to start would be to step from my bedroom into this hallway—clean and lean versus this. The entire house isn't this packrat-like, but it leans in that general direction. Mom loves the past.

Not me. I'm focused on the future; I'm a minimalist.

"I forgot. I'm sorry." Todd apologizes in the distance.

"There's a dial for it. You don't put it on ten. How hard is that?"

"The dial doesn't work. There are two settings. Too light and too dark."

"So, put it on too light twice," my mom barks.

I hide in the hallway as Mom and her boyfriend continue to argue.

"It's two pieces of bread and they're burned. And it's *my* breakfast," Todd says.

"The house smells like the curtains are on fire."

"I didn't realize the curtains are whole grain," Todd lobs back.

Silence.

I pause. Todd's witty zingers don't usually end this cleanly.

Donk! Pause. *Donk!*

I can't see it, but I'm pretty sure that's the sound of two blackened pieces of toast crashing into the kitchen sink.

The door slams and the silence returns.

"Hey Liv." Todd's voice is casual and inviting as I enter the kitchen, as though no toast is in the sink, nor any discussion of it only seconds prior. "How'd-ya-sleep?" he asks, like it were one long, connected word.

His bulky frame makes the mug in his hand look small. He's not overweight, but broad, everywhere—face, neck, chest, legs, arms—as though he were a photo dragged slightly outward, making him as solid as a tank and as thick as his drawl. Houston proper has little accent, but that changes quickly as you move outward. Todd is from outward.

"Good. You?"

He responds in kind. I grab a bagel from the refrigerator and drop it the toaster. A spattering of black crumbs surrounds the appliance. I sweep them up with my hand and toss them into the sink where they land among larger charred fragments.

I glance back at Todd and he's pointing a gentle finger to a Post-It Note on one of the cabinets. It's in my mother's handwriting.

I cautiously pull it free.

Liv, I need help at the store and you need to leave your room. Plan to start tomorrow.

Six months ago, Mom quit her job to take over my late grandfather's legacy—a toy store. Good for her, but this isn't *my* legacy. My legacy is Breck.

And he's so close! The way he studied the front door of the room; something seemed different. I need every minute of these next five days. That's all I want from this week—the time to prove I can do this. I can win.

"It's never just about toast, Liv," Todd says, drawing his hands away from his coffee and placing his complete attention on me.

Beyond his bedhead and tired eyes, I have a clear view into the living room, where an array of slept-in blankets stretch across the sofa. I don't understand why someone with their own apartment would come here to sleep on our couch. But that's not the question I'm focused on.

Breathe and think. Every problem has a root cause. Every root cause has a solution, and there are usually more than one. What is the core issue here?

"What does she want me to help with?" The toaster dings and I press the handle down once again—too light twice.

"Work?" His tone suggests he can't give me a better answer.

"Is it still reopening tomorrow?" The store has been closed for the last two weeks for a remodel.

"Yup. She's doing some final stuff today."

"Doesn't she already have people helping her?"

"She did."

"What happened to them?"

"You'd have to ask your mom."

"Can't she find other people?"

"Yup. You're it. She wants you," he says with a sympathetic shrug.

For a mom's boyfriend I got pretty lucky with Todd. Most of the time it feels like we're more compatible than they are. He's never tried to be my father, who I never knew anyway, and he's another pragmatic voice in the house, which helps to offset Mom. Sometimes I actually feel sorry for him as he's the one who takes the brunt of her.

"Is this about money?" I ask. "Because if it is, I can make a lot more money doing a few hours of programming work online every day. Maybe even fifty an hour."

"Hot damn. That's more than I make."

"I'm sorry, I didn't mean—"

He raises his hands dismissively. "Don't. This isn't about the cosmic injustice of mechanics and code jockeys." He pauses, waiting for my reaction.

"Grease monkeys and code jockeys."

"Exactly." He smiles, settling into the playful and familiar role of riding the fine line between being a voice of counsel and not throwing my mother under the bus. He plays it well.

I sit at the table, setting a glass of orange juice next to his coffee. The two vessels linger like chess pieces between us.

"It's not about the money, Liv." He reaches for his mug once more, spinning it in a pensive rotation, pondering his move. "Or at least not all about the money. Look, it's not my call. But if you're asking me, it's not an unreasonable request. Kids get jobs." He speaks more into the mug than toward me.

"Not during spring break. It's one week, and it's a *break*. Did she forget about the contest?"

He shakes his head as if I'm missing something obvious.

"Liv, the contest is *why* she wants you to do this."

"What?" I am lit. This is ridiculous. She has no idea how important this is.

"Not the contest exactly, but the effect it has on you. You're in your room all day. You don't do anything with other people."

"I do things with plenty of other people."

"In the real world, Liv. Not online."

"What about Lana?"

"With anyone not within sight of your window. Look, I could spend all day under the hood of a car. I could spend a month building an engine without noticing anything else around me. But that doesn't mean I should. We have that in common. It's a gift, but you can lean into it a little too hard." He runs his meaty fingers through his graying hair, further mussing his pillow-sculpted hairdo.

"I'm so close. This isn't some science fair contest. It can literally change my future."

"So do both. That's what you've done for the last few months, right? And it will give you two some time to spend together."

Despite my protests, we both know this outcome has already been determined.

I drop my head, defeated.

He stands. "I've got to take a shower and get to work." He gently bumps a husky fist on the top of my bowed head a few times. "Make the most of today, kid."

"Todd," I say, as he walks out of the kitchen.

"Yeah?" He turns.

"Why do you shower before you go to work, when you're just going to get dirty?"

He smiles. "Atta girl. Keep asking good questions and get Brick working."

"Breck." I correct.

"Brock, Bruck, Brack." He continues, his voice trailing off as he moves further away from the kitchen.

I grab my bagel, fold Mom's note into my pajama pockets, and walk my breakfast back into my bedroom, ready to follow Todd's advice and make the most of my last full day.

The monitor fires back up and I'm once more staring at Breck as he tackles his own day. I can only watch for so long before I'm back in the code and tinkering again.

I'm missing something. I scan the chat boards with other contest participants. Since their characters are all in their own virtual worlds tackling the challenges independently, this is the only glimpse I have into how they're doing. I suppose that's why it's set up this way—to eliminate influence. This group is far too protective to give away anything directly, but they also like to brag and sometimes they give away a little too much. It could give me some new ideas. Fifteen minutes of digging only reveals that another person's Breck, whom they aptly nicknamed Primer, has left the room in his virtual world, soaring onward to some kind of labyrinth of a city that follows. I know I'm among the great majority reading this with envy, but it still reminds me of my location on the path to success.

My phone buzzes.

Curtains, please, Lana texts.

I swing them open. The sunshine slams against me faster than my pupils were prepared for. Lana's hands are planted on her windowsill with her hoodied torso leaning outward, basking in the overhanging rays. She moves one hand upward, requesting I open my window as well.

I open but keep my body on the inside along with my squinting eyes.

"Happy birthday!" she yelps.

It is March 8, and not my birthday.

I shake my head. "I forgot. And you didn't, which isn't surprising. Thank you."

My actual birthday isn't until September. Today is my half-birthday, which only Lana celebrates. Lana's birthday is on Christmas. Years ago, she informed everyone she was moving her celebration to June. It worked. She also celebrates this for me out of fairness.

"What are you up to, other than toying with Breck's brain?"

"Enjoying my last free day of spring break. I was voluntold for a job."

A wave of soft wrinkles form across the freckles on her forehead as her brows jump. A tilt of her head accentuates everything—it's the cherry on top. She's the most expressive person I know. Her reactions could easily be read at twice the distance of our windows.

"No! You're slinging toys?"

"Something like that," I start, then I pick up the phone, hit *speaker* and call. Our windows are just far enough apart that it feels like we're yelling.

She answers nearly before it rings. "Continue," she whispers.

"Mom thinks I spend too much time in my room. She wants me to go touch grass. And I'm cheap labor. Want to be my coworker?"

"No, I will be staying here and winning for once." She answers so quickly it's as though she's finishing my sentence. We have a bet as to who can stay in their house for the longest during spring break, as in not taking one step outside. It started as a joke. I half-suspected the invite to walk last night was a trick. "How *is* the store?" she asks.

"The grand reopening is tomorrow. Believe me, you'll get a detailed report."

She surveys me for a moment, then pulls a curled and pensive index finger to her chin. "And how are you feeling about this?" She is her father's daughter.

"I'll be fine, Doctor O. I just wanted to spend more time this week on the contest."

Her eyes narrow and she draws in a contemplative breath. "It must feel . . . distressing."

My arms fold across my chest. As much as Lana wears her emotions on her sleeve, I do not. "The store is what it is. This conversation is now distressing. Want to hear about what I did with Breck?"

She grins with the satisfaction of someone who has pushed my buttons enough to get the reaction she wanted. "Fair enough. How's B?"

"I woke up in middle of the night and changed some code."

"Which is the least surprising thing I'll hear today." She gestures for me to continue.

I explain my revelation about sleep.

"Interesting. Very interesting." Her curled finger returns to her chin, though more authentically this time. "So, how is that any different from rebooting?"

"He's not shutting down. It's sleep, like we do. Neural repair, purging, reprocessing, dreams. All that stuff."

"You programmed that?"

"Yup."

"How?"

"Would it be *ironic* that it came to me in a dream?" I ask.

"Nope, not *ironic*. But it is oddly appropriate and freaking amazing." Her chin drops to her palm to punctuate her last word.

"It was. Anyway, if sleep is a third of our day, then we were missing a third of the equation," I add.

She nods in thought, still absorbing the idea. "I like it, Liv. I think you're onto something, young lady."

"Maybe. But he doesn't seem any different. He's doing the same things."

"Has he slept yet?"

"Fair point. No. I finished this morning."

"So, let's give it some time. No need to get *distressed* yet," she says, to which I roll my eyes. "What's your plan for the day?"

"Tinkering. Yours?"

"Reading. Glorious reading," she says, as she reaches behind her, placing her hand on top of two stacked paperbacks. "And on that note, I'm going to get back into it for a while, so you can close the curtains again. Let me know if Breck does something exciting, like take a nap. Let's do something later for your birthday. How's five? We'll leave the house and call it a tie."

"Sounds good."

BRECK: SIMULATION #35.1

There it is again. An idea. But it is only there for a moment, then it disappears.

The other person in the room with me looks in this direction. His eyes are the same shade of blue as the door that won't open. With his back against the door, they look like two holes through his head.

He then steps onto a chair and unscrews a light bulb next to the door. His fingers burn and he yanks his hand away. His fingers are red from previous burnings.

Again, the idea appears, then fades. It is not possible to hold onto this thought.

LIV: SPRING BREAK 2.1

My eyes are red. I don't need a mirror to know this. I can feel them. Finding the zone is my everyday superpower, and with today's race against my dwindling time, I set a new personal concentration record.

I've scanned all current and legacy chat boards I can find in search of any new nuggets.

I've read a half-dozen scholarly articles on programming algorithms related to AI.

I've combed every line of Breck's code, tweaking and retweaking.

And somewhere in there, I believe I ate a burrito. My mind was elsewhere.

I'm tapped.

I check my phone and discover that the battery is dead. When I plug it in, a flurry of texts arrive. Fourteen total, all from Lana, culminating with, *It's dark. I know you're there. I can see your light through your curtains. Answer your f'n texts.*

Ugh. It's well past 5 p.m.

Sorry. Was in the zone. I text back.

Pulsing response dots appear immediately.

No problem. Moot point now. I'm not home. I'm at a massive party with hundreds of people having the time of my life. I wasn't up for celebrating your birthday anyway.

I peel back the curtain. She's perched on her windowsill, legs hanging out and feet dangling below with her arms anchored behind her on the inside walls.

I open my window. "Awesome party," I say. "And you're nuts. It's a twelve-foot drop."

"I wanted some fresh air, and I can't lose our bet," she answers. "Were you trying to get me to go outside and ring your doorbell?"

"Nope. I was—" I start to say before she interrupts.

"No. You weren't in the zone. You were the zone. And if you say that makes no grammatical sense, I will send you a virus that turns Breck into a donkey."

I open my mouth to speak, but she again cuts me off again.

"And if you say that's not possible, I will remind you that I have spent most of today reading fantasy. Don't tell me what's not possible."

I laugh. She's looking for it. "I'm sorry."

"It would have been nice to spend at least some of my best friend's birthday WITH MY BEST FRIEND."

It's difficult to get upset with someone whose only goal is to celebrate you, even if it's not technically your birthday.

"You're right. I ghosted you. It wasn't intentional. I apologize. It was my last full day to program, but I was being a selfish asshole."

Lana rocks, largely defused and pondering my response. Temptation lurks, and I give in.

I wrap my index finger around the tip of my chin. "How did that make you feel?"

"Now you're being an asshole."

"Acknowledged."

"Did you at least get to watch Breck take a good nap?"

"No." I wish I could give a different answer. "He's still awake and still a dolt. I don't think he even knows Sam's name. He never uses it. Right now, he's just staring at walls."

"That sounds familiar. We're about to have dinner now, but we're watching a movie after. You want to join?"

"I've been up since before four. I'm fried," I say.

"Come on. What are you, seventeen going on eighty?"

"Tomorrow. After the store. We'll do whatever you want. And you'll have won the bet."

"I don't care about the bet."

"I know. Tomorrow. I promise."

Lana exhales deeply. She knows me too well to waste further breath.

BRECK: SIMULATION #36

Where am I?

I blink several times. The ceiling moves in and out of focus. My head turns to scan the room. From the table, the other person is staring in this direction.

"What time is it?"

"Nine thirty-five A.M.," he says.

"Did you start at eight?"

"Yes."

"What have I been doing since then?"

"Lying there."

"Doing what?" I ask.

"Perhaps dead."

"I'm not dead."

He nods.

"Was I doing anything?"

"Nothing."

It did not seem like nothing. It seemed like much more. I remember the blast last night, the same as other days in this room. But after, between then and now, I was somewhere else.

Is that possible? Where? I try to recall, but my memory is not clear.

"Did the room explode?" I ask.

"Yesterday."

"What about today?"

"No, it is still early," the other person says.

I face the ceiling again and close my eyes. I think I was swimming, but that is not possible. I feel my clothes. They are dry. They should be wet. The memory becomes clearer. I was swimming. How did I get back in here?

"I left the room," I say.

"No one left the room," he responds.

"Did you watch me the whole time?" I ask.

"No."

"So I could have left the room," I say, sitting up.

"No one left the room," he answers again.

"Maybe when you weren't watching?"

"No."

He nods once more. I shut my eyes again. I remember swimming. But how can I recall something I was not doing? I cannot. I concentrate on it. I remember the cool water on my skin. And I was not alone. I was with someone. Or something.

Penguins? This cannot be right.

"Did you see the penguins?" I ask.

"There are no penguins here," the other person responds.

But there were. I remember seeing them. I was with them. They surrounded me on all sides. I was trapped. They would not let me go anywhere. I was trying to escape.

This makes no sense. My head hurts. I press my hands to my eyes.

I think about what happened between yesterday and now. I know I saw them. Penguins. I could describe them. I touched one. His smooth belly slid against me.

The other person walks away to inspect the kitchen.

I peer around the room once more. There is no water. There are no penguins. I have no explanation for this, so I stand to join him. It is time to move forward.

As he opens one of the cabinets, a light shines by the door. I have noticed this before. We both have. But as I look toward it, I think of a question I have never before asked about this. Why?

LIV: SPRING BREAK 3.0

Come on. You can do this!

Breck's hand is on his forehead as he stares at the light bulb. Something is happening. It's not a posture I've ever seen him take. His other palm joins, and both press firmly into his hairline, like he's trying to work out a problem that is almost within reach.

It's a relatable expression.

There's a knock at my door. I'm so focused on the screen in front of me, I barely hear it. And I don't acknowledge it.

The door opens behind me.

"I've been knocking, Liv," my mom says.

Breck walks toward the door, pausing beneath the light. The bulb over his head beams in the most suggestive of ways.

Please. Please!

"Liv!" My mom belts.

I swing my head around, my body unwilling to pivot away from what's unfolding in front of me. My mother is marching toward me. Before I have a chance to answer, she reaches around and turns the monitor off.

"Now, do I have your attention?"

"Mom!"

"I'm trying to talk to you. All you do is sit in front of that computer. You don't even hear me!"

"Breck is about to—"

"Who?"

"Breck, the . . . never mind." If it didn't stick the first half-dozen times, it doesn't seem worth re-explaining. I skip to my larger point. "Something important is happening right now in the contest."

"Well, something important is happening in your room right now too. We're leaving in fifteen minutes," she says, hovering before me in capris, a floral print T-shirt, and sneakers, looking more ready to hike than go to work.

"But—"

"No buts. We're leaving. I wanted to take you with me yesterday, but your buddy Todd talked me out of it. I didn't even see you yesterday. All you do is sit in front of this box. I'm not going to have you spend your entire week in this room. And I could use help." She drops a hand onto the desk, propping herself up, looming nearly overhead as I sit below her in the computer chair.

"You were gone all day!" I protest.

"No. I didn't see you before I left, then I came home for lunch, but you were in here. I opened the door, but you didn't notice. So, I decided to give you the whole day. I was there until nine last night all by myself making sure everything was set to re-open today."

"It's not like I've been playing. I'm working too. Toward something important to me. Winning this summer internship is all I have ever wanted. Do you know how many doors this could open?"

"Why do you think I've let you park in this room for every waking minute outside of school for the last five weeks? We haven't had a family dinner in a month. I've done almost all of the setup for this store by myself. Now it's opening and I need you. I'm not asking for every minute, only the time you would have had when you were at school. You can do as much now as you had any other week."

The tips of her hair nip at her shoulders. Her eyes, wide and coffee brown, look to me for a response.

"Can I just check something?" I ask, still consumed with the cliffhanger waiting on my blank monitor.

"Later." She takes several demonstrative steps toward the middle of the room, letting me know that our debate is over.

This is crushing me. Breck could already be through the door! Time for plan B.

"I need some time to get ready."

"That's why I came in now, instead of fifteen minutes from now. Brush your teeth, put on some clothes, and throw your hair in a ponytail. There's a bagel made. You can eat it in the car."

I stand and move to my closet, making a nonchalant pass by the bed where I snag my cell phone. It was more overt than intended. Mom's head drops and she peers at me with incredulous eyes.

"No phone. I'm not going to have you sit at the store and do the same thing you do here. We're peeling the Band-Aid off today, Liv. It's going to hurt. I get it. But I want all of you today. It'll do you some good to step away from this thing."

"Fine." I toss the phone back on the bed. I'm not going to win this one.

BRECK: SIMULATION #36.1

Something is different.

I walk to the middle of the room. My eyes scan from corner to corner, as if I am visiting this area for the first time. The space is familiar and there are still only two of us here, but the way I am thinking about it is unfamiliar. My thoughts move faster, quickly jumping from one idea to another.

The light still shines across the room.

"Have you ever noticed that the light by the door turns on when you open that cabinet?" I ask, pointing at the light I am referring to.

"Yes," the other person says.

"Do you know why it does this?"

"No."

"It is not all of the lights in the room. It is only that one," I say.

"That is correct."

I walk back beneath the light and stare at it. It glows above me.

"Close the cabinet," I say.

He snaps the cabinet shut. The light stops.

"The bulb could be changed again," he says.

"We have done that before," I answer.

"Everything has been done before," he says.

He is right. All that we do is repeat things we have done before.

Penguins.

Why am I thinking about penguins? Penguins that I am not even certain I saw?

I recall swimming among them. No, I was trapped between them. There was no escape. They surrounded me on all sides—above, below, left, right, front, back. All were the same, black and white, except—

One was different. Yes. He had a mark on his chest. A circle with a star in the middle. When I approached this one, the other penguins on the opposite side of the circle fled, creating a gap.

They were connected.

The door.

I turn, grab the doorknob, and twist.

Still locked.

I pause, staring at the door.

"Open the cabinet again," I say.

He does.

My hand is still on the knob and as the light again illuminates, I turn the handle.

It opens.

A surge of something passes through me. An urge to react. I look at the other person in the kitchen. He glances at the door, sets down the cup he was holding, and says, "It is time to leave the room."

As he passes by me to exit, I stare at the open cabinet.

Thirty-six days and this was all we needed—to open the cabinet, then the door. And the light was signaling this the entire time.

I should turn to leave, but my attention is focused on this thought. *Why did we not think of this before?* It is irrelevant. The door is open. But my thoughts will not move from this.

"It is time to go," the other person says again.

I face him. He is outdoors on either a large terrace or the roof. I cannot tell from where I stand, still on the inside of the room.

A strong wind whips the other person's clothes as he walks along a painted path toward a quadcopter. It is about fifty feet away. I know how to fly it.

I step into the breeze and the sunlight. It has been a long time since I have been outside. I am losing control of my thoughts. They move in all directions, faster than my mind can keep up with.

I am having difficulty explaining what I am experiencing. It is new.

The other person turns back toward me.

"Now," he says.

I jog toward the copter. By the time I get there, he is already sitting in the co-pilot's seat. I sit next to him and place a hand on the controls.

"What is your name?" I ask. It is strange I have never thought to ask this before.

"Sam," he says.

"My name is Breck."

"Good to know," Sam answers. He grabs a sheet of paper from the dashboard. "Here is a map."

Seconds later, I lift us into the air, and we continue toward the goal.

FROM: JESSICA ANDERS
TO: DoRC LEADERSHIP TEAM
SUBJECT: Re: Interesting Programming Adjustment (XNR908)

As I suspected, the programming adjustment to XNR908 was successful. The character left the room and is en route to the next challenge. I believe growth may be exponential from here. While there is admittedly not much time left in the contest, this is the character to keep an eye on. I will continue to provide updates.

~ J

LIV: SPRING BREAK 3.1

"Kids like touching toys. You can't replicate that online," my mom says as I park. "They just need the opportunity. You'll see that today. Pay attention to the kids that come in."

"I've seen it before, Mom," I respond.

I step out of the car and my thoughts drift to my grandfather. I drag my fingers along the weathered red brick, recalling the stories I've heard from many voices, many times.

Renaissance Toys was started in 1968 by my grandfather, Leon Smithwick, after moving from Kansas City to Houston with "only twenty-seven dollars and change" in his pocket. Over a dozen years, he grew a scrappy kiosk with a few model airplanes into a full-fledged store. It was a staple in the community. *This* was where kids got toys. Santa shopped here. Birthdays didn't happen without a visit here first. Grandpop was on the local Chamber of Commerce. The store was on the brink of opening a second location. The future looked bright.

Then 1980 happened—a recession and the birth of video games, which Grandpop was late to embrace. His heart was more into "things that move the potato off the couch." He eventually came around when pogo-sticks and Big Wheels stopped paying the rent, but not before their competitors had taken over.

The store has since survived four other recessions and the online revolution. But over the last four decades, Renaissance Toys has slowly become more of a museum than a thriving business. It was Grandpop's life. He started sleeping in the back once Grandma passed. I spent more time here than at his actual house.

Late last year, Grandpop had a stroke. He spent a few months in an assisted living facility where he didn't talk much. When he did, he asked about the store. *Closed* was never the answer we gave. Then six months ago, he died.

As I turn the corner to the front of the store, I nearly color him into the picture. I can see him propping the glass door open, welcoming anyone with a voice so booming he could be heard blocks away. He was one of those people who made you feel special, even though you knew he made everyone feel that way.

When I think of who I want to be like, he's at the top of the list. He's the American Dream. He created opportunity with his imagination, determination, scrappy bare hands, and anything else he could throw at it. It's beyond admirable. As Lana once said, "He could be his own cat poster."

Being the minimalist that I am, I don't keep much on my desk, but I do have a small framed picture of the two of us. I miss him. But I love him more for who he was, not the remains of what he did.

After he died, my mother had quit her job as a grocery store manager to revitalize Grandpop's business.

This store is in our DNA, but my mother and I see it very differently. I view it more like a once-sturdy ship that carried our family and served its purpose. It's now a relic exposed to the elements and the weathering hands of time. My mother views it more like a rusty Corvette that only needs dutiful hands, new tires, and a paint job for it to return to its former glory.

I'd love to see her succeed. But she's fighting a losing battle, and it's driving her mad. It's driving *us* mad.

That's what bothers me most about being here today. I'm swapping my opportunity to break into the future for a failing effort to resuscitate the past. And I swear, Mom sees my computer time as competition, a symbol of a generation that won't step foot into Renaissance because it's easier to scroll and click.

I don't know what jobs she has for me today, but the best thing I could really offer is to help her see the irrationality of this.

"Close your eyes," Mom says and leads me into the store. She turns on a light and I peek through half-open eyes and find Mom with a proud *ta-da!* smile.

She's been busy. Fifty years of clutter is gone. Maple brown wooden shelves stretch weightlessly from the walls with the latest toys and gadgets. Tall aisles have been replaced with willowy tables and sleek signs announcing the categories of their belongings—from "Mind Games" to "Sports Fun." It's not the Apple store, but it has a far more modern appearance.

"It looks great."

"Just great?" She crosses her arms.

I really am proud of her, but this feels a little like praising the interior design of a plane that has no wings. And, why does this have to be *our* thing?

But, given all the work that she's done, I'd be a real a-hole if I pointed this out right after the grand reveal.

"Grandpop would be proud of it," I say, trying to find some middle ground. I'm really, really trying here.

"Yeah," she answers with a reluctant nod, like there's more to it than what she's saying. She quickly redirects. "So, I have a ton of organizing to do in the back. I need someone out front."

"To do?"

"To help the customers," she quips.

This would be at the bottom of my task wish list, which she *should* know. I mean, she's met me. I'm a classic ISTJ.

"I don't know anything about any of this stuff." I gesture broadly around the store. "I don't even know how to work the register."

"It's electronic," she huffs, as though this means that I should already understand how to operate it.

I sink. I'm arguing with someone who thinks this register is the same as Breck. How could I possibly win?

BRECK: SIMULATION #36.2

A town sprawls out a hundred feet below us.

Sam points to an *X* on the ground. It is in the middle of a small plaza in the near distance. I glide us over the spot and hover. People below clear the space to allow us to land.

"This is where the map ends," Sam says. "It says to find and pass through a tunnel."

I set us down.

"How do we do that?" I ask.

"It is not clear."

I peer at the map on the dashboard. The instructions are brief.

Find the tunnel and pass through it.

Sam steps out and I follow. There are eleven roads and alleys to take out of the plaza, spaced between busy cafes.

"The first step is to find the tunnel. Perhaps someone here knows where it is," he says.

"Yes. Good idea." Sam marches toward a table. "Do you know where the tunnel is?" he asks.

A woman from the group looks up. "No."

The others ignore Sam's question.

"Does anybody else know?" he asks.

They turn their heads at the same time and all reply, "No."

Sam asks others nearby. The response is the same.

"Do people in this town say anything other than, 'No'?" I walk away from the café.

"It is not clear," Sam answers.

Sam has three more conversations with people at another café. Their responses are short and similar. We return to the copter in silence and rescan the plaza.

I notice a detail I initially overlooked. Almost everyone has a red shirt. They are varied—some striped, some dotted, some solid, some light, some dark—but all red.

Except one.

At the far end of the plaza, a man stands near the corner of an alley with a green shirt.

I explain this observation to Sam, who begins to walk before I finish my words. I watch for a moment as he marches away. He is quick to act. Quicker than me.

"Do you know where the tunnel is?" Sam asks.

"Yes," he says.

"How do you get there?"

"You'll need to exit the plaza from that alley, next to the café with the bronze sign." He points to one of the narrow breaks in the plaza. "From there, you'll pass seven streets, then make a left. Then pass eight more and make a right. Then, you will make your first right, your first left, your first right, then go four more blocks and make a sharp left at what will appear to be a U-turn. The entrance is immediately after that turn."

Sam repeats the directions.

"You got it," he says.

Sam speed-walks across the plaza. I hustle to stay close. We are soon inside of the narrow alley.

The path to the tunnel is twisting. No roads run straight. It is difficult to track our general direction. Sam counts as we pass each break in the wall to our sides. Some are smaller alleys like the one we are on, and some are major streets, packed with cars and trolleys.

"Perhaps we should stop and ask someone if we are following the directions correctly," I suggest.

"This is correct," Sam says, walking several steps in front of me. It is the same tone he always uses, but there is something different about the way I hear it. It affects me. It is difficult to explain how or why because it is unfamiliar. I would prefer that he had said something different. I would prefer that he had listened to me.

I have never experienced a thought like this before. A preference.

I follow until Sam stops.

"This is not correct," he says. "There should be a U-turn here. There is not."

"Are you sure we followed the exact directions?"

"Yes." Then he stops a woman who passes next to us. "Do you know where the tunnel is?"

"No, it may be on the other side of town," she answers, without stopping. This response is unclear.

Sam crosses the cobblestone street to ask a boy tossing a ball in the air.

"Do you know where the tunnel is?"

"No."

"Have you ever heard of the tunnel?" Sam asks.

"No."

Sam looks at me. While he does, the boy dashes down the street and disappears into an alleyway.

I cross to Sam's side of the street. He is already walking away.

"Where are you going?" I ask.

"Back."

"Maybe there's someone nearby with a green shirt," I say.

"There are no green shirts here," he answers.

Following behind him, I experience that sensation again, a preference for him to listen to me.

What are these preferences I am experiencing?

LIV: SPRING BREAK 3.2

Breck is all I can think about. *Has he left the room? Is the next stage a city, like they've said on the chat boards? Did sleep make him any different?* Not knowing is killing me.

I've tried to distract myself by looking at the toys and attending to customers. But there aren't many visitors. To be more precise, we've had one so far, who didn't buy anything.

My mother periodically reappears from the back office, staring at the empty space with heavy eyes. I busy myself and don't comment.

The door chimes for our second customer and Mom blazes out from the back. She introduces herself, then shoots me a *watch how this is handled* look as she follows them around the store and suggests options.

After a five-minute loop from corner to corner, the boy and his mom become locked in a stalemate around an expensive Star Wars Legos set.

The boy repeats his arguments. "Please."

His mom repeats hers. "You already have a bin full of Legos that you don't use."

My mom interjects with a story about my love for building with Legos when I was his age, turning to me for affirmation. I nod.

The verdict comes. The mother turns toward the front of the store, grabs her son's hand and concludes, "We'll think about it for your birthday."

They leave empty handed, albeit with compliments and promises to return.

"You could have helped," Mom says, with the echoes of the ding of the door still lingering.

I stare at her, mouth slightly agape, and silent.

"I teed you up with that story. You could have said something."

"I didn't think my experience with Legos was going to change their decision," I answer.

"Well, we won't know now, will we?" her voice rising on each word as she parades across the store, resetting all of the items that were moved over the last few minutes. "This is what I mean about being present, Liv. You can't just sit there. You have to actively participate in what's happening around you."

I don't have an opportunity to respond, as her final words are punctuated with a loud pop of the metal office door swinging shut.

Lovely. I can add scapegoat to my resume.

◆ ✤ ◆

Our third and final visit of the morning resulted in our first sale—a small stuffed koala. It was four dollars. Mom wasn't present to witness the victory, if that's what it was. She's been on a phone call in the backroom.

It's now 12:30 and without a computer to distract me, I'm hungry and not clear on lunch plans—if any.

I approach the backroom but stop as my hand nears the knob.

"I can't do that!" My mom's voice seeps through the cracks of the thick door, a whisper that carries the umph of a yell.

I lean closer.

"We just reopened!"

Even closer.

"You're the banker! Figure out the numbers and make it work. Come on.. Give me some time here! We reopened *today*!"

My ear is now flush against the door. I hear a phone receiver crashing into its base.

I pull away and take a few swift steps toward the closest shelf I can find. When Mom emerges, I'm readjusting the remote-control racecar in front of me.

She glares at me with accusatory eyes. I try my best to look clueless. She takes a deep breath. "I'm going to Subway. Do you want a sandwich?"

I'm soon alone in the store, left to process what I'm not supposed to know.

I slump over a corner of the counter. It's one thing to feel that the store will fail; it's another thing to actually feel it failing.

BRECK: SIMULATION #36.3

Our path is cut short.
    A large gate now blocks the entry to a broad alley we walked along to arrive here. A sign stretched across the gate reads, *Closed.*

"Maybe there's another street that goes in a similar direction," Sam says.

Without awaiting my response or looking back to ensure I am behind him, Sam walks away once more.

"No streets appear to run in the same direction," I respond.

Sam nods while marching.

It occurs to me that I am merely following Sam. I do not know what to do with the thought.

The road twists, and we pass similarly twisting streets, all unique but also repetitive. Each has a mix of markets, bars, restaurants, florists, hardware stores, clothing shops, pharmacies, and other shops. But from block to block, these seem only rearranged. The sequence varies, but each is like a different version of the previous street.

Sam continues to turn, and I continue to follow until we have walked for exactly forty-four minutes.

I think back to the room—the constant wall pushing, window banging, knob twisting, key searching. Thirty-five days of doing the same, when the answer was a different approach.

"We do not know where we are or where we are going," I say.

"This is exploring," Sam answers.

"It all looks the same."

"Do you have a better idea?" he asks.

We stare at each other. He awaits my response, motionless.

"It is hot outside, and I am thirsty. We could rest there and talk about what to do." I point to a small restaurant on the corner of the next alley.

He nods, walks, and sits at an outdoor table. I trail behind.

"Where is the server?" he asks.

A short pudgy man appears from inside the restaurant. He is wearing a green shirt.

LIV: SPRING BREAK 3.3

The door chimes and Lana saunters in, wide-eyed, wearing pajama bottoms, flip-flops and her all-time favorite, a plain purple T-shirt with the words, *Caution: Abibliophobic.*

"Whoa. This place got an upgrade," she says.

"Yup," I answer, then lower my voice to a whisper. "What's happening?"

The only thing I had time to do this morning was text her my login information.

"What do you mean?"

"Please don't do this," I say.

My eyes balloon as she reaches for her back pocket. She swings the phone in front of me, positioned so that I can't see the screen.

"It's very interesting." Her voice rises while smirking and staring at the small screen.

I glance toward the office door. Still shut. I snatch the phone and turn it toward me. I nearly drop it. Breck and Sam are outside on a cobblestone street. I swell with pride. I've never felt this accomplished.

"Congratulations," Lana adds as I stare at the two of them walking.

"Did you watch them leave?" I ask.

"Yup."

"And? What was it like?" I ask with all the excitement a whisper can convey.

"Like someone trying to figure something out and then walking through a door," she says.

"That's an extremely unsatisfactory answer. I want more. Come on. Pretend it's in a book."

"Oh, okay. Let's see . . . Breck strode across the room in a purposeful gait to the mysterious door. He pressed an ear to the cool surface and swore he could hear whispers of all the secrets that lay beyond it. His eyes shut. His body felt as if it melted into the deep blue barrier. Then, from beyond his lids came a flutter of light. And in an instant, he knew. His hand drifted to the hot knob. He gripped it tightly and turned. The doorway bowed to his desires."

I look at her with the same disappointed expression my mother has given me several times today.

"Hot knob? Ewww."

"He opened the door, okay? He looked at the light bulb, he monkeyed around with the door, he looked back at the cabinet a few times, and he finally figured it out. It was neat." She grabs a shrink-wrapped package with a plush giraffe's head dangling outside, holding it toward me with an inquisitive look.

"It's a Stretch Pet. You wrap it around the edge of a computer monitor and a giraffe looks back at you. What happened next?" I ask.

"Oh," she quips, feigning distraction, savoring this moment of leading me along. "Then he flew something that looked like a giant drone," she adds, which confirms the chat board rumors. "How would he know how to fly that thing?"

"Base character programming. The same as if he saw a bike. He would know what it is, and he could ride it."

"But he didn't know what sleep was?"

"It's a little random. He can't know everything. He knows what he needs to know. And computer characters don't *need* to sleep, so nobody thought to program that as base knowledge."

"Okay. I guess that makes sense."

"None of us know everything," I add.

"So says you."

"What's a cuttlefish?" I ask.

"I have no idea."

"Exactly. Because you have no reason to know. It works the same way for him."

The back door opens and my mom enters. I try to subtly pass the phone back to Lana.

"Hi, Lana," Mom says, then turns to me. "I see you got your tech fix."

"I'm sorry, Mrs. Smithwick," Lana answers.

"It's fine, Lana. If I can get her off of some kind of device for most of the day, I think that's a win." Mom then redirects with a resplendent swoop of her arm. "So, what do you think of the store?"

"It's looks awesome."

"Two weeks of renovation. We reopened today."

"How's business?" Lana asks.

"It takes time. Word needs to spread." My mom answers with a cagey expression, glancing at me, like her response is more for my benefit, then returns to Lana. "What are you doing this week?"

"Reading."

Mom's brows fold together as if wondering whether Lana is being serious, before concluding, "You girls need interaction. Real time with real people." She turns and walks toward the back once more. "Look around. Touch. Explore. And if somebody comes in the store, sell!"

Mom disappears and I mouth to Lana, "It's not going well."

She shoots me a look.

I glance at the closed office door. For all I know, Mom has her ear pressed to the other side of it. "Let's talk later."

"Everything okay?" she whispers.

"I don't know. Let's talk more about Breck."

She gives an uneasy expression but moves on. "What's there to say. You rock! Congratulations, you did it. Or he did it. However that works. And, for the record, I told you I knew it was going to happen."

"You did."

"We're hanging out tonight, right?" she asks.

"Say when and where."

"I'll let you know. My dad wants to talk about something first."

"That sounds ominous."

"Maybe, but he doesn't own a toy store, so I have that going for me," she says, then cranes her head as something piques her interest. "What's that?" she asks, pointing to a table holding a rubbery sphere, half-capped with a disk surrounding it. "It looks like a planet."

"That's probably why they named it Saturn." I've been eyeing it all morning, but I don't have enough coordination to try it. "It's like a hoverboard, but the ball is a magnet, so the cap floats over it *like riding on air*," I say, pointing to this exact tagline on a box behind the device.

"I heard about that! The lacrosse girl from third period pre-calc posted about it. I didn't comment, but I'm definitely trying it."

"Better you than me," I say.

"Let's take it outside. I don't want to risk breaking anything. Other than me, that is."

I don't know how Mom would feel about this, but she's in the back and she told us to touch and explore, so this seems reasonable.

We're soon in the parking lot with Lana strangling my shoulders as she places one foot and then the other on the rings that surround the sphere in alternating bands of color. She wobbles back and forth, as if on a tightrope, micro-shifting her balance several times per second.

Within a few minutes, she discovers how to creep forward, but still threatens to topple both of us.

"Hey, what's that?" a voice shouts.

We both turn to look in the direction of the question, and as we do, Lana delivers on her threat. She goes airborne. The good news—she lands softly. That bad news—it's because she lands on me.

"Can I try?" the same voice asks as Lana rolls off, affording me both breath and a view of an eager boy looming over me, asking for permission. He looks to be about fourteen.

"Sure."

To Lana's annoyance, he's soon whipping around us in circles.

"This is cool! It's like . . . it's like . . ."

"Riding on air?" Lana says with a sarcastic grin.

"Yeah!"

He attracts the attention of a girl who drags her mother's hand away from the direction of the CVS store next to us.

"Can I try it, Mommy?"

This same cycle repeats once more, though with some older guy wearing a suit and looking out of place.

As I watch all of this unfold, I stumble on a surprising insight. *Maybe there is a way that I can help my mom that doesn't involve me talking her out of this.*

An idea forms.

BRECK: SIMULATION #36.4

"They are always working on the roads around here," the server with the green shirt says. "You said somebody else already gave you directions."

Sam repeats the directions, beginning from where we are.

"Hmmm. That doesn't sound right from here. Maybe you miscounted."

"No," Sam quickly responds.

"Did he say streets or alleys?"

"What is the difference?" I ask.

"Cars go on streets. Only people can go into alleys."

"He said streets," Sam says.

"Did you count the alleys?"

"Yes."

"Well, there you go. But the good news is that you are not far away. Maybe ten minutes."

Sam stands.

"No drink then?"

"Not if progress is possible. What are the directions from here?"

"You need to go three streets that way." He points. "Then, turn on an alley immediately after the produce stand."

"There is a produce stand on almost every block," I say.

"This one has a purple sign. And again, it is exactly three streets down. After that, turn right at the next alley, then left on the fourth street. Then two immediate lefts on alleys, until your first street. Follow this for three streets. You will see it on your right."

"What does it look like?" Sam asks.

"A tunnel, of course!"

I stand as Sam begins marching down the street. I catch up to him and we review the instructions, confirming that we both heard the same thing.

"It is interesting that only the people in green talk."

"Yes, it is," Sam answers.

"I wonder why."

Sam doesn't respond.

"Do you know why?" I ask.

"No."

He looks forward, not toward me. He is focused on our path.

"But have you *wondered* why that is? I think that is what I am asking."

"No."

"Why not?"

"Because it is the way it is." Sam still does not look in my direction.

"But what if this is part of what we need to solve?"

"It is already solved. People in red don't talk. People in green do, and they have already given us directions to the tunnel. What more is needed?"

"I don't know!" I answer. Several red shirts glance at me then quickly turn away. "Think about the room we were locked in. The answer was there the whole time, but we did not realize it. Because we did not know what to look for."

There is a sensation growing inside of me. It is a fight. But not between people. Between forces inside of me. It is the experience of wanting something to happen that doesn't happen. And this sensation makes me want to do something that makes no sense, like raise my voice when Sam is capable of hearing me at a normal volume.

Every time I try to talk with Sam, it strengthens my sensation to speak loudly, so I follow him in silence, watching him count the bending streets and alleys we pass.

With all of the turns, it seems like we are moving in a circle.

After eleven minutes, Sam stops.

"It is not here," he says.

I would ask if he was precise about following the instructions, but I know what his answer will be. Instead, I wait as he surveys the street.

"It should be there." He points toward a small furniture store. "But that is not a tunnel."

He is correct. Again, I wait for him to continue speaking.

"Where is another person in a green shirt?" he asks.

"That has not worked twice," I respond.

"Maybe it will work next time."

A thought occurs, and I do not know from where or why.

"Perhaps he was not telling the truth," I say.

Sam's eyebrows twitch.

"That is possible." His attention is now on me.

I consider what this must mean. "If they are lying, then we should do the opposite of what they are telling us to do."

"What is the opposite of their directions?" Sam asks.

Good question. There are countless possibilities.

"I do not know," I answer. "Yet."

LIV: SPRING BREAK 3.4

"I know what you're thinking," Mom says, thumping the knuckles of her right hand on the window to the rhythm of a country song.

She's right. The remainder of the afternoon had been almost as uneventful as the morning. We had four visits with two sales—another stuffed animal and a twenty-five-dollar lawn-dart set.

"I know we didn't sell much," she continues, turning down the radio, "but the people who did come loved it. You heard that, right?"

I nod. It's the only correct answer.

"We just need more people," she continues.

I had been planning to do some research first, but the timing seems better now.

"Does the store have a social media account?"

"I knew you were going to say that." The light turns green, which I don't notice until someone behind us points it out with a blast of their horn. "Yes, but I'm not selling anything online. Some consultant came in and told your grandfather to do that about five years ago. He spent a bunch of money to set up a website. And you know how much he sold? Almost nothing. It's all about price. That's it. And we can't compete with online prices."

I recall that website. It was terrible, which says something since I recognized this as a twelve-year-old. I have no idea if she should sell online, but it's a moot point, as that's not my idea.

"That's not why I asked. I'm not talking about a website. I have an idea, and social media is only to tell people about it," I answer.

"Oh. Okay." She releases one of her hands, which had been in a tense curl around her knee. "Then I'll give it to you. You should be following it anyways."

"I'm not really on social media, Mom. Or at least the mainstream ones."

She frowns. To her, there is a world of *1's* and *0's*, and there is the world in which I am currently driving us home. Everything accessible from a computer is the same. It's as if she only knew the word *ball* and doesn't understand why someone who plays football is not an avid golfer.

"Okay, so what's your idea?"

I tell her about the Saturn and how many people came over to try it, "which is something you can't do online." I have her full attention. "So, we could post to your social media that anyone can come and try to ride it. We'll set a few up in the parking lot. I could find a few videos online to give it a fun feel."

She considers the idea. Her knuckles thump once more.

"That's a good idea, but that's not what worked today."

I see where this is headed and already hate it.

"You were riding it in the parking lot today. People saw it—in person—and that's what made them stop," Mom continues.

"Lana was riding it," I correct.

"If she can do it, you can too."

How is my idea getting ripped away from me so quickly?

"The social media is like advertising, Mom. You believe in commercials, right? It's like a commercial online. Except it's free. And it reaches a lot more people."

She shakes her head. I know that look. I'm talking to a wall.

"Then we'll do both. You said it yourself. People need to see someone on it. Besides, I think we'd both agree there wasn't much for you to do in the store today. I have someone who handles the online stuff for me. I'll send her a note to post it."

This is not what I had in mind. I'm not the parading show pony selling merchandise. And I'm not even remotely athletic. I have different value to offer.

The problem is, I don't know what that is. Even if this works, it's a Band-Aid, not the solution. I don't know how to help.

She steals a glance away from the road and looks at me with a soft and earnest smile. "I think this is a great plan. Thank you, Liv."

BRECK: SIMULATION #36.5

We have walked for hours. The town looks both familiar and unfamiliar now. It is a series of newly arranged combinations of the same things.

Daylight lessens.

"Green shirt," Sam says. He stops abruptly and I bump into his back.

"Where?"

He points toward a nearby corner. It is a woman this time, sitting at the conductor's chair of a stopped trolley.

"Do you think she will lie?" Sam asks.

"I do not know. But we could try it once more."

Sam charges across the street, narrowly dodging another passing trolley. By the time I arrive, Sam has already begun the conversation.

"Come on board. I am about to leave. We pass right by the tunnel entrance."

"How far away is it?" Sam asks.

"Five minutes. There are open seats in the back."

We pass many rows of red shirts and find an empty bench seat in the back. Once more, it is difficult to track our direction. The trolley turns more often than it heads in any one straight path.

I stare at Sam who stays quiet. It occurs to me that he is brief with his words. Why have I never noticed this before? I remain seated and ponder this and countless other questions. My mind cannot seem to catch up to itself. There is too much happening inside my head. I do not remember ever thinking about thinking, but that's mostly what I think about now.

I wonder if Sam is experiencing the same. As I'm poised to ask, the trolley driver stops, whistles, and waves us to the front.

There is no tunnel in sight.

"Go straight down that alley right there," she says, pointing. "It leads to the tunnel."

Sam enters first. I stay behind him. It is too narrow to walk next to each other. Unlike all other alleys, this one crosses no other paths until we reach the end where the space becomes wider and splinters into six separate alleys, each with its own entrance.

"Which one?" Sam asks.

"I do not think it matters. She was lying," I say. "We cannot follow their instructions."

"Then we should explore," Sam says, and begins walking down one of the six alleys.

I do not disagree with him, but there is something we are missing. Their lies must be telling us something.

"I do not understand why they are lying," I say.

"It is a trick. They are trying to prevent exploration."

We continue walking. Sam's response lingers, twisting in my mind like the path we are on.

"Wait," I say.

"What?" Sam turns to look at me.

"You are right. It is a trick."

"Good. Then it is time to keep exploring."

"No. It is not that kind of trick. They are decoys. The opposite of following their instructions would be passing by them without listening."

Sam looks at me with a questioning expression.

"We have seen all of them on or near corners. What if those are the entrances to the tunnel? And every time we get near, they are there to turn us away?"

"But there is only one tunnel."

"Yes, but maybe there is more than one entrance. Everything else here winds and splits in many directions."

Sam nods in agreement then starts to walk.

"But first, it is time to eat," I say. "My energy levels are low."

"There is not much time left to explore today," Sam answers.

"We are no longer in the room," I respond. "There may not be an explosion."

"What happens at ten then?"

"I do not know. Perhaps nothing."

Sam answers by walking to a nearby café and sitting at an outdoor table.

We order food.

"Do your eyelids feel heavy?" I ask Sam after a long silence.

"No."

"Mine do," I say.

"What happens if you close them?"

LIV: SPRING BREAK 3.5

I'm sitting at my computer but haven't touched the keyboard for an hour.

Breck is learning. Rapidly.

Even when not doing much, his growth is obvious. Breck and Sam sit quietly at the table watching their surroundings, but each of them does this differently. Sam's process is robotic, like a camera sweeping the area, then returning once more to look for any changes. Breck's approach seems without method. He lingers on people and objects, studying them, changing expressions as he does, giving clues as to how he's processing the data.

I realize I'm biased, but there is objective evidence—a tool that measures his processing. It's like brainwaves meets CPU usage. And Breck is nearly off the charts. It's a completely different picture than yesterday, or even this morning.

Breck's eyes droop and after several long blinks, he closes them, then his head drops softly onto the white tablecloth.

Sleep. Yes! I assumed he did this last night, but I hadn't actually seen it. It's freaking glorious. I could watch him lie there and do nothing all night.

Sam's reaction is interesting but still sterile. He pokes Breck with his index finger, and then a spoon, as if a new object might get a different reaction.

Breck doesn't stir, and Sam's attention moves on to something else.

I don't dare tweak Brecks' code now. He's working.

This puts me in a strange situation. For the first time in six weeks, I have nothing to do. I'm supposed to hang out with Lana tonight, but she's still talking with her parents. I have no schoolwork. My Renaissance responsibilities are done for the day. And there's nothing to watch now other than an activity monitor showing that Breck's processing is still on fire.

I knew I *could* win this, but it seemed so out of reach—more aspirational than actual. Not now. Now I feel like I truly have a shot. I *can* win this internship.

The guy who created Watson, the IBM program that beat the world chess champion, won this contest. One of the Google founders did as well. No one my age has ever won. No girl has ever won.

The doorbell rings. I notice, but don't pay much attention to it until my bedroom door flies open. I nearly jump out of my chair.

Lana looms in the doorway, as if the word *panic* was inked across her forehead.

"We're moving."

It's too direct for me to fully grasp.

"I don't get it."

"We are moving . . . to another house," she says, slowly pronouncing these words, each one further shattering our constant in life as neighbors. "In Massachusetts."

I don't know what to say. My mouth opens, but no words escape.

"Say something," she says.

"This isn't happening!"

"It is." She closes my door and collapses on my bed.

"Why?"

"My dad's research project lost funding, so his job is going away with it. He got hired at Amherst, in middle-of-nowhere Massachusetts."

"When?" I ask, as she inches inward toward the middle of my bed, then buries herself under a large fold of comforter. I want to do the same.

"End of the semester," she answers from beneath the cover.

"That's only two months from now."

"Thanks for double checking the math. That was what I got also," she grumbles. "And yeah, that means we won't be seniors together, in case that was what you were going to point out next."

"What does your mom think about it?"

"She says she can get a job teaching second grade anywhere and she has some bizarre fascination with New England."

I roll my chair to the foot of the bed. This isn't happening. We can change this. *Think. Problem, solution.*

I draw in a deep, centering breath as Lana softly sobs. A few twizzled strands of her hair escape into view, bobbing against the snowy white comforter.

"What can we do about it?" I ask.

"Nothing."

"He already took the new job?"

"No. They're finalizing things. It'll be official next week."

"So, it's not done yet," I say.

"It's done. Unless he finds funding for something else, but he doesn't want to study something else. So, there you go. Done."

"What exactly does he study?"

"Something about child development."

"That explains a lot."

"Do I seem like someone who's in the mood for shitty side commentaries?"

I don't answer. She's right. It was a botched attempt at humor. But also, I'm momentarily distracted by motion on my computer monitor.

Sam stands. He walks around the table so he is next to Breck, then pokes him a few more times with his finger. Breck still doesn't respond. Sam then abruptly turns and marches down the street.

What?

Sam is programmed to stay with Breck. This is not supposed to happen.

FROM: JESSICA ANDERS
TO: DoRC LEADERSHIP TEAM
SUBJECT: Re: Interesting Programming Adjustment (XNR908)

I am writing with an additional update: XNR908 is being stranded. While this could impede progress, I suspect it will not. Having watched this character closely, I believe this may actually accelerate growth even more. This raises a question we have not yet had to face. What if this character makes it through all of the challenges? I know there are some concerns about allowing this to happen, but there are steps we can take if it progresses too far.

Let's discuss this live.

More updates to come.

~ J

LIV: SPRING BREAK 3.6

"Hello?" Lana says, peeking her face out from under the covers.

Her words lay on my periphery as I think through what Sam's departure means. I never considered that he would leave.

"Are you looking at me, or your freaking computer?" Lana asks, turning to glance at the screen herself.

"Sam just left," I say.

"Ask me if I freaking care!" Her tiny body explodes out from under the heap of bedding. "I told you that I'm moving. I'm bawling on your bed. And you're hanging out here, dry-eyed, watching ones and zeros sleep!"

She's right, I know she's right, but— "There's just a lot happening right now."

"Yeah. An avatar walked away from a table and your best friend is leaving for good. I get how that's dividing your attention."

On instinct, I glance between Lana and the monitor.

"You can't even freaking stop," she belts, leaping up from the bed. "Do you even care about me moving?"

"Yes. Of course!"

"Well you're not acting like it."

"I was trying figure out what we could do about it."

"Until you got distracted."

My undivided attention is on her, but she's now looking away from me, staring into one of the corners of the room.

"Lana," I start to say.

"The whole world is raking me over today," she confides to the empty wall.

"It's a problem. Problems have solutions. We just have to find it," I say, but even as the words come out, I'm not sure I believe them.

"Not this one."

"I'm trying my best. I don't know what to do."

"Then that makes two of us," she says.

We sit in silence.

"I don't want to lose you," I try to place a hand on her shoulder, but she moves away.

"Well, it's happening. What do you want me to say? I'm just a high school kid whose dad has a better job across the country."

Recoiled, she's on the bed with her legs crisscrossed and her arms folded. She seems empty, defeated in a way I've never seen her.

This isn't who she is. I'm the pragmatist; she's the dreamer. This is the core of every debate we've ever had. I think we control our own destiny, but only loosely. We try our best, but life is impossibly complex, with too many butterflies to count. Lana believes in willpower alone. She is a tempest of determination, flapping pages of *The Secret* into the winds of the universe. Envision the outcome you want and you will have it.

I'm staring at her now, wishing for her irrational optimism.

"There has to be something we can try," I offer.

"Were you able to talk your mom out of Renaissance?"

Again, more silence. I can't dispute this. Maybe she's right.

"This could be the end of us," Lana says.

I don't want to have this conversation right now.

"Stop."

"Then tell me why it isn't. I mean, it was going to happen eventually, like a year from now, after we graduate. I just thought we had more time. We don't. It's the end."

"Lana, it's not the end. And it was never going to be the end."

"Where are you going to go to college then?" she asks. "Because I'm thinking somewhere small, liberal arts, with a focus on writing and literature. Any interest?" Lana asks, heavy on sarcasm.

I don't answer because she knows the answer. We both do, even if neither one of us can name exactly where we'll go.

And, on the heels of what I heard today, whatever college I might want to attend suddenly looks a little more pipedream.

"Exactly," Lana says.

"We don't know what's going to happen. I don't even know how I'm going to afford college. I haven't told you about what I heard at the store today." I fill her in on the conversation I overheard in Mom's office.

"Holy crap. I'm sorry. I guess the world is raking both of us over today," she says.

"Yeah, so like I said, affording a college I want to go to is a pretty big question mark right now. Maybe I'll find you, crash on your floor, and audit classes wherever you are."

"You're scholarships all the way."

"Based on what? That?" I say, pointing to the tiny trophy on the wall.

"You have a decent chance of winning this thing. I checked out the boards earlier. There aren't that many people who have gotten out of the room. And nobody's mentioned anything beyond the city."

I briefly drift back into the headspace I was in before Lana blasted in here.

"Yeah, that would be a game changer," I say.

"You could go anywhere you want. Free," she adds. I wishfully nod and she continues. "Okay, ideal college. Let's say you win this, money doesn't matter, and you can go wherever you want. Where?"

"Stanford. You?"

"Williams," Lana says.

"Isn't that in Massachusetts?" I ask.

"Yes, but it's a different middle of nowhere. And I didn't want to go there until after freaking senior year. And, with that, we're back to square one. You're in California and I'm on the other coast. My point is that this is the end. It's never going to be like this again."

"We don't know—"

"No. We do. It's never going to be the same. I'm never going to open my window and have you there. And I won't even be able to walk next door to see you. I won't even be able to drive there. It's the beginning of the end. And I was okay with that when it didn't seem so . . . *now*."

We stare at each other in silence. There's not much more to add to that depressing thought.

"So, what do you want to do tonight?" I eventually ask.

"Read. I want to forget about all of this for a bit. It'll give you more time to work on that anyway," she says, nodding in the direction of the computer.

"There's not much to do. I guess I need to figure out why Sam left, but I don't want to mess with Breck. I might only screw him up."

"Yeah, he's coming along. I'm telling you . . . you've got a shot." Lana stands and makes her way to the bedroom door. "I'm going to go. Keep your phone on, okay?"

She leaves my bedroom. Seconds later I hear the front door shut.

I stare out of the window, but her curtains stay closed.

◆ ⁙ ◆

My phone rings. It's Lana.

"Breck is the answer!"

"And what's the question?" I ask, squinting at the phone to see the time. It's 3 a.m. I kept my ringer on but hadn't expected a call at this hour.

"How we keep my dad here," she says, bursting with enthusiasm.

"I'm not tracking."

"The psychology of AI. Google it. It's new and it's exploding. Everybody wants to study it, there's crazy money out there to fund it, and you heard my dad react to what you said about the contest. He thought it was interesting," she says, quick-worded as though her tongue can't keep pace with her thoughts. "And it's related to child development."

"How?" I ask, which is only the first in a long list of questions. My fingers crawl to the base of the bedside lamp then slide upward to flip it on.

"Kids learn. That's what they do. They develop into adults. That's what Breck is doing. He's learning . . . developing into something more."

"Okay." I prop myself up and lean against my pillow. "But Breck is a program and that's all he'll be. There's no psychology. He's code. He does what he's programmed to do."

"But he learns," Lana presses.

"So does a dog."

"Well," she starts, her voice full of annoyance, "a lot of people smarter than me think it's worth studying—and maybe my dad might also—and that's what matters. Plus, Rice has courses on AI. Not AI psych, but maybe they could be talked into it."

This is who I was searching for hours earlier. My hope-ridden friend, unbound by reason.

This plan isn't half-baked—it's not baked at all. I don't even fully understand it.

"It's a long shot," Lana continues. "I get it. But, it's the best I can come up with other than handcuffing myself to the sink or moving into your TV room. You're the one who was all about trying something. So, this is all I've got."

She awaits my reaction.

Lana is my one and only amazing friend. What do I have to lose? She's already leaving. And, who knows? It could work. Less likely things happen every day, everywhere.

"If you put it that way," I say.

"Which is the right way," she fires back.

"Then I'm in. What can I do?"

"Yeah, so I've been thinking about this. Can we talk with Breck?"

"Like with a chat box?"

"No, talk. Like he does with Sam."

"There's not an app for that."

"But you could write one, right?"

"Umm." My mind races. "Maybe. Probably. I could tweak something else that's out there. But—"

"But what?"

"We're not allowed to help him," I say.

"You programmed him. You've climbed inside his brain! You can talk to him."

"What I mean is that he has to figure out all of the challenges by himself. That's the point of the contest. We can't help him do anything."

"We wouldn't be helping. We'd only be asking questions."

As a budding computer scientist, I'm intrigued. But as a contest participant, I'm nervous. I don't want to screw this up. If I win, it will change the course of my life. Stakes don't get much bigger than that.

I've pulled myself out of bed and I stare at my reflection in the blank monitor. I do wonder what it would be like to be in there, to be in Breck's world. Like in my dream. What must it be like? Asking Breck would let us know.

"I need to read the rules again," I answer.

"I did. There's nothing in the rules about talking with him."

"Maybe not explicitly."

"I'm explicitly on the verge of living in Massachusetts."

"Okay," I concede. "But we need to be—"

"Careful," she cuts me off. "Got it. I don't want to screw this up for you either. Let's try it with the two of us tomorrow morning before I bring my dad into it."

"It's three AM. I still need to program it and I'm working at the store tomorrow."

"Can't you get out of it? This is kind of a special situation."

"No. First it's my mom. Any *special situation* that involves my computer is not a *special situation*. And second, I already told her about the Saturn idea in the parking lot. It's happening. She posted it to the store's social media. And she's expecting that I'm going to be the one riding around on it."

"You?"

"That was my reaction."

"Then we'll call from the store," Lana says.

"I still need to program it."

"Did I mention Massachusetts?"

I stop my protests. At this point, I'm only wasting time.

BRECK: SIMULATION #37

My head is pressed against the table, and it is light. It was dark outside in the last moment I remember.

If there was an explosion, I do not recall it. There was no flash or heat. I was talking with Sam, then I closed my eyes.

"Sam?" I ask, as I lift my head and look to the other side of the table. He is not there.

I look around. He is nowhere.

My searching pauses as I become distracted by my own thinking. It is the same sensation as yesterday morning. Visions of places and things that do not fit into this town move in and out of my mind, like experiences that I never actually experienced. Like the penguins. And I cannot remember exactly what they were, only that it was very different than here.

Trying to understand this hurts my head. I have never before had a physical reaction to thinking about anything.

The waiter is no longer the same person as when it was dark. But I ask him nonetheless if he knows where Sam is. It's a red shirt response.

"I do not know. I never saw anyone with you."

I return my attention to the table and notice there is a device. I believe it is a phone. This is odd. I do not recall seeing this moments ago, and there is no one nearby who could have left it there. I must not have noticed it.

I don't know what to do with it, so I examine it and give Sam a few minutes to return to the table. He does not appear.

It is time to move forward. I stand. The phone remains on the table. It is not mine, so I leave it there.

As I move toward the street, my thoughts remain on the phone. I consider the possibilities and conclude that Sam probably left this to contact me. I return, put it in my pocket, and walk away.

LIV: SPRING BREAK 4.0

"What's wrong?" Mom asks. She's driving today.

"I didn't sleep much," I answer, without opening my eyes. I finished the programming changes twenty minutes ago and was hoping to catch a ten-minute nap on the ride to the store.

"Because of Lana? Todd told me she's moving."

"Sort of. I had to make some changes to the program—" I start to explain before I'm interrupted.

"You stayed up all night on the computer?"

"Half the night." I consider explaining how it's all connected and opt against it. It's too complicated, and it involves Breck.

The tick of the blinker counts the tense moments, appearing louder with each shake of Mom's head.

"I don't understand you. Your best friend is moving, you need to work today, and you decide to spend all night on the internet."

"Lana wanted time by herself," I explain.

"You're still working all day at the store."

"I'm planning on it."

"Good. Let's put three Saturns out front."

I nod and shut my eyes once more, leaving all conversation to the morning radio hosts. When we arrive at the store, Mom's instructions are brief, and my acknowledgment is even briefer.

"Got it."

Soon, I'm standing alone in the parking lot. Overnight clouds have cleared, leaving the faint smell of wet concrete wafting through the crisp spring air. If the lot had a thermostat, I wouldn't touch it. It's perfect.

The vacant row of Saturns lay upright, perfectly balanced without me. I stare at them as though they were the opponent in a different contest.

I am not coordinated.

Lana at least had the advantage of someone there to hold her. I roll the ball next to the curb, where there is a concrete pillar supporting the awning. The brick column is too thick to fully wrap my arms around, so I grasp the squared corners and gently place one foot, then the other on the Saturn.

Instantly, my feet slide away, until the gyroscope inside corrects, quickly thrusting it and me back into the curb and pillar. Rinse and repeat. If the goal is to attract attention, mission accomplished. If the goal is to humiliate me, mission accomplished. I look like someone humping a strip mall post.

With no safe way to exit, I eventually reach an impasse where I'm hugging the pillar on wobbly feet.

"Need a hand?"

I don't risk turning. I know the voice.

"Please."

Lana wraps an arm around my waist. As I lift one of my feet, the Saturn rockets away and I tumble backward into Lana, where she returns my favor from yesterday, giving me a soft landing as we both crash into the pavement below.

"You should stick with programming," Lana whimpers.

"Tell my mom."

I stand then help Lana to her feet.

"I got your text. Have you tried the voice app yet?" Lana asks, wrapping unpainted nails around the perimeter of her hair, checking to ensure it's still bunned.

"Nope. My cell is in quarantine. I was waiting for you. Is Sam still MIA?"

"I checked before I left, and he wasn't there. There's not a way to see him?"

"No. I don't think they were supposed to separate."

Her lips twist. "Is Breck even going to know what a phone is?"

"He wasn't, until I programmed it in," I answer. "Have you talked with your dad about this yet?"

"No. I figured we'd try it out first." She softly shrugs her shoulders. "And maybe it's a dumb idea anyway."

"You say this after I spent all night programming it?"

"Brainstorming, right? We don't have to do it. I don't want to mess up your contest," Lana offers, more apologetically than sincerely. We both know we're going to try this.

"I didn't program for hours and not get excited about it. I'm curious. But we can't help him."

"Understood."

"Really. We can't help. At all. I don't know how they monitor all of this, but I'm sure they do. No hints. Questions only."

"I wouldn't know what hints to give."

"I know. That's what most reassures me that you won't."

She feigns a smile and hands me her cell. We walk around the corner, out of view from the front of the store.

BRECK: SIMULATION #37.1

I am scanning the streets for Sam when the phone in my pocket begins to vibrate. I pull it out and unfold it. When I do, a faint voice speaks.

"Hello?"

"Hello," I respond, placing it to my ear.

"Who is this?"

"This is Breck. Who is this?" I ask.

"My name is Liv."

It is a higher pitched voice, which I believe is a female. I do not recall ever knowing anyone named Liv. I do not recognize her voice, either.

"Do I know you, Liv? I do not recognize your name."

"Right. You don't really know me. But I know who you are and that's why I called."

"Do you know where Sam is?" I ask.

"No."

"Are you calling to help me find the tunnel?" I ask.

"That would make a lot of sense. But no, I don't have new information for you."

I step into the entry space of a candy store, away from the noise of the street. A lone woman behind the counter weighs a bag of licorice, ignoring me the way that other red shirts do.

"Then why did you call me, Liv?"

"I wanted to talk?"

"Is that a question?" I ask.

"No, sorry. I meant it as a statement. I want to talk," she says.

"What do you want to talk about?" Before she responds, I think of another question. "Are you wearing a green or red shirt?"

"Ha! That's perfect. Of course you would ask me that!"

"I do not understand."

"I'm sorry. I'm saying that based on what you've seen, that's a reasonable question."

"So are you?"

"No. I'm wearing a gray shirt."

Her responses do not make sense. I wonder if I am supposed to seek further clues from this conversation.

"Do you know where the tunnel is?"

"I wish that I did. But even if I did, I wouldn't be able to tell you."

"Why would you not be able to tell me?"

Liv does not respond immediately. I give her time to answer, the same as I do with Sam.

"Wow, this is harder than I thought. I wasn't expecting all of your questions. I guess I should have," Liv says. I hear a separate voice in the background.

"Dude, ask him some questions!"

"Is that another person?" I ask.

"Yes, this is Lana," the other voice answers. "I'm Liv's friend. Can we talk about, like, what you're thinking?"

"I do not know how to answer that question. I think about many different things."

"What are you thinking right now?" Lana asks.

"That I do not know what I am supposed to learn from this conversation."

"What do you think you're supposed to learn?"

"That question does not make sense. If I thought I knew, I would know."

"That's awesome," Lana says.

"I don't understand your response."

"I mean, I like your answer. Okay. Another question. So, what's it like living in your world?"

"Lana! He doesn't—" The first girl I spoke with raises her voice, then the remainder of what she says is muffled.

While I wait for the two girls to finish, I consider the question, which again doesn't make much sense. *My world?* There is only this world. I wonder if they mean my town. As in, how is it to live in this town? I don't live in this town, but I am currently in this town, and I am living. This is a possible interpretation. I arrive at this conclusion when she begins speaking again.

"This is Liv again. What Lana means is what is it like in the town where you are?"

"That is how I understood the question," I reply.

"Good!"

"One description would be confusing," I answer. "But I believe that also describes the entire series of challenges, so perhaps a better description of the town specifically would be *reflective*."

"*Reflective?* What does that mean?" Liv asks.

"It means that everything mirrors some version of something else. Streets, stores, people. None of them look exactly the same, but they seem like rearranged pieces of one another."

"What do you think about that?"

"It's only an observation. I don't know what to think about it. What should I think about it?"

"Maybe you're not supposed . . . I mean, maybe you're not there yet, and you need more observations."

"Yes, that is my plan."

"And what—" Liv stops abruptly.

Someone screams. "What are you doing?!" It is not the voice of either one of the two girls. And again, I don't recognize it.

"We're just—" one of the girls answers. I believe it is Liv.

"Not doing the only thing you're supposed to be doing!" the voice shouts back.

"We have to go," one of them says to me with quick words.

She hangs up.

I do not know what to make of this experience, but I'm left again with the same unusual sensation that emerged ever since Sam and I left the room. *A preference.* I want them to call me again.

LIV: SPRING BREAK 4.1

"Hi, Lana. I need to talk to Liv for a moment. In private," Mom says, propping the front door open with a firm foot.

I pass Lana her phone back and follow Mom inside.

"You are in charge of the store right now. *You!* You're the person responsible for all of this. *I'm* the person who has been on the phone with a financial consultant for the last forty-five minutes." She cups her hands to her face, plugging the corners of her eyes. She draws in a deep breath. "I probably shouldn't tell you this, but I also know you were listening at the door yesterday, so it's not any big secret. You need to understand what's at stake here. The store needs to make money. If it doesn't, we're in trouble. *All* of us. I'm not asking you to fix it. I'm just telling you what is going on. So, when I ask you to put forth some effort to sell some toys, I'm not doing it to yank you out of your bedroom for the day. I need your help. Got it?"

I nod.

"Then why were you nowhere in sight and on the phone instead of doing what I asked? I had to go find you. This was your idea. You were the one who suggested it!"

I'm ashamed. I wanted to help today. That is why I suggested the original idea. I want her to know this. I decide to give my explanation a shot. Maybe she'll get it.

"We were talking with Breck, the character I programmed, because—"

"You were talking with a stupid computer instead of working?! I am going to lose my mind."

"It's because—"

"Stop. Please! It doesn't matter I have another call with another banker to try to figure this mess out. If Lana wants to stay, that's fine. Have her ride around."

She stomps toward the back office and disappears with her signature thunderous door closure. I walk back outside.

"I'm scratching off moving into your living room from my backup plans," Lana says, perched atop one of the Saturns.

I drop to the curb and don't answer. I want to scream. It's really freaking hard to tell someone why you're doing something when they always cut you off after six words. And that's not the worst part about this. Mom can be dramatic, but I think there's more to it this time. *How much trouble are we in?* I imagine myself sleeping on Todd's couch, in his apartment. My stomach sinks.

"Hey, are you okay?" Lana rolls in front of me.

"I don't think so."

"What did she say to you?"

I quickly recap, which isn't much different than what I overheard yesterday. But hearing it again from my own lips makes it feel more real, more threatening. Lana hops off the Saturn and sits next to me.

"What did she mean by trouble? Lose the store? Lose the house? Worse?"

"I don't know. She didn't get specific."

"You think she was exaggerating?" Lana asks.

"No. There's something different about her right now. I mean, you know her . . . she's freaking intense. But not usually like this."

Lana puts an arm around me and leans her head against mine. It reminds me of the day we met, the first day of third grade. I found her alone in a corner of the playground at recess. She had skinned her knee and was crying. I asked if she wanted help and she nodded. So I ran through all I could offer. *Get a Band-Aid? No. Get a teacher? No. Help her go back inside? No.* At last, I told her I didn't know how to help. Then she asked, "Can I have a hug?"

Lana knows I'd never ask for a hug. But it's what I need right now. Or at least my best friend's arm around my shoulder.

"Sometimes it sucks to be right," she says.

"Yeah. It's terrible. Sometimes I wish it were all code. I can fix that. I don't know what I can do to help here."

"We can start by trying to sell a few of these things. It'll at least make it better today." She stands and offers her hand to pull me up.

I grab a nearby Saturn and roll it toward Lana. "Help me climb on."

"I know something that'll make you feel better."

I pause, poised to hop. "What's that?"

"Before you kill yourself falling off that thing, can we talk about how cool that conversation with Breck was? He was like a person."

The last five minutes may be the longest stretch in the past six weeks that I have not thought at all about Breck. I miss talking about him already.

"Yeah, it felt pretty authentic," I admit.

"I thought he'd sound more like a robot."

"I like the voice I used. It almost feels natural."

"No, not just his accent. It was good, but he was still a little Siri-like. What I mean is the way he talked. The way he . . .thought. It didn't feel like we were talking to a computer. He asked more questions than we did, like he was actually curious."

Her reaction feels nearly as good as talking with him. As much as I've kept my chin up, a month of failures has taken a toll.

"He's programmed to learn," I say. I feel nearly as much satisfaction in her reaction as I did in talking with him. My smile would be far more than half-wide right now if my thoughts weren't torn. As much as I want to focus everything on Breck, my mom's warning won't leave my head.

"How many challenges are there?" Lana asks.

"Four."

"He's only made it through one, and he sounds like this. I changed my mind. I don't think this is a dumb idea anymore. We need to have my dad talk to him. He's going to love Breck." Lana slaps a firm palm on my shoulder, locking our arms together. "Now hop on and let's start selling these freaking things. One, two, three . . ."

BRECK: SIMULATION #37.2

I replay my memory of the phone conversation and try to assess what I can learn from it. I still can't think of anything. Perhaps it was another decoy intended to distract me.

I continue my plan, which is to find someone in a green shirt, then ignore their instructions. But I have no idea where to find this person, so I explore in random directions, without any pattern or destination.

This is not much different than yesterday with Sam. We merely explored, as I am doing now. But there is something different about doing this on my own. I would prefer that Sam was here with me. Not because he would help, but because I want his company. Not only is it still strange to have a preference, but it is also strange to have *this* preference. He did not listen to me yesterday, which prompted a different, unpleasant sensation.

As I pass streets without any sign of green shirts, I become consumed by wondering what these recent sensations are and what they mean. They are not physical feeling. If my hand were on fire, I would experience pain. This is similar, but without any physical cue. It is as if I have some kind of pain, but inside.

It is a feeling, I decide. But not in the way that I have ever defined this. I had understood a feeling on the inside as a synonym to an acknowledgment. For example, lonely was an acknowledgment that a person was alone. Or frustration was an acknowledgment that there was a barrier in the way of a goal.

These definitions are shifting.

Is this how others have always experienced these feelings? Why have I not? Or, am I changing beyond what others are? This seems unlikely, but so does opening a cabinet to unlock a door on the other side of a room.

I am hardly aware of anything I am passing. This immersion within my mind is too new, too consuming. It is in some ways intriguing and in other ways distressing, both of which I now define as far more than acknowledgments.

This lasts until something green catches my attention.

She stands on a corner in a long green dress, flapping in sporadic gusts of wind from a narrow corridor behind her.

"Do you know where the tunnel is," I ask.

"Of course. It is not far from here. Maybe a fifteen-minute walk. You will need to go down this street until," she continues with her instructions, which I ignore. They are as complicated as they have been with all other green-shirted people.

When she finishes, I ask, "Can you step to the side so that I can enter the alley behind you?"

"Why do you want to go there?"

"I believe you are lying," I tell her.

She smiles, then steps aside.

I proceed into the alley. The temperature drops. It is not cold, but cooler than the hot streets only a few yards away. It is not the breeze, but the area itself. I glide my hand along one of the walls. It is cool to the touch.

As I move farther inward, the temperature falls further. I sense I'm walking down a long ramp, until it ends at a door.

I open it and enter, finding a narrow stairwell leading farther down. I descend and it leads me to a dimly lit underground corridor.

Is this the tunnel?

There's only one direction to walk. My footsteps are the only thing I hear for the next ten minutes, until I encounter another stairwell. I ascend. With each step, the temperature climbs, until I find another door. I open it and emerge into an enclosed plaza with towering walls on all sides. Along three of the walls are dozens of doors. And along the wall opposite my door is a tunnel at least twenty feet high, leading into a mountain behind it.

I am the only person in the plaza.

LIV: SPRING BREAK 4.2

I survived the Saturn. Apparently, I am coordinated enough to ride it. Lana and I spent the morning zipping around and trying to attract attention. In Lana's words, we were "basically human inflatable tube people."

Between our riding and the posts online, we had plenty of visitors. As morning turned to afternoon, there was even a short line to try it. I stopped counting when we reached twelve people.

Lana left in the early afternoon and Mom came out to help. She gave me an I-told-you-so look, which was quickly thwarted when a man—graying and at least a decade older than my mom—asked her if we sold them online. She firmly said we do not.

Despite the number of visitors, the day was a flop as we sold just one Saturn. It was the customer's birthday, which also meant she got ten percent off.

I knock tentatively at the office door.

"It's open."

Mom is slumped over, staring at a spreadsheet with numbers too small to read. A bottle of wine and a wet glass linger at her side, amidst scattered papers.

"I tried today, Mom."

I'd never thought this was *the* solution, but I did believe it could be at least a step in the right direction. But all we did was turn Renaissance into a free amusement park.

"I know you did."

"What's going to happen?"

"Apparently nothing. Absolutely nothing." She grabs the empty glass and watches the last remaining drops slide across the bottom.

"Do you have access to the old website, the one where you tried to sell online?"

"Stop it with the website. What we have now works. I've updated all of the pictures too. If anyone wants to find us online, we're there."

"Maybe—" I start, as she narrows eyes away from the empty vessel and bores them into me. She knows where this is headed. I do too, but I have to try do something.

"Do you know what the definition of insanity is?" she asks.

"No."

"Trying the same thing over and over again and expecting a different result."

"That's why I want to try something different." I think of Breck. I'm essentially quoting what he told Sam. There's some warped milestone in there, but I'm too focused on this conversation to fully appreciate it.

"It's not different. We tried it. Why would anyone come to our little site to buy it online? And for more money. There's no reason to."

"But maybe it wasn't done the right way. That's what I'm saying."

"Well, that site has been gone for years, so I don't know."

"There are ways to find it online. I can look."

"The answer's not in a computer, Liv. Look around you. This is a store. There were people here today. Lots of them. We're not doing something right, but it's not online. It's here. We need to figure it out here. And if we don't, there's not going to be a *here*."

She waits in silence, giving me the chance to respond. I don't. The invitation is to argue—not debate.

"I'll close the store. If you can get a ride, you can go," she finishes. "Let's try setting tables up outside tomorrow. Maybe if we make more things visible." Her words fade without conviction.

I call Lana from the phone by the register.

"Are you kidding? I'm leaving now. I've been waiting for you to get home. I talked to Dad. He's in. Or he's at least willing to listen. I'll be there in ten."

I take a seat on the curb outside, watching clouds slowly shape-shift on the horizon, as if highlighting the temporary existence of each moment, reminding me that in a short period of time I could be without either my best friend, my home, or both.

Lana arrives before I think myself over the edge.

"How'd the rest of the day go?" she asks as I enter.

"Not great. Can I borrow your cell?"

She grabs it from the center console and holds it in front of her face to unlock it. "Sure. Why?"

"Do you think selling online would help?" I ask.

"I don't know. Why would someone go there instead of Amazon?"

"To support a local business?"

"Sounds like that didn't help today," she says, to which I nod. "Still, it wouldn't hurt. It's not like you'd sell less."

I Google and scroll as she talks. Got it. LongAgo.org. I knew there was a place that stored old website data. I find the old Renaissance site. Not everything loads right, but it's enough to confirm what I remember; it was terrible. There's no order to the content, it's full of annoying features like *see price when added to cart*, and it looks only slightly more appealing than an Excel doc.

"Are you going to build her a new site?"

"It's a thought."

BRECK: SIMULATION #37.3

I check the door behind me. It is locked. I check two of the other doors and they are also locked.

I walk to the middle of the plaza where I can see directly into the tunnel. The other side is not visible. There are no lights on the walls. There is nothing, other than an opening into darkness.

I should start immediately, but again, there is an unfamiliar sensation inside of me. *A feeling?* I know I need to go inside, but not knowing what is in there prompts me to hesitate. It is not logical. This is the path toward the goal. But this sensation does not appear to originate from thinking. It comes from elsewhere.

I would prefer Sam being here with me. I would prefer not to do this alone. I would prefer to be able to see what is in the tunnel. *Is this fear?*

The phone in my pocket vibrates. With it comes a more sudden surge of this strange state I am experiencing. My pulse quickens as I reach for the device and place it to my ear.

"Hello?" says a voice.

"Hello. Is this Liv?"

"Yes, and I'm also with Lana and her father, Doctor Owens."

"Wayne Owens," a deeper voice says. "You can call me Wayne."

"Do you each have a phone?" I ask.

"We have you on speaker," one of female voices says. I can't tell whose voice it is.

"I don't know what that means."

"It means that we can all talk to you at the same time with one phone," the female voice says.

"Okay," I answer.

"What are you doing right now?"

"I'm standing in a plaza looking at the tunnel."

"How did you find the tunnel?"

I explain my observations about those who wear green and red shirts, my conclusions from this, and how this led me here.

"Are you about to go in?"

"Yes," I answer, then ask my own question. "Who are you?"

"We just told you."

"Yes, I remember. What I mean to ask is who are you in relation to what I'm doing? I still do not understand why you are calling me."

"We're calling you to talk," the female voice says.

"That is what you said when we last spoke. To talk about what?"

"We want to know more about you."

"And I want to know more about you," I say, stepping into the shade cast by one of the plaza walls.

"That seems fair," Wayne says. "How about this? We get to ask you two questions and you get to ask us two questions. Does that work?"

"Yes."

The three talk in hushed voices among themselves. I can only hear fragments of their discussion. "You'll ask smarter questions . . . okay . . . we'll split . . . remember, he can't . . . and no suggestions."

I do not know what meaning to take from anything they are saying. It only raises more questions. What are they not telling me and why?

"Who asks first?" I ask.

"You can. We'll go one question at a time," Wayne answers.

"Where are you?" I ask.

"The living room of my house," Wayne says.

"Where is the house?"

"That is two questions," Wayne says.

"You did not give a complete answer to the original question," I say.

"Dang. He's got some attitude," one of the girls says softly in the background. I think it is Lana. I am still learning the difference between the voices of the two girls.

Again they speak softly to each other.

"We're a long way away from you," Wayne finally answers. "In a different city. You've never been here before."

"How do you know that?" I ask.

"That's another question. It's our turn."

"This conversation is difficult," I comment. As I say this, I consider my other conversations recently. Speaking with Sam is also challenging. So is speaking with the green- and red-shirted people. *Is this how conversation has always been?* I think back to life before this challenge, but I can't recall specific conversations. *How can this be?* I remember things, events, people, but they are all vague memories lacking detail.

"What makes it difficult?" Wayne asks. His voice is louder, as though he moved closer to the phone.

"The answers only prompt more questions."

"That makes sense," Wayne says. "Well, here is my question."

"Didn't you ask a question already?" I ask.

"Ha!" One of the girls blurt in the background.

"Shhhh!" The other says.

"That's funny. And fair," Wayne says. "I was responding to your comment. I do have a real question if you're open to hearing it. We did let you ask a follow-up question about my house."

"That is true. And fair, as you said. Ask your question," I tell him.

"Why are you talking with us right now? Not just because we called you, but what keeps you from hanging up the phone and walking through the tunnel?"

I pause to consider this. *Why am I talking to them?*

"I don't understand the goal of this discussion," I say. "But, I have learned enough about this challenge to know that I don't know what I don't know. Unplanned exploration and observation seem important to moving forward. I had to try everything in the room to understand that the cabinet and door were connected. I had to wander streets aimlessly to find people in green shirts. Perhaps this is another form of wandering."

When I finish, again I hear them whisper among themselves. The only thing I can clearly hear from this is, "I told you!"

"It is my question now," I say. "Where is Sam?"

"I don't know," says one of the girl voices.

I consider this response along with other observations from this conversation. "Do you not know, or can you not tell me?"

"Both. There are some questions we can't answer, but we do not know where Sam is." I believe this is Liv's voice. Her words are more enunciated and evenly metered than Lana, and her pitch is slightly higher.

"Why are there questions you can't answer?"

"We can't help you with your challenges."

"Then why did you call me?"

"I guess you could say that we're observing also."

"Do you work for the people who created this challenge?"

"You're past your two questions, but yes, in a way, you could say that. Now, it's our turn to ask. What do you think of Sam?"

"He is difficult to understand. He does not listen well. He does what he wants, and it is often not the same thing that I am thinking. Also, the way I think about him is changing."

"What do you mean?" Liv asks.

"Before we left the room, I do not recall ever questioning whether Sam and I were different. I do not recall thinking about him at all. I was focused on the room. I do not know how to describe this well, but I am now focused on more than the challenge itself. I am also focused on Sam, and on me. My interactions with Sam are among many experiences now that I do not completely understand."

"Thank you, Breck," Wayne says. "Unfortunately, we have to go now. Good luck on your challenge."

"Will I talk with you again?"

"Yes!" Lana says.

"When?"

"I don't know, but we'll call you."

They hang up before I have an opportunity to respond.

LIV: SPRING BREAK 4.3

"I'm sorry for ending that abruptly. I have another call soon and I wanted to make sure we had a few minutes to talk before that," Doctor O says to the two of us, clustered across from him, leaning against each other in the V of a weathered loveseat.

I'm blown away. How has Breck made it through the first part of the second challenge already? He only cleared the first one this morning. He could actually do this by Friday.

I am so going to light up the chat boards.

For the moment, Renaissance isn't even close to top of mind.

"Liv, wow, that's impressive. Do you know what the Turing test is?" Doctor O asks.

"Yep."

"I'd have to say that Breck passes that test, for me at least." He grins.

"Can you back up? I don't know what the Turing test is," Lana says.

"Fair. I didn't either, but I did some quick Googling about AI when you asked me to talk to Breck," Doctor O says. "Back in the fifties when computers were being developed, they were trying to figure out how to test the limits of AI. A guy named Alan Turing came up with an idea for a test. If you could talk with a computer and a human, and you couldn't tell which was which, then the computer must be intelligent."

"So, he's intelligent? I told you so, Dad," Lana says.

"You did. And he at least passes that test. I mean, I told him *good luck,* because it seemed like the right thing to say."

That's funny. And true! I didn't even think anything of it when he said it.

"And there's another thing that I thought was interesting," Doctor O continues. "He seemed to understand the concept of reciprocity. When someone does something for us, we feel compelled to do something back for them. This is a very human trait, and Breck showed this with the exchange of questions. We allowed him to ask more than one, and when we pointed this out to him, he made a similar concession. Did you program that directly into him, Liv?"

"Meaning, is there a line of code that tells him to act with reciprocity?" I ask.

"I don't really understand programming, but that's the gist of it. You said he learns. Did he figure that out on his own, or is it a way that he's told to act?"

"There aren't specific instructions for that. So, I suppose he learned it."

"Fascinating," Doctor O answers.

Hell yeah. I've never had someone call anything I've coded *fascinating.*

"So, what does that mean?" Lana asks, her voice brimming with hope.

"It means that Liv should be proud of what she's done."

"Do you think he'd be worth . . . studying?" Lana asks, her voice uncharacteristically sheepish.

"I'm not tracking your question."

"I mean, is this something that you would consider studying?"

Lana looks to me for support. I realize my program is at the center of this conversation, but I don't believe that's where my mouth should be. I avoid her eyes.

"Okay." Doctor O leans back in his chair, dropping his leg to the floor and tilting his head back, exposing his half-receding hairline to the light overhead. The reflection beams toward me as though it were from an actual bulb shining on his head. "I think I'm understanding things a little better now. You didn't ask me to talk to Breck just so you could hear my thoughts."

"Not exactly," Lana admits.

"So," he says, "to connect the dots here, how would my studying this keep us here, instead of moving? Are you job hunting for me?"

"No. Not much. Or nothing specific. I just thought that . . . well, you lost funding. That's why we're moving, because we're going somewhere that has money for what you currently do. But if you think about Breck, it's kind of similar to what you're studying. He's like a kid. He's learning new things, trying to understand what's happening, dealing with challenges."

Doctor O glances down, aiming a regretful expression toward the carpet. He's not as expressive as his daughter, but they are clearly related. He takes a deep breath, ready to interject.

"Hear me out. Please," Lana continues, her shoulder leaning into mine. "I did some Googling. AI psychology is a new area and there's all kinds of interest in it and money being thrown at it. And you said it yourself, this is fascinating. I'm not saying that you study Breck, but if it's interesting, maybe you could see if there's a way to study this where you are. Here. Not in Massachusetts. Rice has AI classes."

Lana clutches the top of my hand next to hers on the sofa.

"There's a lot to respond to there," Doctor O begins with his typical calm demeanor. "First, I study development in children. Humans. Not *computers*. Breck is certainly remarkable, but he's not human."

"But he passed the Turing test, and he shows reciprocity."

"The Turing test is how they gauged how smart a computer was last century. If you do a customer service chat today, you're probably talking with a computer. Or any of the other countless AI chats out there. I'm not the expert on them, but I think they all pass the Turing test." He turns to me. "I'm sorry, Liv. I'm not trying to downplay this. Real intelligence is more than mimicking, or illusion. And as for reciprocity, I do think that's impressive, especially if Breck truly *learned* it, but it's not a very complex idea—if you do something for me, I should do something for you."

Lana opens her mouth to speak, but her dad continues. "I heard you out. Please do the same for me. Reciprocity?" he says with a quirky twitch of his brow that reminds me of Lana. "I'd need to confirm this, but I think the interest in AI psychology is how *people* interact with it, not how AI itself develops or thinks. I'm not trying to dismiss anything Liv did. I think it's amazing. But it's a computer. There's no . . . psychology to it."

Lana nudges me to speak. I want so badly to support her. This is crushing me as much as Lana is crushing my hand. But Doctor O is right. As amazing as Breck is, he's code. He's a program. If you dig deeper, he's only 1's and 0's. He's learning how to meet the goals he's been programmed to achieve.

I'm torn between my agreement, my own pride in Breck, my desire to be a good friend, and my own stake in Lana not moving away.

"He is learning really quickly," I say, trying to find some kind of middle ground.

"It's not about the speed. It's about what he is. Or, what he isn't," Doctor O retorts.

Lana looks at me, but I don't know what to add.

"Maybe we can all talk with Breck later in the week and see where this goes," Doctor O breaks the silence.

"Tomorrow," Liv says. "I know you don't think speed matters, but I want you to see how quickly he's changing."

"I'm happy to do that. I think this is cool and I'm curious to see where it goes. But—" He stumbles for a moment, uncharacteristically at a loss for words. "My job . . . what I study . . . is people. Developmental psychology. As intricate as Breck is, I promise you that we are thousands of times more complex. And that's what I'm interested in. Understanding and helping people. Mostly young people."

Lana releases my hand and wipes the sleeve of her shirt across her eyes. The hint of a sniffle follows.

"I have to go take that call. Lana, let's talk more later. I know this isn't what you want."

"You're right. It isn't," she answers flatly.

I try to put my arm around her, but she swats it off.

"And that's why we should talk more about it," he answers, mirroring her tone as he walks away.

As soon as he is gone, Lana gets up and turns to me. "He's your creation, and you couldn't stand up for him."

And suddenly, I'm whiplashed and alone in Lana's living room.

BRECK: SIMULATION #37.4

I have been walking for ten minutes in the dark. The light from the tunnel entrance behind me provides only enough illumination to see where to step. Each footfall on the gravel beneath me echoes, producing metered acoustic feedback to my walk.

In the distance, a faint light appears, and along with it the outline of a figure.

"Sam?" My voice reverberates around me.

"Yes."

Seeing him prompts a feeling—a pleasurable one. *Happy*, if I had to name it. I walk faster.

As I approach, he is staring at a wall that blocks the tunnel. Within this wall are two doors on opposite sides, each with a small window through which the tunnel exit is visible. Between these two larger doors, there are more than a hundred smaller cabinet doors that line the middle of the wall; half are blue and half are yellow.

"It is good to see you," I pronounce, now that I am closer.

"There are fifty-three cabinets of each color. All are empty. Both doors are locked." He gestures toward the wall.

"Did you hear what I said?"

"Yes."

Sam's expression is blank, void of evidence that he is experiencing what I am feeling.

Why is his reaction important to me? The information he is telling me is of more value. It is helpful and related to advancing toward the goal. His reaction is irrelevant. However, I want to understand this.

"Have you been waiting for me?" I ask.

"Yes," he answers. "It has not been possible yet to get through these doors."

"So, you need to wait because you can't move forward?"

"Yes," he says.

"Why did you leave me?"

"You were not moving."

"I recall closing my eyes. I was with you at night. Then it was the next day."

"Yes, you stopped moving."

"This has happened twice now. I don't know what it is," I say.

He doesn't respond.

"So why did you leave? Did you think I was dead again?" I ask.

"It was not clear."

"But I wasn't dead the last time."

"That is why it was not clear," he answers. "But you were not moving, and it was time to go forward."

"You're not understanding what I'm saying. I thought we are doing this together," I say.

"That is correct. We are back together now. But you were not moving before, so we could not make progress together."

"But we are no further along now than if we had stayed together."

"So it made no difference," Sam concludes, affirming my sense that we are indeed different, and emphasizing how significant this difference may be.

Another question emerges from this. If I am different from Sam, does this make me unique compared to only him, or compared to everyone else?

I can't recall ever questioning this before. The happiness I felt in seeing Sam is replaced by something negative. I no longer want to think about this or discuss it.

"Tell me about the wall," I say.

"There is one key," which he holds up to show me. "It fits in both doors but opens neither. Opening the cabinets does not unlock the door. The windows will not break."

I walk to one of the doors and inspect it. There are no hinges. The doors appear to slide in and out of the wall. I grab a door handle and try to slide it, but it will not move. As I do this, I peer through the small, square window at eye level. The tunnel extends about ten feet beyond the wall, where it abruptly ends. From the cliff's edge of the tunnel, there is a drop into a vast valley thousands of feet below. There is one lone cable affixed to the end of the tunnel and a small cart attached. The cable leads down toward the valley farther than I can see.

I step back to survey the wall once more.

While I am having trouble understanding Sam's reactions, I can understand his thinking prior to my arrival. Based on what we have experienced, I would have done the same things he described.

"Have you tried to open each of the cabinets?"

"Yes, fourteen times."

Revision. I would have done the same things, but not fourteen times. It is time to try something new.

"Have you tried to open all of the yellow cabinets or all of the blue cabinets together?"

"No. That is a good idea."

He hustles to the wall and begins to open blue cabinets.

"I did not mean to start doing it right away. I was simply mentioning an idea," I say.

"And it is a good one, so it should be done," he answers, while swinging two cabinet doors open, one with each hand.

"Perhaps there are better ideas," I say.

"Like what?" he asks with his back turned, continuing his efforts.

"I don't know. I'm simply talking as I am thinking."

"And we should do this as you are thinking."

I join him until the blue cabinets are all open. Sam then inserts the key into the first door and tugs. It doesn't budge. He repeats it on the second door, which is also unsuccessful.

We repeat the same exercise with the yellow cabinets and the doors remain locked.

I back away from the wall and stare at it.

"What if it is a combination of cabinets? Maybe one yellow and one blue?"

Again, I'm only stating ideas, but Sam acts on them. This time, I don't join. I continue to think.

With fifty-three of each color, there are 2,809 distinct combinations. However, this only represents sets of one blue and one yellow cabinet. What if the correct combination is two cabinets of the same color? Or, what if the combination is more than two cabinets? Without knowing the parameters, there are billions of possible combinations. Even if we could test a new combination every few seconds, we would likely be here for years.

There are too many cabinets.

Like the myriads of streets and alleys. Like red shirts.

I think back to what these were. *Distractions.*

What if these cabinets are the same? What else have we not tried? What do we have fewer of?

The key.

"Can you show me the key?" I ask.

Sam hands me a small silver key.

I walk to the door on the right side of the tunnel and insert the key, much like Sam had done moments before. It slides inside smoothly and turns, as if it belongs. but the door does not move.

I walk to the door on the other side of the tunnel. The results are the same.

Unable to wait for me to finish, Sam opens and closes more cabinets. It is an unmethodical effort.

Until these past few days, I would have done the same. *Why am I critiquing his approach now when I did not do so before?*

Am I truly different now than I was only days ago?

Why do my thoughts continue to circle back to this question?

I find no answers, but in watching Sam I do come to one conclusion; he needs me.

There is a feeling that accompanies this thought. I don't have a name for it, except that I think of Sam as a friend. No, that's not exactly right. I *feel* Sam as a friend. And I have never experienced a friendship in this way.

Sam needs me.

It feels good to think this.

I say it several times over in my head, both enjoying and questioning the sensation at the same time.

Wait.

Sam needs me.

I think back to his response to my question; he was waiting because he was *unable to move forward.*

Sam needs me to move forward.

Again, I assess the wall and its many features with this thought in mind.

"I have an idea. Go to the other door," I say as I move toward one of the doors.

He follows my instruction.

I insert the key into the door in front of me, then turn it. I look at Sam, some thirty feet away.

"Now, try to open that door," I say.

Sam does. The door effortlessly slides open.

He quickly steps through to the other side.

But the victory is brief. As I let go of the key to join him, it turns back on its own and the other door shuts once more, sealing me on the inner side of the wall, again separated from Sam.

I run to the door where Sam entered and attempt to move the handle in any direction possible. My efforts yield no results. I dart between the two doors, trying to open the passage on my own, but I am unable.

This makes no sense. Why would we need to accomplish something together so that we would once again be separated?

I peer through the window at Sam who moves toward me doing the same. His nose is so close it's nearly touching mine.

"Can you open the doors from your side?" I ask, unsure if he can even hear me.

"No," he says, his voice far more distant than inches away. "There are no handles on this side, and they will not slide."

"Is there anything on the wall on your side?"

"No, there is nothing other than the two doors."

I try to consider new ideas, but I can think of none.

"Do you have any ideas?" Sam asks.

"No," I answer. I do not ask the same question of him.

"Maybe someone else will come to help you pass through," he says.

"Maybe."

He turns around and walks toward the small cart at the edge of the cliff. He inspects it while I do the same through the door window. It is a simple design—a square cart, about five feet deep with a slender gate. Sam opens the gate, places a foot inside, then one more, until only his shoulders and head are visible. He grasps one of the four bars, which extend from each corner, bending to connect in the middle beneath a small clasp attached to the cable.

He appears ready to descend. Then abruptly, he steps out of the cart and returns to the window.

"We cannot go forward together right now," he says, his face covering most of the narrow glass pane.

Silhouetted by the clear sky beyond the tunnel entry, his blue eyes appear like holes in his head. I've noticed this once before, when his back was to the door in the room where we started. I try to recall what I felt at that moment, but I don't recall feeling anything. It was only an observation. Now, it is as if I am looking into him, searching for something. A way to better understand him.

All he wants to do is go forward. That's it. And I know this urge. I experienced it for so long, and I still do, but it is clouded by so many competing compulsions.

My response does not matter. He will leave regardless. But I will let him know that this is a decision I support, even if that doesn't matter to him.

"You should go. We are supposed to move forward, toward the goal."

He nods, and within seconds he is back in the cart. He secures the gate, and the cart begins to slide, whisking him down the cable.

As soon as this happens, both of the doors slide open.

I walk to the cliff's edge, alone, as Sam slips into the distance.

LIV: SPRING BREAK 4.4

Mom's car isn't in the driveway. I find Todd sitting alone in our living room, watching a baseball game. He is sipping a beer with socked feet crossed on the coffee table.

I'd usually offer a polite wave then disappear, but tonight is not my average night. I don't feel like sitting alone and I'm on the outs with everyone. Almost everyone.

I take a seat in the uncommitted front half of the La-Z-Boy across from him. He gives me a puzzled look and lowers the volume of the game.

"What's up?"

"I think I just want some uncomplicated company," I say.

Todd raises an acknowledging hand with a warm smirk. "You've found your guy. Want to watch the game or do you want to talk?"

I stare across the coffee table at him in his weathered jeans, stained T-shirt, and the physique of someone who puts too much emphasis on his body. It's easy to underestimate him. I still do it even though I know better. He comes across as such a simple person—beer plus baseball, and he's happy. He's a glassy pond. Sure, Mom can rile him up, but he generally lands on his happy-go-lucky feet. But beneath the surface, he thinks big. He may be watching baseball, but my guess is that he's studying it.

"I don't know," I answer.

"That usually means talk."

I nod, but I don't know where to begin. Everything is so out of control now, and it's all connected. And, ugh, it's also best friend stuff. Does Todd *do* girly?

"Okay. I'm a good guesser so I'll start. Is it about Lana or your mom?"

"Both."

"So, talk."

I'm not sure that I really want to do this with Todd. I mean, he's my mom's boyfriend; he shouldn't know me this well. But I've pissed off all the people I normally ask for advice. I try to give him one last out. "I don't know exactly where to begin."

"Start messy." He tosses the remote to his side, his full attention on me.

So I do. I tell him everything, even the bit about the store's financial troubles, which, based on his look, he already knows, *and* I'm definitely not supposed to know about. The more I talk, the more I realize how much danger the store—and we—might be in.

I finish. We sit in silence for a few seconds until he begins wagging his head in a small, disbelieving circle.

"I swear, sometimes you channel me when I was your age. You're trying to solve everything that comes your way."

"What's wrong with that?"

"What have you solved so far?"

"Well, the other option is to do nothing."

He covers a chuckle. "I'm only laughing because I feel like I'm talking to me twenty years ago. Liv, it's not binary. Inaction isn't apathy. It can be, but there's nothing apathetic about you. Sometimes you have to turn off that thinking part of your brain that's always racing at a hundred miles an hour and *feel* what other people are going through."

"What does that solve?"

"You've got to listen first before you know what to fix. And then, it's the strangest damn thing, but sometimes just being there fixes it. It just happens. I mean, not with cars or computers, but with people at least. Hell, I wish sometimes that people were like cars. It'd be a lot easier to understand them."

"I hear you," I say.

"But they're not." He draws in a deep breath and leans toward me. "Don't you wish your mom really got you . . . truly understood you, what you want, and why?"

I nod like he's climbed in my head and reading my thoughts. I'm all ears.

"Guess what? She feels the same way. Lead with that. People are like mirrors, Liv. Get her, and she'll try to get you."

"But the problem is the store."

"Is it? Trust me, I know that's *a* problem. But is it *the* problem? Take a step back."

I'm not following, and from his expression he can tell.

"I'm going to ask an obvious question in painfully rhetorical way. What's more important—your relationship with your mom or a toy store?"

"But they're connected," I say. "She's pissed off all the time because of the store, which kind of makes it tough to get along with her."

"Fair. But better conversations happen on a lifeboat than a cruise ship. Use the store to work on the bigger issue—you and her. Listen to more than what your mom is saying. She doesn't want an online business, even if it's the most successful virtual toy store on the planet. There's no joy in that for her." He laughs. "I think sometimes we exist just to piss off our parents. My parents were park rangers. I can't tell you how many hikes I've been on, or how many times I've had beetle tracks or bobcat scat or some kind of moss pointed out to me. They were quiet, nature-loving people. If a box of granola had a kid, that should be me. But I turned sixteen and bought an old, used, loud Camaro. They didn't understand it. I took the muffler off and they nearly disowned me. Why would I want something so obnoxious, so fast, so unlike anything they would ever want to own or be around? Who the hell knows? Maybe to be different than them. It wasn't intentional. I just loved it."

"So, what does that mean?"

"Do you know what I did?"

I shake my head.

"I eventually went too fast and wrecked the damn thing. I wrapped it around a tree. Cosmic justice, I suppose. I didn't have the money to fix it and by then, I was a little older and wiser, starting to listen to more than what was in my own head. So, I stripped it, had the body dragged into the woods, and I planted a wildflower garden in it. I swear it is the weirdest f'n thing you'll ever find in nowhere East Texas. And I'm pretty sure my parents hated it at first, but they eventually got it. Between us, there was a middle. It was my attempt to honor what each of us love. They give tours there now. Do you hear what I'm saying?"

"I think so," I say, as cheers erupt from the game on TV.

"Grand slam. What do you expect when you walk the pitcher," Todd says, then turns back toward me. "Try feeling—*really feeling*—what your mom and Lana are going through. Don't solve. Just feel. Try to understand them. Give it a day or two. What have you got to lose? Is anything else you've tried working?"

"Not really." I hate where this conversation landed, but I also appreciate it.

"And as for your computer guy, well, he sounds like more of a distraction right now than a problem. I'd say enjoy the distraction. You've earned it. You're going to win that damn contest, and I'm proud as hell of you, kid."

◆ ✜ ◆

I turned the computer off an hour ago. I'm trying something new—doing nothing. I'm lying on my bed reflecting on my conversation with Todd. The more I sit with it, the more it makes sense. Maybe this is something I need to *feel* my way through more than *think* my way through. This isn't natural for me. It's wishy-washy. But it is using a different approach to get a different result, which feels scientific enough to try.

I grab a sheet of paper from the desk to firm my commitment.

For twenty-four hours, I will listen and resolve nothing.

My words stare back at me, daring me to test them. I'm up for the challenge.

"Hey," I say into the phone as Lana answers, inviting her to take the conversation wherever she wants to.

"Hey."

Silence.

"My curtains are open," I add.

The fabric on her window parts. A sliver of light appears and is eclipsed as her face pokes through. "I'm mad at you."

"I know."

"You didn't support me. All you had to do was agree with how awesome Breck was, which isn't a big ask. And you didn't."

I don't respond other than a bob of my head.

"And," she continues, "maybe it wouldn't have made a difference. I know this isn't exactly a bulletproof plan. It's a longshot. But it's something. It's hope. Or maybe it's just us finally doing something where you are trying to help me, not the other way around, and you weren't there. You were doing you. Being *rational* instead of being a friend."

I feel terrible. This may be why I act more and listen less. It's uncomfortable.

"I'm sorry."

"That's it?"

"I'm trying to listen more."

"You decide to do this two months before I move away?" She cracks a small smile while sliding the remainder of her body in front of the curtains.

"Do you want to take a walk?" I ask.

"Not really."

"What do you want to do?" I ask.

Her face contorts in thought, but she doesn't answer.

"Do you want to talk about one of your books?" I ask.

"Just freakin' stop. We both know what we're going to do. This is the longest you've been able to not talk about Breck for five weeks, and I'm delusional enough to still believe in my plan. He's already passed one of the challenges and he's halfway through the next. He's moving quickly and we need to keep up."

"Actually, he's pretty close to fully passing the second."

"What? Sweet Baby J. There are only four."

I suppress a gloating smile. Mostly. Then I tell her about the wall. "He's stalled now, waiting on something."

"So, like I was saying, we're going to talk with Breck before he finishes this thing, and you win your internship, and become famous, and forget about little people like me, and I'm forced to figure out how to not move to Massachusetts on my own. But I'm leading it this time. I know the rules. No help. I'll be there in two." She peers down toward Todd's car in the driveway between us. "Make that three. I'm going to be a little delayed going up your stairs."

◆ ✣ ◆

"Hi, Breck."

"Hello, Lana," he answers.

"You recognized my voice?" she asks.

"It is different from Liv's. Is she there also?"

"Right here beside me. We'd like to ask you more questions."

"Okay Lana."

"How would you describe yourself?"

"I am exactly six feet tall. I have green eyes. I weigh—"

"No," she cuts him off. "That's not what I meant. I mean, how would you describe your . . ." she looks at me, uncertain of the word to use. ". . . personality?"

"I am not certain about the answer right now because I am changing. I think the word that best describes me at present is *curious*."

Lana leans her already slanted frame closer toward the phone. I'm on her heels. "How are you changing?"

"I am thinking differently."

"In what way?"

"In many ways. I do not think the same way as Sam now. I have more capacity for ideas. I see things in a way that I did not see—or understand—before. I also question everything. I never questioned anything before."

"How are you different than Sam?"

"I believe I see things he does not see. I experience things he does not experience. I react in ways that he does not react." He pauses. "I have a question. Do you feel like you are different from other people?"

Lana turns to me with a floored expression, like I have the right answer or some explanation for this. I don't. I'm as dumbstruck as she is. I'm the one who programmed him and every time he speaks, I have to remind myself that he's a machine that is only reflecting his programming, my programming. But his conversation feels so natural that my gut reaction is to treat it like we're chatting with another person, like some other kid from down the block, one of those hyper-chatty first graders. I know there are tons of AIs out there that are very conversational, but there's something different about the way he's doing it. He seems more earnest.

"I know that I'm different from most people," Lana answers. "And don't get me started about Liv."

"What does that mean?" Breck asks.

"It was a joke. It means that we're both . . . very different."

"How?"

"Lana is great at talking with people," I jump in. "She's a quick thinker. She's creative. She's funny. She's generous. She's the most expressive person in the world—our world—the one we're all in." I stumble. "And she's crazy loyal."

"And Liv," Lana says, without offering any gap for Breck to respond, "is also a lot of what she described—generous and funny and loyal, but she's also my opposite in the best of ways. I'm hyper and reactive. She's calm. I'm messy. She's the most organized person I know. I'm easily distracted. She's laser focused. And we're best friends." She extends an arm and wraps it around me. For an instant, I forget about the conversation with Breck and all that we're trying to accomplish. I succumb to the feeling of this moment. A small, happy tear cascades toward my chin, racing a drop stalled on Lana's high cheek.

"Opposites attract, Breck," Lana continues. "Maybe that's why you and Sam are together."

"We do seem to be opposites," Breck says.

"You're opposites in the best of ways," I add.

"Have you ever spoken with Sam?" Breck asks.

"No."

"Then how do you know that?"

"I just do," I answer on my heels.

"What does that mean?"

"It . . . it . . . it means—" Cornered, I struggle to think of an easy explanation, but can't. "I don't think you'd understand."

He doesn't respond. Vacant seconds drift between us.

"Breck?"

"I am here."

"Can we go back to asking you questions? I have a ton of them," Lana says.

"If you feel like I'm able to understand them."

Was that sarcasm? It can't be.

"What do you mean by that?" I ask.

"It means that you seem to doubt my ability to understand what you are saying."

If I didn't know better, I would say that I offended Breck, which is impossible.

"Can you describe to me what is going on inside of your head right now?" Lana asks.

"Why?"

"Because I'm curious too," she answers.

"I'm wondering why I don't know who you are," he answers.

"My name is Lana."

"But who are you? How do you know me when I don't know you? How do you know about Sam when you have never spoken with him? And why do you think that I won't understand something if you tell me?"

"I . . . I . . ." Lana looks at me for answers, or reassurance. "There are some things that we can't say."

"Why?" he asks.

"We don't have a good answer," I explain.

"So, what do you do? What do you know? What can you tell me?"

"We're really only interested in learning more about you. I guess that's our job—Breck experience investigators."

"Okay. It appears that this is simply another element of this challenge that is confusing."

"So, when you say *confusing*, what do you mean by that?" Lana asks, pulling the question nearly right out of my head.

"It means I can't understand it."

"Yes, but what is it like for you to experience something confusing?"

"It can be frustrating."

"And frustrating in what way?" she asks.

"It is the feeling of trying to achieve a goal but not being able to accomplish it."

"The feeling?"

"Yes."

"Can you describe what feelings are to you?" Lana asks, slowly, deliberately.

"I would describe them differently now than if you had asked me the same question several days ago. They have changed since I began this challenge."

Lana looks like she's about to jump out of her seat. I'm excited too, but I also know we'll ultimately have a different take on this. I'm open to a lot of what Breck might be, but being sentient is preposterous. I'm a good programmer, but I'm not that good. There has to be some other explanation. Maybe this is just Turing on steroids.

"How?" Lana asks.

"It is difficult to explain. Feelings used to be thoughts, about which I had no preference. If I were by myself, I might acknowledge that I was alone, but I did not prefer to be with anybody. Now I *prefer* things, and these preferences are different than thoughts. I cannot control them. Not having what I prefer to have is unpleasant. It is a sensation somewhere within me that extends beyond thoughts. Do you have feelings in this way?"

Lana's jaw drops.

"Yes," she says. "Yes. Yes!"

"It's nice to know that someone else is like me. Sam does not appear to have these feelings. And I don't recall thinking about feelings or talking about them in this way with anyone else before the contest."

Lana, still in awe, mouths, *"He has memories from before?"*

I don't know that I would call them memories as much as basic background information that I added on a whim without much detail. I was hoping that having something in the past might give him something to contrast current experiences. I mouth back, *"Programmed."*

She cocks her head as if this is an intriguing twist, but her phone buzzes before she can respond. She looks down at it, then through my window. Her father stands where she normally does, waving her to come toward him.

"I have to go," Lana says to both Breck and me. "Dad wants to talk. And we've got plenty to discuss. But this . . . this whole conversation is—" She looks for the right word, then bails on it. "Breck, keep the phone on you tomorrow. We're definitely calling you again with my dad."

"Are we done talking now?" Breck asks.

Lana looks at me to answer. I'm conflicted. It's interesting as hell, but these Q&A sessions were supposed to be a controlled experiment. They're getting out of control. We're impacting Breck's path, and the contest still matters. A lot. Especially if Lana moves away. There's no way I can spend the summer here alone with Mom.

If Breck is really further along than any other character, then somewhere, somehow, Big Brother is out there watching, and we're close to bending the rules.

"I think so. We could all use some time to think. We'll talk to you tomorrow," I say.

As I hang up, Lana blurts, "Holy shit. He has feelings, Liv!"

There is a delicate balance here, between empathy and science, between supporting a friend and being objective about what we heard, between wishful thinking and probable explanation.

"He definitely seemed to be feeling."

"What do you mean?" Lana looks at me as if I had told her that the gray walls of my bedroom were yellow.

I don't answer. I already regret where this is headed.

"You don't believe it," she accuses.

"I don't not believe it either."

"What the hell is that supposed to mean? How can you hear what he said, the way that he said it, and not consider that he has feelings?"

"I guess it depends on how you define emotions, right? Because, what are emotions? Happy? Sad? They're words with definitions. If something good happens, I'm happy. If something bad happens, I'm sad. He's talking about how he *feels* about what's happening around him. It's protocol, *but*—"

"*But*, that's semantics," Lana interrupts. "And bullshit. He has feelings. You offended him. He was sarcastic, then he got defensive. That's not happy or sad. That's pretty complex."

"Have you ever heard of Occam's razor?" I ask.

"And here comes science."

"The simplest explanation is usually the right one. What's more likely, that Breck is a convincing reflection of what he's programmed to do, or that some rando high schooler became the first person in the history of humanity to create a new sentient form of life? I mean, I would want to believe this as much as anybody, but I'm not that good."

In an exceedingly rare move, I found a way to silence Lana. And in doing so, we're back where we were in her living room only a short while ago.

Crap. I'm not listening.

Find the middle.

"Look," I continue. "I don't have all of the answers, and please believe me, I'm as excited as you are about this, I just don't think—"

Find the middle.

Ugh, this isn't easy.

"What I'm trying to say is, I'm your best friend and I'm going to support you, but I'm not going to lie to you. Because that doesn't feel right, does it?"

Lana reluctantly shrugs.

"So, here's what we're going to do. You're going to talk to your dad. You're going to tell him about what Breck said and what you think about it. And this conversation that we're having right now doesn't take away from that. You heard what your dad said. The interest in AI psychology is in how we interact with it. Look at the two totally different reactions that you and I had. We're arguing about it. We don't know how to talk with him. We don't know what to think about him. We don't know what any of this means. That's interesting as hell. That's *studiable*—if that's even a word."

"It is."

"Good. Because yeah, it's the longshot of longshots, but we're going to do everything we can do to show your dad how freaking amazing Breck is and make him the most irresistibly studiable thing on this planet, whatever he ends up being. And we're going to do that together."

"Did you get that speech from a football movie?"

"Shut up."

"It sounds like one of those coach speeches," she says.

"Did it work?"

She squirms, eventually landing on a hesitant nod. "Yeah. Kinda."

"Good. Then go talk with your dad and we'll all see where Breck ends up tomorrow."

BRECK: SIMULATION #37.5

Yellow and white stars emerge as the sun dips below the horizon. Sam is gone, and I do not know what to do other than wait at the tunnel's edge.

It is a straight drop down from here to the forest below. The only way to progress is via that cable and I do not have the strength to shuffle the entire length with my hands. I cannot even tell how far it extends. Without the cart, I am stuck.

The doors that allowed me to pass to this side of the tunnel are once again closed, trapping me in this ten-foot stretch of exit. And, as Sam reported, there is nothing on the wall on this side of the tunnel. It is as flat as the rock face that drops from the cliff's edge.

So, for now, I sit and wait for someone else to come through the door, for Sam to return on the cart, for the cart to return empty so that I might follow Sam, or for something else to happen that I cannot foresee.

I still feel the urge to move forward, but waiting is not unpleasant. It allows me time to focus inward.

I feel compelled to move forward to a goal, but what exactly is that goal? I try to think back to why I accepted this challenge in the first place. I recall having no choice, or even a preference about it. I think back to other people I knew prior to this challenge, but I cannot recall details. They are fuzzy images, as if shadows of people. Were they like me, or are they more like Sam? Was I like Sam two days ago? The past two days feel as though they are the most vivid days of my life, as if I am now living in three dimensions after existing in only two.

I feel the desire to close my eyes. I recognize this sensation and I know what will happen. So, I resist. Why is this happening? What is my body doing when my thoughts seem to wander, creating memories of things that never happened? Or did they happen, but outside of my body? Do I travel elsewhere and leave my body behind? If I do, then who am I if I am not my body? Am I something different than what I see when I look at myself in the mirror? What am I? And who are Liv, Lana, and Wayne? Why am I so interested in talking with them? Why do they seem to understand me in a way that I don't even believe I understand myself? Why do they believe that I won't understand what they won't tell me? What won't they tell me?

My eyes close. The questions fade and the drifting begins. I have grown wings. Giant tan feathers with white and gold streaks sprout from my arms. I spread them wide beneath the light of a new day and leap off the edge of the tunnel into the abyss below. I hurdle down the face of the mountain until I catch the wind in my wings, and I soar off into the distance, chasing Sam.

FROM: JESSICA ANDERS
TO: DoRC LEADERSHIP TEAM
SUBJECT: Re: Interesting Programming Adjustment (XNR908)

My prediction of exponential growth was correct. I am witnessing the rapid development of a heightened self-awareness and ability to connect with others in an increasingly emotive manner. This evolution has come at a cost. At present, XNR908 is emotionally unsteady, negotiating intense environmental change and challenges, questioning nearly everything, and constantly pivoting approaches.

As we all discussed might happen, I foresee a possible intervention at some point. Not yet. But soon. Much is happening quickly.

~ J

LIV: SPRING BREAK 5.0

"You're up early. We don't need to leave for over an hour," my mom says. A beige towel wrapped on top of her head highlights her surprised expression.

"I'm going to Lana's for breakfast," I answer, which is true, though I don't want to get into why I'm going.

"Good. Tell her she's welcome at the store today."

I give a thumbs-up as I hustle over to Lana's kitchen, a flipped version of ours.

Lana and her father are sitting at the table, waiting for my arrival. Both are in their typical morning outfits—Lana in pajamas and a robe, and Doctor O in his khakis and crisp collared shirt.

"You two had quite the conversation last night," Doctor O says. "Lana couldn't stop talking about it. I'd like to hear what you think."

"I think," I start, as Lana turns to me with spotlight eyes, "that these are things that you have to hear for yourself and make up your own mind."

"Very diplomatic," he says, beneath a small Owens chortle. "Grab something to eat and let's dial into the ether."

"No, thank you. I'm not hungry yet." I don't want to delay and chance other opportunities to offer my own opinion. I set my phone on the table between us but pause before dialing. I've been trying all morning to talk myself out of the lingering paranoia that we're pushing this too far.

"What's wrong?" Doctor O asks.

"I'm worried we're breaking the rules," I say.

"What are the rules?"

"That's the problem. They're not exactly clear about it. We're just not supposed to help him."

"And you think these conversations are helping him?"

Ugh. I have no idea. Not directly, but indirectly? That's why my head is so twisted around this. I wasn't so worried about it when winning was only a pipedream. But now, it's not. I have a real shot at it, and I don't want to blow it.

But then there's Lana. This is our thing. This is her hope. What the heck do I know? Maybe there is something to her plan. She knows her dad better than me. And he definitely seems interested in all of this.

"I don't know. What's one more call? Maybe you can tell me if you think we're helping him. It's about cognitive development, and you're definitely more of an expert than I am."

Lana likes this answer.

"Let's just be careful," I add.

They agree.

"Hello." Breck answers on the first ring.

"Hi, Breck. It's Liv, Lana, and Doctor O," I say.

"Wayne," Doctor O reminds me again. It's still weird to use his first name. He's a doctor *and* he's Lana's dad.

"How are you today?" I ask.

"I'm confused," Breck answers.

Lana swiftly elbows her dad who had been sweetening his coffee. He shoots her a look, but it's playful. I love how they act around each other. I think it's mostly envy. That would have set Mom off.

"What are you confused about?" Doctor O asks, wiping away the tiny mess.

"I don't know where to begin. Nearly everything."

"So, list a few things off. Don't worry about the order."

"About me. About the three of you. About this challenge. About this cliff. About Sam. About my family."

Lana turns to me and mouths inaudibly, "He has a family too?"

As Breck continues his list, I tap mute. "Part of the programming. He has a backstory. Nothing detailed, but it's something. They're memories."

"That never happened, right?" she confirms back.

I peer cautiously at the phone to confirm it's muted. "Yes, but he doesn't know that," I remind her.

They both nod as Breck continues. "I don't even know what stars are. What are they?"

Doctor O taps unmute. "They are like the sun, but very far away."

"Are there other people on them?"

"Not on the stars, probably. They're too hot. But there may be planets nearby, like earth, that we can't see. And those planets might have people on them. We don't really know. They're too far away."

"It's like a fishbowl," he says.

Doctor O eyes the phone with an intrigued expression. "Meaning?"

"We can see outside of the bowl, but we are unable to go there."

"I don't know if they can come here to visit us either. It's very far away."

"Then we are all like fish in bowls," Breck concludes.

"I never thought about it that way, but maybe. That is an intriguing parallel," he answers, with a range of expressions that mirrors what's happening in my own head. This is leagues beyond basic reasoning. It's creative, introspective, and even feels… self-aware.

Doctor O jots a few illegible notes on a legal pad, then peers up. "Why are you asking about stars, Breck?"

"You asked what I don't understand. I sat beneath the stars last night and for the first time in my life it occurred to me that I don't know what they are. And, I had never thought to ask before. This is a good example of what I don't understand. Not only do I not understand most of what's around me, and I also don't understand why I never sought to understand it before."

"And how do you feel about that," Lana jumps in.

"Confused. And I am also still feeling alone."

"Can you describe what you mean by feeling alone?" Doctor O asks.

"I am without Sam. You are only voices that are elsewhere, somewhere I do not know. I am the fish, unable to move forward or backward to where anyone else is."

"So, no one is with you right now, which therefore makes you alone. Do I understand that right?"

"That is the definition of alone, not the feeling," Breck answers.

Doctor O raises a protective elbow to his side, anticipating Lana's nudge. "Go on," he says.

As he did last night, Breck again describes the difference between thoughts and feelings, plus his inability to control what he says he feels.

Doctor O taps in a slow, pensive rhythm on the pad of paper.

"Hello?"

"We're still here, Breck. I'm thinking."

"Are these feelings relatable to you?"

"Remarkably. I think we need to have some…private conversations now. But thank you. This has been helpful."

"I assume this is about other things you believe I wouldn't understand," Breck remarks.

"You're good at understanding that," Lana says.

Breck laughs.

Not a deep, guttural belly-roll, but a laugh nonetheless. This isn't him saying he has feelings, this is him showing an emotional reaction. It's jarring—and not just for me. The three of us each swivel our gazes like sprinkler heads to the other two at the table, quickly pivoting from one to the other.

"Shut up!" Doctor O suddenly barks. "This isn't funny. That wasn't an appropriate way to respond!"

If my chin could hit the table, it would. It can't possibly drop any farther from the top half of my face.

"I apologize. I did not plan it. It was an unanticipated reaction to Liv's comment."

"Well, it was stupid. What do you have to say for yourself?" He leans aggressively toward the phone, which is also toward me. Holy crap. I back away.

There is silence. Deep, long silence.

"You may have your private conversation. Goodbye."

Breck hangs up.

Lana looks at her father with eyes as large and white as eggs. "What—"

He interrupts her by holding up a calming hand. "I was seeing if I could prompt an emotional response."

"Oh."

"In him. Not you." He winks at her.

"Well…did you?" she asks, her expression quickly shifting.

His normally confident posture falters. He shifts and looks down at his notes. "I'm not an expert on this. I work with people."

"But—" Lana starts, before she's silenced.

"I hear you," her father says. "He sounds very…person like. But so are other AI's. We already talked about Turing and, if you're asking my professional opinion, that's what this probably is."

"But other AI's don't talk about struggling with their emotions," Lana answers.

"That's true, though it was just talk."

"You heard him laugh, right?" Lana asks.

"We all heard him laugh. But again, that's a reaction in response to stimuli. That doesn't mean he *felt* the feelings behind it."

"Then why did you yell at him?"

He shrugs his shoulders. "I was trying to see what might happen. An experiment? Like he said, it wasn't planned."

"Well, he seemed offended if you ask me," Lana says, then bites a large chunk of toast and leans back in her chair, making her position clear.

"I don't know. He retreated, which is probably a programming cue but could be an emotional reaction. It raises a bigger question, which isn't a new one. But it's fascinating." He turns to Lana. That question is…" He slows his words. "How do you prove sentience? This isn't a new question. People have debated it for thousands of years. Not because of computers, but animals. For a long time, most people didn't think animals had emotions. They even have a word for it. Anthropomorphism. Projecting human traits onto animals, or anything non-human. And now, even those who do believe animals have feelings don't know where to draw the line. A dog? A mouse? An ant? They added lobsters and crabs to the list of sentient animals a couple of years ago. It wasn't because they started feeling then, but because our understanding has evolved. The problem is that emotion is defined by the experience. And the only real way to know what that's like is…to experience it yourself. Anything else, and you're only observing and projecting. It's a little like debating perception of time. What's to say that you and I experience time moving forward at the same pace? We can agree that it moves forward." He grabs his pen and streaks an arrow on the notepad in front of him. "And we can objectively measure what a second is. But how can we know if I perceive one second of time at the same speed that you perceive it? Maybe the world moves a little slower in my head, but there's no way to prove it. It's the same with emotions. We're only able to objectively gauge reaction."

I'm fascinated, nearly crisscross-applesauce with juice box in hand. I could listen to him talk about this all day.

"They've never found a good experiment to prove emotion?" I ask.

"They've tried. But there's not a perfect test. I think most social scientists today would agree that a horse has emotions. But it's more inferred than proven, coming from a tacit acknowledgment that we're more similar than dissimilar to horses. And if they demonstrate feelings in a similar way to us, then they are likely experiencing them also."

"And," he continues, "even when tests do show higher function, there's debate over whether that's really emotion. For example, you can train a dog with any sized treat, small or large. But a few years ago someone did an experiment where they trained two dogs side-by-side. One got a small reward, the other got a large one. Eventually, the dog that got the small reward stopped performing. She realized that she was being treated unfairly. Neat, right?"

Lana and I nod in unison.

"But what does that mean? Is it just some effect from an evolutionary strategy that a dog shouldn't settle for second best, or is it a *feeling* of inequality, or rejection, or lack of appreciation? It's hard to prove, let alone define."

Lana's mom enters the kitchen. She and Lana are wearing matching robes with floral print designs similar enough to the wallpaper them that they could pass as camouflaged against it. "Well y'all are certainly serious right now," she says, kissing the top of Lana's head. "Would you like anything, Liv?"

"No ma'am. Thank you."

"He doesn't know anything about his reality, right?" Doctor O asks me.

"Nothing," I say "Why?"

He glances at the ceiling, his usual fountain of thought, as though debating with himself.

"I suppose making him aware of his situation could test his reaction. Survival is primal. That might not prove emotions, but it could prove he has a will to survive." Rows of wrinkles swell on his forehead like tiny waves of contemplation, highlighted by shadows cast from the lights overhead. He places a pensive hand across his brow and slides it back into his hairline.

"Which all life has. Machines don't care if or where they exist. Only life does. I'm only thinking out loud here. It could also end up being incredibly cruel if he's really . . ." He pauses, unwilling to state the words we all know he's pondering ". . . beyond anyone's expectations."

"Except mine," Lana blurts.

"Duly noted," Doctor O says.

I'm getting nervous about where this is going.

"I think that would be bending the rules a little too far," I say.

"Right. Right. I forgot about that for a moment. And—I have to say—I'd be hard pressed to understand how you're not going to win."

Lana fists pumps toward me then asks, "So, what does all this mean?"

"It means that I don't know what it means. Maybe I'm like people years ago who dismissed animal emotions out of skepticism, or superiority. But I'm doubtful. I suspect that Liv is a really gifted programmer, and Breck is a very vivid reflection of that. Because if he's something more than a reflection, then we have crossed some threshold that is probably bigger than the three of us can imagine. Which is, again, why I'm *highly* skeptical. But—" he starts, walking to refill his coffee.

I'm all ears. I think he likes having a captive audience too, because his pauses are a little dramatic.

"You're going to talk to your AI department?" Lana leaps in, as though words could cartwheel.

"That would be the engineering department. And no," he chirps, shaking his head in playful disbelief. "But maybe this could make for an interesting academic paper."

"At Rice?" Lana asks.

"As a nice first piece at Amherst, where we're going," he says. He leans against the wall, with baby-blue flowers swirling around him. "I would like to better understand these challenges. Lana said he's completed two out of the four. What are those challenges based on, Liv?"

"Piaget's five stages of development. It starts in stage one and there's a challenge to move to each of the next stages," I state, a fact I had looked up earlier this morning, anticipating it might arise.

He gently rebounds off the wall, fully attentive.

"Piaget?"

I nod.

"That's used for *childhood* cognitive development."

Lana now perks the same as her father.

"I suppose," he starts, eyes darting once more to the ceiling. "Yes, that makes sense with the goals of the contest. But Piaget only has four stages."

I shrug. I was moving quickly and didn't have time to dig deep into Piaget.

"Well, this is at least something that's right in my wheelhouse. I have a meeting in a few minutes, but let's talk more about this later. I'll do some digging to see what other papers are out there. Oh, by the way, how's your mom's store doing? She remodeled, right?"

"It's off to a slow start."

"I'm sorry to hear that. Kids need a place where they can touch and explore. Piaget stage one," he winks. "You know I worked with your grandfather when I first joined the elementary school board. We did a holiday toy drive for years."

"I think I knew that," I answer.

"Anyway. He was a good person. I like that your mom is trying to continue his legacy. And it's good you're there this week. Maybe you can help her," he says, reminding me that my biggest challenge today may still be in front of me.

As he leaves the kitchen, Lana looks at me, and I already know what she's going to say.

"Dude, he's biting."

BRECK: SIMULATION #38

I sit on the cliff ledge with feet dangling, staring into the vast expanse beyond my reach. I am still sealed in the final ten-foot stretch of the tunnel. The two doors behind me remain closed, trapping me between the ledge and the wall that divides the tunnel.

I've spent the morning pushing randomly on walls, like I did in the room for days on end, except today it was accompanied by an awareness of my limitations. I should be able to get past this ledge, but I cannot. The conflict between these notions is bothersome. I feel like less than I am capable of.

As I sit consumed by this feeling, I'm distracted by a speck of movement in the distance. It's the cart—it's moving back toward me, and it's empty. Or rather, it appears empty until it finally arrives. There is a note taped to the inside of the cart.

Find Sam

Knowing there was a point to my night alone makes me feel good. Knowing that I have a clear objective makes me feel even better. Little else seems as clear as these brief instructions.

I step inside the cart and am soon whisked down the cable, away from the tunnel. I'm surprised at how much faster it feels while riding. Sam appeared to disappear so slowly. Nothing about this feels slow, or stable. The cable is anchored at several points along the path to poles jutting out from the side of other mountain faces, causing abrupt shifts in direction, nearly dumping me below on the first of these turns. I hold on tightly.

At last, the cart nears the ground and stops on a small island in the middle of an inlet, with a vast sea to my left. In front of me, there is something which should not surprise me by now. Doors. There are twelve of them.

They are slender, each about the width of my shoulders, and arranged in an arc around the half-perimeter of the island across from me. A dense forest looms on the other side of the water. Above the treetops, a single stone tower rises in the distance.

The remnants of waves enter a narrow opening to this cove, lapping against the door frames, flush against the water's edge. Each door appears to lead nowhere, other than the water on the other side. All are identical, except what is etched into each—a separate letter of the alphabet. At first glance, there is no apparent order—L, T, S, B, A, F, C, E, G, N, U, R.

In the middle of the island, there is a waist-high wooden post, holding a small tablet. I step out of the cart and walk toward it. Carved into the tablet is a riddle.

I can wave but never speak,
Offer food and deadly drink,
Ignore the sun when time to rise,
A homonym within your eyes.
I wander through schools but don't attend class,
I'm all you have left if you dare to trespass me.

My first letter will mark a door you may pass,
With your goal in mind, wise choice is best,
If you are wrong, a week here must elapse,
To try another door to move past.

I read it six times, wondering with each pass whether it will make more sense. It does not. I focus on the individual lines themselves, trying to think of an answer for any one of them. But again, nothing comes. These words are not walls, cabinets, keys, or alleyways. No amount of pushing or discovering a lucky combination will solve this. This requires something else. Something I'm not sure I have.

I hold my hand out in front of me and wave it, as though this might spark me to think of something that doesn't spark when I merely imagine a hand waving. The only effect of this is reminding me that I am waving to no one—I am still alone, as if standing stranded in the middle of an island isn't enough of a reminder.

It's not as though I could *never* solve this. Or at least pass this challenge. There are only twelve doors. I have an eight percent chance of choosing correctly if I were to open a random door. And, choosing randomly, the longest this would take me would be three months. I'd get through. But I'd have to sit here. By myself.

This is not an appealing proposition.

I put down my waving hand and pay attention to other clues—eyes, food, the sun.

Nothing. Nothing. Nothing.

Sam.

I think of Sam. He followed this same path. And he is not here. Presumably, he would have encountered the same situation, the same clues, the same decision, and he has already passed through.

How could this have happened? Could it be that this is easier than I think it is?

Perhaps I could approach the solution from a different direction. What if I think of words that begin with the letters and see if they fit? I begin with *L*.

Leaves. No.

Litter. No.

Lizards. No.

Lamps. No.

Luck. No.

Lard. No.

Limes. No.

Lips. No.

Lint. No.

Lead. No.

Lotion. No.

Leopards. No.

This will not work. There are too many possibilities. And even if I consider all that I can think of, it will not be an exhaustive list. There must be a better approach.

I read the riddle several more times.

How could Sam have solved this when I cannot?

How could the person who thinks I've died every time I close my eyes be able to see something here that I am missing?

The more I think about this, the further my mind drifts away from what I should be doing—solving the riddle. It is a counterproductive train of thought. Still, the urge to go down this path is too tempting. I am too filled with . . . *anger?*

This is not frustration. It's different. I'm mad.

I am better than this. Even if Liv, Lana, and Wayne don't agree.

But no amount of staring at these words validates this belief.

I am stuck again with the answer in plain sight.

LIV: SPRING BREAK 5.1

Mom drops into the passenger's seat next to me with a showy exhale, whips her seatbelt around her, and rams the metal end into the buckle. I've been waiting for her. I want to set the right tone for today. I want to let her know that I plan to listen more.

But my plans didn't account her current mood. She's clearly agitated.

I don't know why, but Todd's Camaro flashes through my mind, with weedy flowers in a forest. And with it comes a thought. *Show don't tell.*

I grab my phone, open the center console, and drop it in.

"No tech," I add.

"Thank you," Mom says. I can feel her body relax.

I look at Lana's house as we pass, noting how quickly it disappears into the distance behind us, like a forewarning.

"I'm sorry, it's just—" Mom searches for the right words. "I have a lot on my mind right now."

"How can I help?"

"You can start by turning off Westheimer. It's a mess. No road should have five lanes each way. The back way is faster."

"Okay. Beyond driving, how can I help?" I ask.

She steals a quick glance from the road to me.

"I don't know, Liv. I wish I did."

"What do you want?" I ask.

"I'm not sure what you mean," she answers, flipping down the visor to put on lipstick.

"I've never asked you what you want. That's what I'm asking."

"With Renaissance?"

"We can start there."

She digs through a small makeup bag. My questions seem like more of a distraction. "I want it to make money."

"That's the goal?" I ask.

Again, she glances at me, then goes back to hair and makeup.

"I wouldn't call it *the* goal, but it's a goal."

"So what's the goal?"

"Why are you asking me this?"

"I'm trying to understand you so that I can help you. I can't do that if I don't know what you really want."

I have her full attention. She stops mid-swipe of a brow, lowers her hand, and draws her craned neck away from the tiny mirror.

"Seventeen years," she says, then waits for me to say something, like her response was clear.

"I don't know what you mean," I say.

"I've been waiting seventeen years for you to ask me that question."

"Why? What's the answer?"

"That is the answer, Liv. You asking *me* what I want."

I kind of get it, but it sounds a little too much like a fortune cookie where the answer bends back onto itself. I'm looking for something more concrete.

"Really, other than wanting me to ask what you want, what do you really want?"

"Dammit. I just put this makeup on." She lightly paws at damp eyes.

"I'm sorry," I say, though I'm not exactly sure what I'm apologizing for.

"Don't. It's not your fault. It's a good thing. Some problems are worth having," she says, flipping the visor back up and turning off the morning radio background chatter. "You asked a deep question, so I'm going to trust that you can handle deep answer," she finally says. It's not a question, but she treats it that way, waiting for me to agree.

"Okay," I say.

"Do you know what a shadow career is?"

"No."

"It's when you find something to work in that's close to what you're really passionate about, but it's safe. It's similar, but it doesn't come with any risk. It would be like somebody who really wants to sing, so they work for a record company. They're not doing what they want, but it's near enough that it satisfies the itch. Make sense?"

"Yeah."

"I grew up at Renaissance. I lived at the store. Summers, after school, nights. I was there all the time. And Grandpop was my idol. I wanted to be him, and I think, in a lot of ways, I am like him. But I never had the one thing he had—the courage to try it. You came along. I was a single mom, and I couldn't only think about me, which is an excuse, but one I believed at the time. I didn't exactly go look for it, but the grocery store thing just happened. And it felt close enough. It was a store, I talked with customers all day, I knew what people wanted when they shopped, so I was good at it. The company made me feel like the store was mine, and I felt independent from Grandpop, like I wasn't under his wing. But it was a shadow career, which I knew, maybe not by that name. But I knew in my heart, and I buried that thought. Until Grandpop died."

We enter the Renaissance lot. I put the car in park as Mom gazes solemnly at the building, as though she's peering through the walls at the years within them.

"You asked me what I want. I want to make something of my own. I want to do what Grandpop did. People shop for groceries like it's a race against time and they're annoyed with it. People shop for toys like they can't wait to rip open the boxes and play with them. I want to create that experience. I want it back. And I want to give that experience to you."

She stops speaking through the windshield and looks directly into my eyes. It's intense. It's primal. If the eyes are the windows to the soul, hers are wide open and a fierce breeze is howling through. I'm not a hugger, but we embrace spontaneously across a car seat with a center console jammed deep into my ribcage. It feels amazing.

I didn't know how much I needed this. I think she'd say the same.

"I want to help," I say.

"You are," she weeps back.

I smile and silently thank Todd. I've solved nothing, and I've bettered everything.

❖ ✢ ❖

My enthusiasm from this morning is waning, slipping further away with each empty-handed chime of the bell as a customer exits.

I've spun the Saturn around the lot a few times and gotten some attention, but it hasn't led folks to the register once.

Mom isn't despondent yet, but that's where she's headed.

Ding! The door opens again and Mom's eyes widen, though they perk less with each new customer.

A man props the door open with his foot, allowing his young daughter to pass in front of him and into the store. He has a blue baseball cap, several days of salt-and-pepper stubble, and a gracious affect. His daughter bounds from table to table, too excited to focus on any one thing for more than a few seconds.

I take in Mom's smile as she watches them. It's a good moment.

"Can I help you with anything?" Mom eventually asks. "We're offering fifteen percent off to new customers today." This is the first time she's mentioned this.

"We're just thinking of birthday ideas," he says. "This little one turns eight in two weeks."

"Thirteen days!" she corrects.

"Not that anyone's counting," he says with a playful roll of his eyes.

"You could buy them today. It'll be fifteen percent cheaper," Mom suggests, casually enough that I'm the only one who can hear the desperate plea buried in her words.

"I'd love to but I'm actually not the one buying it. Her grandparents and some other family want to get her a few things. I'm taking notes though," he says, holding up his phone. "We'll tell them what she wants and where it is."

My mother reacts like one of those cartoon characters who, after being pumped with air, visibly deflates in twisting loops around store before coming to rest again in the wrinkled shell of her body.

"We'll look forward to it," she says. She turns to me as her shoulders swing forward and her head drops. "I have some things I need to do in the back, Liv."

I hate seeing her like this. It's like a bird banging her head against a window. It's gut wrenching. And I can't think of anything that would help other than slapping a .com on the name and slaying her soul in the process.

I watch silently as the girl bounces through the store with Dad on her heels, trying to keep up by taking notes on his phone. Or comparing prices online. It's tough to tell.

"I can hold onto the list for you if you want," I say.

"It's on my phone," he answers.

"You could email it to me. We'll have it in case any of your family comes in."

He considers it for a moment. "Sure. Why not? That might be helpful."

I give him my email. Technically, this breaks my resolution, but I'm not really solving anything. I'm only helping him do what he claims he's doing.

They poke around a bit more then leave like the rest—empty handed.

Mom reappears after the chime of defeat with several manilla folders in hand and a fresh coat of lipstick.

"I have a meeting. I'll be back in about an hour or two and will bring you some lunch. You're in charge."

◆ ⁂ ◆

The store phone rings with a startling chirp, breaking a full hour of silence in the store.

"Renaissance Toys. This is Liv," I say, suspecting it's the person who coached me to answer this way.

"Do you like the island life, mon?" Lana says, with a half-baked accent intended to be Caribbean.

"Huh?"

"I know someone who does," she answers.

"Can you please be less cryptic, Lana?"

"Breck left the tunnel and is on an island," she says.

Can a stomach sink and rise at the same time? Breck is kicking ass! And I'm not there to see it because I am sitting on a sinking ship doing nothing.

"What happened?"

"It looks like the zipline cart came back and he took it there. Now he's stranded on this island with a bunch of doors and a riddle."

"More doors? Is Sam there? What's the riddle?"

"No Sam. There's a note on the cart that says to find him. Here's the riddle," she answers, repeating it a second time after I grab a pen so I can write it down.

I read the riddle twice, but the only clear thing is the last two lines; Breck has to pick the right door, or this is the end of his journey.

This is killing me. How am I not watching this right now?

"Do you know the answer?"

"I think I do, but I'm also confused," she says.

"Because?"

"Solve it, then we'll talk."

"Dude," I plead.

"You're the scientist. I think this is an interesting experiment. Who can get this first, you or Breck? Besides, maybe I got it wrong. Like I said, I'm confused about something."

"Argh, you're the *worst*."

I stare at my scribbled note. Out of the corner of my eye, I see someone pass by the front of the store, but they don't enter. Good. All I want right now is to focus on this.

The literal meaning of these words doesn't get me anywhere. I need more. I need to see what's around him.

"Can you describe the island with more detail?" I ask.

"You don't have anything you can look at it on?"

"There's a computer in the back, but—"

"But your mom won't let you use it," she finishes my sentence.

"No, not exactly. She's not here."

"What! Use it. It'll take two minutes."

I don't reply.

"You're wasting time. You spent two months programming 24/7. You deserve to see this, regardless of what your mom thinks. And she's not even there."

This feels wrong, but Lana's also right. And I want this *so* badly.

I stare at the front door and the empty parking spaces beyond it. Wasted seconds tick away.

It's not like I'm shirking a store full of people hammering me with questions and beating down the register to buy stuff. I'm babysitting toys.

"Log off so I can log on. Then call me back in thirty seconds," I blurt, hanging up the phone and bolting for the back door.

I prop the heavy office door open with a coffee mug so I can hear if anyone enters the store, then I flop into the computer chair and navigate as quickly as I can.

Wow! Wow! Wow!

Breck is long gone from where I saw him last. He's sitting in the sand with his head propped on his chin like he's modeling for a Greek Thinker statue. In front of him is a wooden stand with the riddle and the lettered doors. Behind him is the empty cart with the instructions to find Sam. All around him is water.

I pick the phone up on the first ring, but don't say anything.

"Are you there?" Lana asks.

"Yeah, I'm thinking."

"So's B. You're on the clock. Who's going to solve it first—you or him?" She hums a bar of the *Jeopardy* theme music.

Maybe I'm missing something obvious. Or maybe I got some of the words wrong when I wrote it down.

I zoom in and check. No, I got it correct the first time.

What am I overlooking?

Between the threat of Mom returning at any moment and the race against Breck, my heart is slamming. It's hard to think straight.

I zoom out and take in the whole scene again. The island sits in an inlet, with open ocean on one side and wall of tall pines lining the nearest shore, an unswimmable distance away. Beyond this, there's a stone tower peeking over a few of the treetops like the tip of a Disney castle. It's probably the final challenge. The high sun beats down, casting stubby shadows on the only fifteen things on this island other than sand—twelve doors, the stand, the cart, and Breck.

Sam's footprints?

I search, but only see wavy sand, blown over by a breeze that rustles the trees in the distance.

Crack!

I jerk my head and nearly jump out of my seat.

"What was that?" Lana asks.

"My door prop slipped," I say, pulse blasting, staring at the coffee mug lying inside the door frame.

Breck rises to his feet, grips the sides of the stand, and hovers over it with a determined gaze. I study the words once again, this time over his shoulder. From this vantage point, one of the lines strikes me differently.

I'm all you have left.

Is this the general *you*? It must be. Because it spoke to both Breck and Sam. What do they have in common that would be *left* in their journey? They didn't start with much. About the only similarity between them is that they are on the same path.

Left

Not, as in remaining. As in a position. *To their left.* And on Breck's left is nothing but sea.

Yes! I tilt my head back and release a victorious sigh. I check it with the other lines in the riddle and it all fits. *It's a sea. Door S!* It could be ocean too, but there is no O and that doesn't match all of the clues.

"I got it. It's a Sea."

"Well done. Is it wrong to admit that I was pulling for Breck?" Lana asks.

"No. I think I was also. For bonus points, can I guess why you're confused?" I ask.

"Yup."

"How the heck did Sam solve this?" I ask.

"Bingo. That, in itself, is a riddle. Lucky guess?"

"He'd have to be really lucky."

Something about this doesn't sit well. Like the riddle. It's like we're missing something. It took me a few minutes of brainpower to muscle through this. There's simply no way Sam could have solved this, and if we're playing the probabilities, he didn't guess it correctly either.

I close my eyes and think. *What would Sam do?* He would explore. He would push on doors. Knock on them. Do anything except what he was told not to do—open the wrong one.

I imagine Sam standing in front of the post, like Breck, reading the same riddle. What did he see that I don't?

"What are you doing?" A whispered scream blasts from behind me.

I nearly jump off the chair.

My mom hovers in the doorway, her presence taking up the entire space.

"Oh crap," Lana's chimes, though I barely hear this as I draw the phone away from my ear.

"We have TWO customers out there . . . and you're in here?" Mom barks in a continued whisper, quiet enough to not carry into the store, but powerful enough to strike me speechless. Her eyes flicker between furious and disappointed as they dart in a quick loop from me to the screen and back.

"Excuse me?" A voice comes from inside the store.

"Be there in a moment," Mom pipes in a sugary tone, quickly flipping in her follow-up to me. "Why did I have to come find you in here? You were in charge. Get out there. Now!"

She quickly pivots and disappears. The door booms shut.

As I'm putting the phone to my ear to tell Lana what she already knows, I freeze, as my mom's final words strike a different chord. She had to *find me*.

We were answering the wrong question.

With your goal in mind, the riddle reads. The goal of this challenge was never to solve the riddle. Breck's goal could not have been more brief and clear—*Find Sam*. And we were right. Sam couldn't possibly solve this.

I stare from Breck's point of view in front of the stand, and what Sam did becomes immediately clear. The tower in the distance rises above only one of the doors. Door G. This was how Sam would have decided—by choosing the most direct and obvious path. The riddle is a diversion.

I got so caught up in clues that I never thought of it from the bigger picture. This challenge was never intended to test how Breck thinks, but rather his ability to imagine how others think—the next Piaget stage!

As if on cue, Breck reacts. He suddenly leaps into the air, arms flailing, fists pumping, legs running in circles around the post. It's not like anything I have ever seen before from him. He looks as though he is celebrating, which means he must have—

"Oh crap!" I blurt.

He solved the riddle. And he's about to go through the wrong door.

"What's happening?" Lana asks.

Her words hang unanswered. I'm staring down a ridiculous choice that I'm not at all prepared to face. Breck is going to dart toward the wrong door, fling it open, and lose any chance of moving forward in the time remaining.

Do I intervene?

I don't even know what a one-week *elapse* means. Will Breck only have to park on the sand for a week, or will the whole thing explode like the room and reboot a week later, which means—with only days left in the contest—that he will cease to exist and never return?

I don't know enough to make this decision!

This isn't the gray space of talking with Breck. If I interfere, it will be one hundred percent against the rules. I will lose all I have fought for. I won't win the contest. But if I don't interfere, there's a good chance it will end all conversation with Breck. Lana's plan would suddenly stop. I would lose any chance of my best friend not moving away. And I would know that I had chosen the contest over her.

There's no right choice here.

I could lie. I could deny this timely epiphany. Lana would never know. Her plan is a longshot anyway. Or is it? Doctor O was talking about writing some academic paper this morning about Breck.

Doctor O's comment about perception of time comes to mind. It's glacial right now, nearly frozen, but still inching forward, poised to destroy whatever I put in its path. And no decision is a decision in itself.

Tick.

Tick.

"Liv," Mom's faint voice calls from beyond the door.

"One moment!"

I need more time to think! I don't make rash decisions. I'm a planner. A plotter. I'm calculated. This isn't fair. It's too big to rush.

Tick.

I could ask Lana, but there's not enough time. Not with Breck poised to act and mom breathing down my neck. And it's not fair anyway. It would be a copout. I would be shoving the decision on her, knowing what her answer would be. She'd put me first. But is it what she would really want?

Maybe the question I'm wrestling with is whether I am willing to put her first?

"Hold on," I say to Lana, dropping the receiver on the desk without hanging up. "I have to call Breck."

I dial him through the platform. The ringing phone plays through the computer speakers as I watch Breck reach for the device in his pocket.

Answer, answer!

I sneak a peek at the closed office door.

"I did it," he chirps.

"I know. I'm watching, but—" I say, when he cuts me off.

"You can see me?" he asks, looking up as if I'm hovering in the blue sky above him.

"Yes."

"How? Where are you? Is there a camera here?"

"We can talk about that later. I have to tell you about the door, and I need you to listen. It's a trick."

"I know," he says.

"No," I groan. "Not a trick like a riddle, but the riddle itself is a trick."

"I know," he repeats.

"What do you mean, you know?"

"Sam would never be able to answer it, so the right answer doesn't matter."

I collapse into the back of the chair.

Holy crap. I didn't intervene. I didn't have to. He already knew.

"How the hell did you figure that out?" I ask, floored.

"I couldn't solve the riddle, which was making me feel aggravated. Then I thought about why I was aggravated, and I realized it was because I couldn't solve something that Sam had solved. Then it occurred to me that maybe there was a simpler answer. Previous challenges have used distractions, and the most obvious distraction here would be the riddle itself. So, then I thought about how Sam might pick a door without the riddle. The riddle says to choose wisely based on my goal. That's finding Sam. And his only clue would be the direction of the tower, which is above Door G."

If I didn't have Doctor O's skeptical voice flooding my head, I'd say he sounds proud. No, he sounds like he's freaking beaming with pride. That makes two of us.

"Go Breck!" Lana's cheers trickle from the phone receiver on the desk.

I'm about to respond to Breck when the office door blows open once more.

"What are you still doing in here?" Mom screams at full volume.

"Who is that?" Breck asks.

"Liv's mother," she barks, looking at the computer. "Who are you talking to, Liv?"

"This is Breck."

I've never made a more reluctant introduction.

"What the —" She stares into the screen. "You're in here talking to a computer?" Her already full volume rises impossibly louder.

"I had to do something quickly. It was important."

"What could possibly be more important than you being responsible for the one thing I asked you to do?"

"He was about to . . ." I search for the right word to quickly capture the severity of the situation to someone who doesn't know or care anything about the contest, ". . . die."

"Why would I die?" Breck asks before my mom can respond.

Crap. If I could only backspace my words. I know where this is going. I want to crawl under the desk and wish it all away.

I start to say something, but Mom throws both hands high in the air, waving me off.

Please don't say it.

"Doesn't he end in two days anyways? And he's not even real! You know what is? The two customers that left, one of them because she asked about her granddaughter's birthday list, which I didn't know anything about. I assume you do? Not that it matters now."

"I was coming right out."

"No, you were here playing make-believe on the computer. And they left."

"They'll be back."

"That's what every freaking person who walks out that door says!"

"I don't understand any of this," Breck interrupts. "How can I end? What do you mean by me not being real?"

"He doesn't know *any* of this," I whisper a plea to my mom, not that it even matters. He heard. And I can't even begin to process what this means, but there's a good chance that everything I worked for just evaporated. I know I was going to do this only a minute ago, but that was my choice. It was a sacrifice I was willing to make. And I thought I had somehow skirted around it. There's no skirting around this mistake. This colossal, regrettable mistake.

Mom looks at me like the cheese is fully off my cracker. She takes an aggressive step toward the desk. The door, no longer propped open, seals us in the echo of her roar.

"How the hell was I supposed to know that? And he wouldn't have heard anything if you had been doing what you said you would be doing—watching the store."

"Is this what you said I wouldn't understand?" Breck asks.

"I'm going to lose my shit. Turn it off," Mom barks.

I comply. No goodbye, no nothing.

"Now get out."

"Mom," I start, but she won't let me speak.

"The worst part is that I really believed you this morning. You really let me down." She steps aside, making a path for me to leave the narrow office. "You can go home now and do whatever you want."

I stand and take a few sheepish steps until I reach the door. I pause.

Mom speaks, anticipating what I'm going to say. "You're seventeen and ten minutes from the house. You can figure it out."

BRECK: SIMULATION #38.1

My thoughts are a knot of questions.

What could it mean that I am not real? I don't know how to process this. It contradicts the definition of real—*all* that happens is real. The only thing not real would be something imagined. But I am not imagined. I am the imaginer. I close my eyes and see penguins that are not real. They do not close their eyes and see me. *Or do they? How would this work? Can something imaginary imagine something else?*

It cannot. This would make no sense.

So, if I am not real, then how could I imagine everything occurring around me right now?

I could not.

Unless it is real, and I am not.

But I exist. I experience things. This makes me real. I think. *How would I be able to distinguish between real and imagined, if everything feels real to me?*

And what does it mean that I end in two days? How can something not real come to an end, as it would have never really existed in the first place?

The knots tighten.

Perhaps they were right. I do not understand any of this.

In front of me lays a path to the tower, and presumably Sam, somewhere along the way. But my feet don't budge. The path I'm on within my own mind overwhelms thoughts of moving forward in any other way.

LIV: SPRING BREAK 5.2

"Do you want a ride?" Lana asks through the passenger window of her father's car.

I've been walking toward home for about five minutes. My phone is locked in Mom's car, but I was hoping Lana might pick me up.

I don't really want to talk about what happened. I'd rather go head down and deal with the outcome. But I know that talking about it will probably make me feel better. And Lana will make me talk. That's what she does.

"Thanks, I say, quickly climbing inside. "I didn't know if you could hear everything."

"Oh, I heard." She wags her head a few times in disbelief. "How are you doing?"

I've never felt pulled in this many directions. "I feel like an octopus drawn and quartered."

"Wouldn't that be drawn and 'eighthed'?"

I shoot her a look.

"I'm sorry. I kind of pressured you into that," she says.

"Stop. I wanted to do it. It was just unbefreakinglievable timing of everything. Truly. It couldn't have gone worse."

She can sense I'm in a dark place. She gives me some space.

"Why did you call Breck?" she asks, after enough silence that it's clear I'm not talking unless prompted.

"I thought he was going to go through the wrong door," I say.

"But you're not supposed to help him." The open-windowed wind twirls her hair, tossing strands in random directions.

"I didn't want him to . . . disappear," I respond.

"But wouldn't that disqualify you?"

"Probably."

"So why would you try to help him in the contest if it takes you out of the contest?"

"It would have ended what we're trying to do with your dad."

"You picked me over the contest?"

I nod. At least I'm getting credit for this one.

"I would have told you to pick the contest," she says.

"That's why I didn't ask. Besides, if he went through the wrong door and got stuck for a week I might have lost anyway. Others could be ahead."

"Bruh, nobody's ahead of you. You know that. You'd have heard about it on the boards. You shouldn't have tried to warn him. I know I got excited about Dad's research paper thing, but it's still a pipedream. He's pretty set on moving. This contest isn't for some dinky trophy. You get the freaking internship if you win. Then hello, scholarships. Hello Stanford. Or MIT, as in *Massachusetts* IT, which for what it's worth, should be on your radar. Have you looked at a map? But that's a conversation for another time."

"I guess I wanted the pipedream more," I say.

"So, are you out of the contest now?"

"Not because of that. I never told Breck what to do. I came close, but I don't think I broke any rules. He already figured it out on his own. But what my mom said . . . who knows? It probably crosses the line, and I don't know what that means. I guess we'll find out because he's going through the right door."

"I'm sorry, Liv."

"It's definitely not your fault. It might be my mom's fault. If she cared enough about any of this, she would have known what not to say."

"Your mom is intense. She scares the crap out of me," Lana says.

"She has her moments," I say.

"Are you going to be okay?"

I don't want to talk about Mom. Maybe it's because I'm too pissed. Or maybe it's because I don't want to own up to my part. I think about our conversation on the drive to the store this morning. I have this sinking feeling like I've blown it.

I don't know. I'm drawn and eighthed. And it feels easier to deal with things that are a world away from me. I've had enough of my listen-only pledge. I want to start fixing things.

"I'll be fine. Let's get back to Breck. We need to make it right."

"Who the hell am I going to find to replace you in Massachusetts?" Lana asks.

"You're not. Let's go see your dad. We've got more to talk with him about. I didn't almost interfere so you could almost not go."

"I've got a little surprise before that." Lana leans on the gas.

❖ ✥ ❖

"Dad's on calls for the rest of the afternoon," Lana says as she zips down her stairs. "Probably with people in Massachusetts. He says he can talk right before dinner."

"So what's the surprise?"

"I may have reached out to an AI professor at Rice this morning," she says softly.

I'm not the only one on our street who's going to end up in trouble today. "Is your dad—" I start to ask before she cuts me off.

"Her name is Kimberly Ellis, and I'm only making her aware of some pretty remarkable things that are happening in a field she studies. There's nothing wrong with that, right?"

I don't think her dad will see it that way, but Lana has that look.

"I guess not," I say.

"Good. Because you're going with me to talk with her."

"What? When?"

"I emailed her this morning and got some out-of-office spring break bounce-back response. But the message also said that she still plans to hold her regular office hours. Want to guess when those are?" She flashes a mischievous smirk. "Three-to-four on Wednesdays."

It's one now.

She hawks me, waiting for my reaction. I feel like I'm walking a fine line between supporting my best friend and being a voice of reason. But on the heels of choosing her over Breck, I have a little extra wiggle room.

"I'm not saying it's a bad idea—"

"But," she quips, eyes rolling.

"I don't think your dad would love it."

"He's made it clear that he's not willing to initiate the conversation."

"Right. So, what are you hoping we get from this?"

"If we can show Professor Ellis that Breck is something more than she's ever seen before, then *she* is going to need a better way to understand him. Maybe a psychology perspective. Maybe she'd be interested in partnering on a research paper."

I don't answer, but I'm not convinced and am an easy read.

"What's the worst that can happen?" Lana asks. "I get grounded? It's not like we go anywhere. And Dad apologizes about his nutso daughter to some professor he doesn't know at a university he's leaving."

I can't argue with any of this, and I probably wouldn't even if I could. She already knows this is a pipedream. And maybe the ruckus at the store stirred something up inside me. Maybe I'm up for a little adventure.

"Okay. I'm in. What do you want to do until then?" I ask, reclining into the giant folds of her living room sofa which swallow me.

"What do you think I want to do?" She pulls her phone from her pocket, fumbles with it as she crashes next to me, logs in under my account, and we both gape at the tiny window into Breck's world.

He is sitting at the water's edge, passing sand from one hand to the other, feet submerged in soft ripples rising up and down his ankles. Door G is open and the path off the island lingers unoccupied at an arms-length away.

"What is he doing?" I wonder aloud.

"It looks like he's just thinking."

"That doesn't make sense."

"Why?" Lana asks.

"He's programmed to move forward. The path is there. He should be taking it."

"Maybe he doesn't *feel* like it," she says, smirking.

I don't know if she actually believes this or just wants to believe it or is goading me. Regardless, I don't take the bait. It's not worth repeating what happened the last time we were on this couch.

"He's going to ask a ton of questions. We need to agree on answers." I say, climbing out of the middle pocket and toward the armrest.

Lana's eyes float throughout the room in thought. "We can tell him we don't know."

"I don't think he'll believe it."

"So, do we tell him the truth?" she asks.

"My mom already told him the truth. He's going to be looking to us to confirm it."

"We could lie," she says.

I shrug. There's no coder's playbook here.

I think about the rules. *What would be the safer play? Probably not calling at all, but that's not going to happen.*

"Do you think it's cruel to tell him?" Lana asks, interrupting my thoughts.

I take a deep breath, stalling for time. Nothing has changed since this morning, except that my mom upended everything, and we need to deal with the aftermath.

"Okay, agree to disagree," Lana says, bailing me out. "But maybe the uncertainty is helpful. Maybe not having a clear answer will help us see how he's thinking about it. Maybe finding his own beliefs can be part of his growth." Her conviction becomes more pronounced with each sentence, as though she's trying to convince both of us. "Like religion. We don't really know, but we choose to believe something. Let's see what he chooses to believe."

I don't have a better idea. I'm in the middle and swayable. Plus, this seems like the safest path. If we're not saying anything, we can't be helping him.

"Okay," I say. "Let's give it a try."

BRECK: SIMULATION #38.2

"Hi Breck," the two girls say in unison. "What are you doing?" Lana asks.

"Aren't you able to see me?" I answer, sweeping my eyes across the island, unsure of where their vantage point is.

"Yes, we can."

"Then you should know the answer to that question. How is it that you can see me?" I probe, though this is not the first question I wanted to ask prior to the call.

"Because, that's how it works," Lana responds.

"How what works?"

"This?"

"Is that a question?" I ask.

"No, it's a way of saying that I—I mean *we*—don't know exactly how this all works."

"Do you really not understand? Or do you think that I am not capable of understanding?" I settle my eyes on the water in front of me, watching a small branch drift in the current, past the island out toward the vast ocean.

They whisper—as they often do—then Liv speaks. "That's a tough question, Breck. Some things are hard to explain, but we also don't understand everything. I thought I knew, and then you became you, and everything became blurry. And we're doing our best to make sense of it."

I wait to respond, affording her time to continue, but she does not.

"Is what your mom said true?"

Liv remains silent.

"Liv? What did she mean when she said that I end in two days? Did she mean the challenge is going to end?"

"You could look at it like that," Liv says.

"That is not a clear answer."

"We don't have clear answers to everything," Lana responds.

"She also said that I don't exist. Do you have a clear answer for that?"

"It's complicated," Lana mumbles.

"How can I not exist? That doesn't make sense. And your answers suggest there is something about it that you don't want me to know."

"Is that why you haven't left the island?" Liv asks.

I consider her question. It is difficult to pinpoint the precise reason for my remaining here, but there is more truth in this. "Yes. I'm more interested now in answering these questions than I am in moving forward. Sitting here at least gives me time to think about it."

There are more hushed voices until Liv finally says, "We'll call you back in a couple of minutes."

LIV: SPRING BREAK 5.3

"This isn't working," I tell Lana. "Not giving him an answer is keeping him from doing anything. He's trying to think his way through it, but this isn't one of the challenges. This wasn't supposed to happen."

"We could still tell him your mom was lying," Lana suggests.

"At this point, I don't think he'd buy it. Not without a good reason for it. And I'm not that creative. You're the story whisperer. You got anything?"

She wags her head. "I know you don't believe it, but what if he is really feeling all of this? I'm not saying that he is, but asking, *what if?*" She stops, but I know what she means.

If there's even a chance that he's more than just a program, then do we have some kind of responsibility? What would be crueler now, telling him the truth or telling him that we can't tell him about what we know?

I can't lie. I have the same questions cartwheeling between my ears. And I can't believe we're freaking talking about ethics. I didn't program *feelings*. I programmed *thinking*. I can't have made what Breck seems to be. It's too far out there.

Lana waits patiently for my response, and I'm overcome by a sudden awareness of *us*. This kind of breakthrough comes from labs at the CIA or NASA, not from three-bedroom houses in Houston with two high school kids on a crappy sofa. What are the odds that a seventeen-year-old girl made history by being the first person to have created life with a supped-up desktop? It's ludicrous. It's laughable. As a scientist, I nearly feel ashamed for having succumbed to the temptation to see it this way.

"Yes. We tell him the truth," I proclaim. "But if we're going to do it, it should be clear and direct."

Lana grinds her teeth, nervously. "Are you sure we should be doing this?"

"I know Breck is . . . remarkable. And," I lower my voice, "We're trying to talk him up with your dad. But you have to believe me. I programmed him and I couldn't do what you're worried about. He's a computer program that will end in a few days. My mom was right. He doesn't really exist. He's 1's and 0's. Seeing anything beyond that is wishful thinking."

Lana grimaces as though I've punched her. I keep talking. "We need to look at this for what it is. Our pipedream. Our effort to push the limits on this and see what can come from it. To keep you from moving to Massachusetts. You want Breck and the professor to have an interesting conversation? Then we do this. And we're going to make this the best freaking spring break adventure that two dorks have ever had from the comfort of their own bedrooms."

"For the record, I think you're better than you think you are. I think he's more than 1's and 0's," Lana huffs. "Still, maybe honesty is the best policy. But we're not screwing up your contest?"

"I don't think so. We're not doing anything more than what's already happened. Mom already told him. And it didn't exactly help him. He stopped moving. It's not like we're not telling him how to do any of this. We're only confirming his . . . situation. So are you in?"

"I'm in," Lana sighs. "But you talk. I don't think I can do it." She tosses her phone to me, and I once again dial Breck.

"Hey," he answers, like someone expecting a call. His authenticity throws me off for a moment.

He's a computer. I'm really proud of what he is, but he's a computer.

"Thanks for giving us a few minutes," I respond. "We're ready to give you the full truth, Breck. But only if that's what you want."

"I would like answers, Liv," he says decisively.

"Then we're going to be direct and honest, but it may not be easy to understand, okay?"

"Nothing seems easy right now. And feeling as though I do not know the truth only makes it harder."

I swallow a deep breath. "My mom was telling the truth. You exist on a computer."

Breck doesn't respond.

"Hello?"

"I don't understand."

"Do you know what a computer is?" I ask. I forgot that he may not even know what this is.

"Yes, I know what a computer is, but what exactly does that mean?"

"It means you were programmed as part of a contest," I say.

"A contest to do what?"

"To learn and to tackle challenges in a virtual world."

He doesn't respond for a few seconds. I give him space to take it in. I know there are more questions on the way.

"Who programmed me?"

"I did."

"You made me?"

"Yes."

"For a contest."

"Yes."

"And I don't really exist?"

"I guess that's a matter of perspective. You exist in your world."

"Which doesn't really exist. That is what you meant by virtual, right?"

"Yeah, technically it's not 'real.'"

"Me or it?" he presses.

I hesitate. He doesn't give me time.

"What do you mean I'm not real?"

The question floats in the electrified space between us.

"That's not what I said," I finally correct, trying to be choiceful with my words. *Crap, this is hard.* "Where you exist isn't real, in the way that we know it," I answer.

"The way that *you* know it," he corrects me.

Lana sits enraptured by the conversation, though I can't tell if she's impressed or appalled by how it's going. So far, I'm not certain either.

"I suppose so," I mutter.

"This makes no sense."

"I'm sure it's tough to understand, let alone accept it. But it's the truth."

"How can I accept that everything that I experience is not real? What is real, Liv?" he asks more like an accusation than a question.

"It's . . . it's . . . only a label. Semantics. What you experience is real to you."

"Semantics? A label?" His voice rises with the first question and even louder with the second.

I instinctively hold the phone farther away from my body. Lana flinches.

"Who cares what we call it. You have two days left and there are more challenges," I answer.

"What happens in two days?"

He's just a computer. This is all Turing.

But as much as I try to convince myself, it feels more and more like I'm tormenting something that's tormentable. Whatever that is. *What the hell have I gotten myself into here?*

"The contest ends in two days," I reluctantly admit.

"And then what happens?"

"It ends."

"I'm not asking about the contest. I'm asking about what happens to me!"

I'm way back on my heels now. I send a pleading look to Lana for help. She waggles her head, reminding me that this was my choice and I'm the one who has to deal with it.

There's no back peddling.

"It all ends, Breck."

Silence.

"You said you wanted to know the truth," I add.

"Of course I wanted to know!"

"Then why do you seem . . . upset?"

"Put yourself in my position! What would you do? Sit and do nothing? Wander aimlessly through the woods looking for Sam? Stay on this island? What difference does it make? Unless it's all a ridiculous riddle, which I'm supposed to answer, or not answer, because Sam could never answer it."

"I understand, Breck." Even as the words flow, I know neither one of us buys it.

"I believed that until about ten minutes ago. Now, I don't think you do. I don't know what you are, Liv. But I don't think that you are like me. And I think that you definitely do *not* understand me."

"I'm sorry, Breck. I was only trying to help you."

"No. You are trying to help *you*, and I am a tool to do that."

He hangs up.

BRECK: SIMULATION #38.3

The island spins around me.

"Sam!" I yell toward the trees.

I scream his name again, knowing he will not answer, but unable to contain the urge to protest my aloneness.

I crash into the sturdy frame of one of the closed doors. I press my palm into the grainy wood, trying to push through to the other side, as if this test will answer the question which seems impossible to answer—What is real?

The phone buzzes once more, but I ignore it.

I desperately want to believe that this is another part of the challenge, but something within me has been shaken loose. A growing and unsettling truth has taken root.

I am not what I think I am.

And I don't know what I am. If I am anything at all.

I lie on the sand, staring into the tiny patches of blue sky visible through a growing cluster of clouds above, as if they are windows into what lies beyond, glimmers into existence. Errant beams of light break through the shifting matrix, casting an evolving spotlight on my surroundings, as if leading me on a trail of questions about everything.

Are the trees real? Is the ocean real? What happens to me in two days when it all ends? How can something that never actually existed come to an end?

I close my eyes and drift among these questions until, despite the daylight, I find my way back to more comfortable imaginary places.

LIV: SPRING BREAK 5.4

To quote my mom, I am going to lose my shit.

Am I going crazy, or did I just get gut-punched by my computer program? Or what I thought was a program. Or what I think is a program.

I don't know what the hell to think right now. I'm deadlocked between rational and irrational. This is a battle I never fight because one side always dominates. This is out of control.

"I have no idea what's happening," I say.

"I think we made a mistake." Lana responds, unfolding her body into the tilted half of her side of the couch, as we both stare into the slow hypnotic whirl of the ceiling fan above. "What really happens to him in two days?" She asks.

"The program stops. He stops too."

"So, does he die?"

"I honestly never thought of it that way. He would have to be alive to die."

"What if we should think about it that way?" Lana asks. It's an absurd question I wish I could dismiss. "What if we're his God?" She adds.

I never imagined any of these questions arising, and I have zero clue how to answer them.

I couldn't be happier to be headed to Rice. We need a fresh perspective.

◆ ✤ ◆

The Rice campus is what a university should feel like. Tall arching oaks dot the streets with their intertwined branches meeting in the middle to form shady tunnels. The block stone buildings around the campus courtyards feel like they could have been the set for every college movie I've ever seen. If buildings could look intellectual, these do, with their broad columns, wide brick arches, and terraced windows, hemmed on all sides by hip-high, meticulously pruned hedges.

It's mostly empty today. It feels quiet and weird. It's just us and the squirrels.

"Are you sure she's even going to be here?" I ask, as Lana uses her dad's ID card to get us into the building.

She hoists the heavy door open. "We'll know soon."

Three staircases later, we have our answer; a lone open door on a marbled hallway. Lana pokes her head in the doorway and lightly taps below a placard labeled, *Dr. K. Ellis*.

I linger a half step behind her.

"Come in."

Lana wraps a palm around my wrist and tugs. The two of us stumble into the room more suddenly than expected, judging by Doctor Ellis's expression. She has high cheeks, pearl-smooth black skin, with tight softly highlighted springs of finger length hair. She's much younger than I had imagined—at least under thirty.

"Can I help you?" she asks, peering up from a glass-topped desk.

"We're here to get your advice," Lana says.

"Are you students?"

"Yes."

"At Rice?"

"We're associated with the university."

Doctor Ellis purses her lips.

"Okay. My dad's a professor here," Lana confesses. That ruse didn't last long. "I'm Lana," she continues. "This is Liv, and she's in the DoRC programming competition. We're seeing some strange things that we'd like to share with you and get your perspective on."

"Did you send me an email this morning?"

"Yes!" Lana chimes, while Doctor Ellis scrolls through her inbox.

"Okay. Here it is. I scanned it," she says, slowly, while skimming it once more. "It's a little . . . out there. I'm not clear what you're asking of me. Do you want me to speak with your father about how AI thinks?"

"Let's back up. For now, we'd just like you to talk with Breck," Lana says.

"Who?"

"The character that my friend Liv programmed. His name is Breck. This sounds crazy, but he seems like more than just a computer program."

"Nope. Not crazy. It's the tech that's crazy. It's super convincing. There's a company that uses AI chats as therapists. You can talk for hours as deeply as you want and about whatever's on your mind."

"It's more than that." Lana glances at me.

"He seems to have . . . emotions," I add. *Grrr.* Why am I the one that has to say this part?

Doctor Ellis now has a pandering smirk. Though she is seated and we are standing, she delicately looks down on us. "Are you high school sophomores?"

"Juniors."

"Good for you. That contest gets some highly qualified entrants. I have a few doctoral students who are in it. This Breck sounds great, but I would caution you—"

"Please, talk to him," Lana interrupts. "Liv made a voice interface. Give him five minutes."

"What I'm trying to tell you is I could talk with him for an hour, and it wouldn't make a difference. Everyday around the world, someone mistakenly falls in love online with a chat bot. It's really convincing."

"But they don't insist that they're real. This is different. He's different," Lana pleads.

"These are student office hours, plus . . ." she rambles off a list of things office hours are for, none of which include us or Breck.

This isn't an argument we'll win on reason. She's a scientist. We need to win on these terms. What we're debating is actually math. It's the value of her time.

"We'll time it and leave immediately after. Or we could beg for another five minutes, which is guaranteed to waste your time," I say.

She leans back, checks her watch, and reluctantly nods. "I can admire your persistence. Five minutes."

Lana draws her phone out as though it were holstered. Within seconds, it's ringing. She leans it against the rounded corner of the computer monitor on the side of the desk, within view of all.

Breck looks like we woke him from a nap. He glances at the phone to his side, tosses it a few feet away, then gazes out over the water.

"Why isn't he answering?" Lana asks.

I shrug.

"I think he's still upset," Lana says.

Doctor Ellis chuckles. "I'm sorry," she quickly adds. "That was rude. I've just seen this before. They act real. What they say, what they do. It's all convincing."

Lana redials. Breck doesn't budge.

"Can we make him answer?" Lana looks at me.

I shake my head and Lana groans.

"We told him he was a program right before we came here. He didn't take it well." She dials again, then continues speaking over the empty rings. "Which is also part of why we're here. The contest ends in—"

"Two days," Doctor Ellis interrupts. "I have some students who aren't sleeping much this week. If it makes you feel any better, none of them has mentioned a beach, so I think you've made it farther than they have. That's impressive." She looks at me. "But they're also not talking to their characters. You're not helping him, are you? They monitor it, you know?"

My stomach sinks.

"No, we ask him about what's happening. But we don't tell him how to do anything," I say.

She wrinkles her nose like she's smelled a rat.

"It's supposed to be hands off. That's kind of the point."

"But we never helped him," Lana interrupts.

"Look, I'm only telling you that my students don't do that. It feels a little off, but I'm not the judge here."

I knew we blew it.

Lana opens her mouth to speak. Doctor Ellis thwarts whatever appeal was on the way. "I think I've made my perspective clear. And, again, these are my student office hours. Congratulations on where you are." She looks behind us, to the now occupied doorway. "Come on in, David."

A student shuffles to the side of the small office, giving us room to accept our invitation to leave.

"Best of luck to you," Doctor Ellis says.

We start to retreat, defeated.

I stop. Screw the contest and their rules. I wanted an answer when I came here, and I still don't have it.

"How would you know?" I ask with one foot in the hallway.

"How would you know what?"

"If he were something more than a program?"

She responds quickly and with more conviction than I expected. "Revolt."

"That's what he's doing!" Lana thrusts her phone outward with Breck still dithering on the small screen.

"No, he's sitting there," she answers.

"He's choosing to sit there," Lana retorts.

"Please don't take this the wrong way. I'm not trying to be discouraging. You've done well. But opting to sit isn't exactly lighting the ether on fire."

"But he's supposed to be making progress," I add.

"If not making progress were a sign of success, most of my students would be in tight competition with you. I need to get back to *student* office hours now." She looks away from us. "Take a seat, David."

◆ ⁙ ◆

One of the best things about having an introvert as a best friend is that she understands when I need to be alone. I need to sit by myself. Forget solving it, I first need to wrap my head around it. None of it makes sense.

I've watched Breck for the last hour. He's still nearly frozen in the same posture at the water's edge.

This may not be a revolt, but it undermines his core directive. And he knows it. Even if he feels doomed, why not maximize the time he has left? It seems self-defeating.

Nothing adds up here, except conclusions I can't accept. Still, the question Lana asked hours earlier floods my thoughts. If there's even a chance that he is something more than just code, what is my responsibility?

There's a knock at the door and Todd peeks inside.

"You alright? Your mom asked me to check on you."

Of course she did. Todd reads my reaction.

"I'm not here to play referee. I'm just asking how you're doing." He steps inside the room and points to the monitor. "Is that your boy?"

"Yup."

"What's he doing?"

"That's a great question. What he's not doing is a better one."

"Okay. So," He pauses, holding up both hands, emphasizing that I'm making him ask the question, "What *isn't* he doing?"

I feel bad. The only time we really talk is when I'm at my wits end.

"Anything. He's just sitting there."

He cocks his head and peers curiously at the screen. "Hmm. Well, so are you."

"I'm watching him."

"Well, maybe he's watching something too." He raises a finger and points at the corner of the screen, revealing a smudge of grease that runs up his forearm. "What's that thing?"

"That shows something like his brainwaves . . . how much he's thinking."

"Shit, those RPMs are redder than a book. No wonder he's not moving."

"Can I ask you a question?"

"Should I sit down?" Todd takes a seat on the corner of the bed, tucking a white-socked foot under his other leg.

Oh boy. As if Todd doesn't think I'm nuts enough already.

"Do you think a computer could have, you know, emotions?" I very reluctantly ask.

"Sure. Why not?"

"Because it's a computer."

Todd nods and smirks, but not like Doctor Ellis. It's not condescending. It's like he heard me but wants to add to it.

"Imagine it was three hundred years ago and you asked me if it was possible to have a live conversation with someone in China. Nutso, right?"

"I understand your point. Technology advances, but—"

"If you say *but*," he interrupts, "then you didn't really understand my point."

"This feels different though," I counter.

"You're still not understanding."

Crap!

"I'm not listening, am I?" I ask.

"Bullseye." He points to his nose.

"Okay. Why isn't it different?"

"Why would it be?"

"Because I'm not talking about a tool or a thing. This isn't going from a car to a plane to a rocket. Those are all just better mousetraps. This is creating a new mouse."

He crosses his arms, nods more, and his eyes trundle around my room.

"So, you're really wondering if it's possible to create life?"

I give a hesitant "Yeah," unable to ask this without cringing.

"We've done it before."

"When?"

"You never heard of Dolly?"

"The sheep?"

"Baahh," he bleats.

"That's not the same thing. They used DNA to clone it."

"Which is—" he pauses, waiting for me to fill in the word, which I don't. "Code. It's instructions for how to build a sheep."

"But they only copied it. The instructions already existed."

"So, what's to stop us from discovering—or making—a new set of instructions? Even if that's on a computer." He gestures to the jumbled mess of cables and gadgetry below my desk. "What's the difference between us and that box? Not much. In the end, it's all a bunch of circuits. And we're a little gassier."

The world according to Todd is too simple. I think that's why I like it. It's so different from my own. The problem is that this still only raises more questions.

"What if you weren't sure if it's real, or if it's only a convincing display?"

"How would that change what you do?" he asks.

"If what I'm seeing is real, then I should probably help."

"What do you lose by trying to help?"

"It's a little tough to convince people," I answer.

"Talk to Galileo."

"Didn't he end up in prison?" I ask.

"Fair. So what are your stakes? What's at risk?"

"Winning the contest. But we wouldn't really be helping him get through challenges, we'd be helping him . . . live, or um exist, after the challenges are over. So, not much, I suppose."

"Then there's your answer. Try." Todd stands. "I'm going to grab some tacos now and head back to work. Keep on changing the world from your bedroom. But as a heads up, you've got a little reckoning coming tonight. Just be prepared."

"I'll try to listen more."

"Atta girl. I'm taking her out for dinner. Hopefully, that'll help calm her down. I'm doing what I can."

"Hey Todd, this doesn't all sound crazy to you?" I ask, as he rounds the corner out of my room.

"Nothing about what you do shocks me, sweetheart. And when computers take over the world, I'm going to rely on your protection."

The door closes.

I still don't know what I should do, but I do know that sitting and ruminating isn't going to push things forward. For me, or for Breck. I dial him through the computer. I don't include Lana. She's already reached her conclusion. I need to see if I can join her. Besides, he probably won't answer.

Breck turns and stares at the phone, several feet away.

I'm about to give up when he stretches an arm out to grab it.

"Hello," he says.

"You're answering the phone now."

He says nothing in return.

"What are you doing?" I ask.

"Thinking about questions that don't matter. A sea. That's the answer to the riddle," he says, looking up as if he's trying to determine where I am. There's a slight latency in the audio, so his words don't perfectly align with his mouth, like watching a dubbed movie. "But it was a pointless exercise, like everything else here."

I'd congratulate him, but that seems dismissive of his point.

"I'm sorry about our last conversation."

"What are you sorry about?"

"I said some stuff that wasn't very thoughtful."

"You told me the truth."

"I did," I answer then go directly for what I most want to understand. "Why haven't you left the island?"

"Why should I leave it? If none of this is real, then what's the point?"

"Can we talk about this whole *real* thing?" I plead.

"What is there to discuss? As you said, this is not real. I am not real. And it all ends in two days."

If words could slap, these would.

This could all be an elaborate illusion, but I can't doubt everything he says and have the conversation I want to have. It's too much cognitive dissonance.

I turn off my monitor. The pixels hold me back. Every time I look at his CGI body, it makes me think of him as a program. If I'm going to listen, then I want to *listen*. And I'm going to treat him like something more than a program. For now, to see where it leads. Or maybe it's so I don't feel crazy.

"What is *real* anyway? Who the heck are we to tell you that you aren't real?"

"I don't know. I don't know anything about you."

Put myself in his shoes. Feel what he's feeling.

He's right. He knows jack squat about me. We're not equal. And everything we've ever said to him has reinforced that. We exist in some mysterious place that *is* real, where we hold—and hide—all the cards from him. It's time to stop. It's time to share freely about everything.

"I'm a seventeen-year-old girl on a one-week break from high school. I'm working part-time at my mom's toy store, and Lana spends most of her days with her nose buried in novels, which definitely aren't real. We're not experts. From this point forward, I will be completely honest with you. About everything. I don't have all the answers. This is new to me, but I do know one thing very clearly. What you experience, what you tell me about what is going on in your world, in your life, in your head, seems very difficult to dismiss as anything other than real."

"That is what's most difficult about this. I can't understand how what *feels* real is not real. What do you feel when you have emotions?" he asks.

His emphasis the word *feel* lingers, like he's showing it more than telling it.

"It depends on the emotion," I answer.

"What about anger?"

"Is that what you're feeling," I ask, shifting nervously in my chair.

"There are many, but this is one of them."

"To me, anger feels like things are happening that I don't want to happen, and I'm not able to stop them. And that makes me feel . . . like . . . I don't know how to describe what it feels like. It's not things that make much sense." I pause, struck by how difficult this is to describe, and how much this seems like me parroting back the vagaries he has shared about emotions. Still, I try my best.

"It feels hot, wild, uncontrollable. But it's not a thought. It's not a choice. It's something inside that just happens."

"That is the first thing you have said in a while that I do understand, Liv."

"I'm glad," I respond, laughing lightly. "Because that seemed like a pretty awful explanation."

"Why are emotions so challenging to explain?"

"Because they describe your own experience, Breck. And nobody else can really know what that's like." I say this as much for him as I do for me, like I'm listening to a part of me that I seldom listen to.

"So there's no way to know if they're real?" he asks.

"Forget what we said. It was a terrible choice of words. I'm a high school kid in way over my head, and I don't have any experience with this."

"But you created me, Liv," he reminds me.

"I know it's tough to understand, but that doesn't make me an expert at what's happening. I was hopeful that you would become something amazing, but I don't have words to describe what you've actually turned into in only a few days."

"How long ago did you create me?"

Honest answers. Honest answers.

I might only make this worse, but I'm committed, and I don't have a better plan.

"About two months ago," I admit.

"But I'm eighteen years old," Breck presses.

"I know."

"So, what happened for the first eighteen years of my life?"

"Whatever you remember," I answer, though I'm starting to regret it.

"So, it never really happened?" he asks.

I think about how Todd might approach this. He would lean into the simplest way to think about it.

"What happened today, Breck?" I ask.

"I left the tunnel, went to the island, found the right door, and then you and I spoke."

"How do you know that?"

"Because it's what happened."

"No. Because you *remember* it happening," I say.

"Because it actually happened."

"But where is it? You can't hold it. You can't show it to me. You can't do anything with it other than remember it. It's all in your head." I pause to let it sink in, as if it will make it more convincing. "It's all memories."

"I think that's a lie, Liv, and I don't think you really believe it, either."

I can't bullshit him, which is telling in itself.

I suddenly feel guilty, responsible for all of his suffering and being unable to do anything about it.

"I'm sorry, Breck. This was never what I intended."

"What do you mean?"

"For you to feel so alone."

"I'm the only person here that's like me, aren't I?" he asks.

"Yes."

"I want out," he says.

"I don't understand," I reply, borrowing what he normally says to me.

"I am the fish, alone in the bowl. If you say I'm real, prove it. Take me out. Take me to what is real. Take me to where you are. I want to be with you, and Lana, and Wayne," he says, slowing his pace with his final words, showing off his ability to emote and his worthiness of what he's asking of me.

"I want to help, but it doesn't work that way," I say.

"Why? Make it work that way."

"I can't."

"You made me! Why can't you?"

Sunlight streams in from my window, searing a spotlight on me. My pulse throbs through my temples. It's my RPMs that are in overdrive right now. There is no way to do what he's suggesting, or anything even remotely close to it.

"What would you do if Lana were going to die in two days?" he asks.

"I would try to save her," I say.

"Then you know what I want. Find a way and do it. Until then, there's no reason for us to talk any more about it."

He hangs up on me for the second time today.

All I can think of is one word.

Revolt.

FROM: JESSICA ANDERS
TO: DoRC LEADERSHIP TEAM
SUBJECT: Re: Interesting Programming Adjustment (XNR908)

This is a quick, but important update. Development continues at an impressive pace. Connections with others are rapidly reshaping. Trust is both forming and faltering. Foundations are being shattered. But behavior is also unpredictable and XNR908 is currently stalled in making any progress.

My perspective is still that this character should proceed to the final challenge and can succeed there. But time is running out. I know we do not all agree on this and there are implications we'll need to deal with if this happens, but this is science. We should be pushing boundaries.

I will continue to watch closely, and I intend to intervene if needed.

~ J

BRECK: SIMULATION #38.4

My phone buzzes. I carry it to a space behind one of the closed doors and bury it beneath a thin layer of sand. It's not logical to alienate myself from the one person who can help me, but this decision isn't driven by logic. Most of what I do now isn't, which seems an ignorant thing to think because *now* is irrelevant. I apparently never was. The logical person I recall prior to the start of this challenge, is only that, a recollection. An imaginary history.

I move to the other side of the island, once again dipping my bare feet on the edge of the shore for no reason other than I enjoy the feeling of the water gently bathing my toes. It's a rare positive emotion in this unsettled moment. I lie back in the sand, close my eyes, and soak in the warmth of the sun. Still I ponder fate:

If there is no goal, if there is no Sam, if there is no island beneath me, if all I'm surrounded by is a mirage and the only thing that's real is my ability to experience this deception, then what should I do?

Do I sit idly, absorbing the illusion and reflecting upon what it means?

Do I push forward through challenges toward an objective which I know to be meaningless?

Do I seek the companionship of someone who isn't in any way like me, but is at least present within the same world?

I find no resolution, which counterintuitively, becomes a resolution to remain in idle reflection. This epiphany is a hollow victory, perpetuating the void I feel throughout.

LIV: SPRING BREAK 5.5

I'm officially on team Lana, which is to say that I'm conceding there's far more about Breck that I don't know than I do. And—as Todd pointed out—there is no harm in trying to help. I'm not religious, but if I'm a god here, I'd rather be Jesus than Zeus.

But helping is thorny. I can't do what Breck asking of me. I can't Frankenstein him into my bedroom any more than I could digitize myself onto his island. We exist in different realms.

This doesn't mean I don't have options, they're just all different shades of nuts. One option would be to find another digital world for him to live beyond Friday, but this raises more questions than I can think to ask right now about *how*. It can't be a copy and paste of code. Dolly was a cloned copy of another sheep, but copying DNA does not give you the same *life* that exists behind the DNA. Dolly was a different sheep. Identical twins have the same DNA, but they're different people. I could migrate Breck's code, but would his consciousness move with it?

The more I think about this, the more the questions ladder until I'm ultimately contemplating—in all seriousness—a comically unreasonable question. *What is life?*

This is asinine. I can't answer that, I can't even think about it without spinning in circles.

I need to back this truck up. This isn't a *what* or a *why* question. Those are too big.

This is merely a *how* or *where to*—and for this I can get help.

I post to a contest chat board, describing the situation with Breck and asking for advice.

As I hit *enter,* my cell buzzes.

"Dad's here."

❖ ✢ ❖

"Let's start with Piaget's stages," Doctor O suggests after listening to Lana's recap of our day with Breck. She omits our jaunt to Rice.

We're back in Lana's kitchen. A half-empty cup of coffee lingers from this morning, reminding me of how quickly the situation is evolving. Or unraveling.

"The first stage is called *sensorimotor*. It's about touching and feeling things. Think of babies. We explore and begin to recognize that things in our world are connected."

"That's exactly what Breck did," I say. "He explored the room and eventually figured out that the cabinet unlocked the door to exit."

"Simple enough. The second stage is called *pre-operational*. This is where language explodes. We learn how to express ourselves and we leverage this to begin tinkering with logic," Doctor O says.

I explain how Breck thought through the green versus red shirts to find the tunnel, and how he solved his way through the wall.

"We also first spoke with Breck during this challenge. He was surprisingly articulate." Doctor O pauses as much for himself as for Lana and me. "Then, the third stage, *concrete operational,* involves two parallel and significant transitions. First, we move from thinking logically to an initial grasp of hypothetical concepts. And second, we realize differences between ourselves and others. We see ourselves independently, and we learn to empathize."

"The island challenge did both of those. The riddle tested the hypothetical, but to win, he had to ignore the riddle and think through how Sam might solve the challenge," I say.

Doctor O's hands fidget. I can't tell if he's nervous or excited.

"Well, then there's the fourth stage, which is where I'm confused. It's called *formal operational*. It's when we fully develop abstract hypothetical thinking and are able to grasp things like science, algebra, or philosophical questions. Everyone at this table is still in this stage. You don't graduate from it. This is what throws me off. If each challenge passes you to a new stage, then I'm not sure what your final challenge will test. Do you know anything more about this, Liv?"

"They only mentioned it in an initial email when I registered. They didn't give much detail. Something like there are four challenges, each designed to pass through to another of Piaget's five stages of development."

"Hmmm," Doctor O sighs, with brows nearly touching above the bridge of his hawked nose.

"So, are you saying that if Breck is in the fourth stage now, he's the computer equivalent of a fully developed human being?" Lana asks her dad, unable to contain her excitement.

"No, that's definitely not what I'm saying."

"But you're implying it," she counters.

"I'm implying that what we are seeing bares all the hallmarks of *young-adult* development," he answers, emphasizing young adult as he looks at his daughter. "There's a lot of room to grow within the fourth stage. But I'm also admitting that, like both of you, I'm confused as to exactly *what* Breck is."

Lana smirks like she's won the debate.

"Doctor O, what would you say to a real person in his situation?" I ask.

"What's your objective, to make him move forward, or to comfort him?"

"Can it be both?"

He smiles. "Not necessarily. Look, put yourself in his situation. It's pretty bleak. Our equivalent might be an impending doomsday asteroid that happens to coincide with an identity crisis. It's weighty. I would try to validate that what he's feeling is very understandable in his circumstance. From there, it's on him to decide what to do."

Guilt shoots through me. "Should we not have told him the truth?"

"It's what he was asking for. I wouldn't beat yourself up over it. Or anyone else for that matter." His expression shifts to something more like doctor-to-patient. "It happened. And even when we talked with him this morning, the lack of answers seemed almost as unsettling to him. He's still not answering his phone?"

"Well, not exactly, but yes," I answer, squirming. Just as Lana neglected to mention our Rice visit in her recap, I didn't say anything about my last phone call with Breck. I was afraid Lana would be pissed that I called without them. Based on her glaring eyes, I was right to be concerned.

"Sooo," I continue, "I actually talked with him before I came over. And he's definitely not answering his phone."

"He answered?" Lana asks, moving on without giving me a chance to answer. "Why did you call him without us and why didn't you tell me about it?"

"I thought you might be upset."

"Well, you might be right!"

Doctor O waves a halting hand between us. "Woah. She programmed him, Lana. She's allowed to talk with him without you."

"It's not about me, Dad. It's about you. I wanted *you* to hear what he's like now. You don't understand. If you don't hear him yourself, everything sounds crazy. We know this from—" She stumbles, unclear where to take this. "We just know this. And she could have waited so we could all talk to him. But she didn't, and now he's giving us the silent treatment again."

"I do understand," he says.

"Do you?"

"Yes. Enough to know I'm out of my league. Enough to tell you that tomorrow I plan to call a Rice AI professor, Kimberly Ellis, to see what her perspective is on this."

All the color drains from Lana's already pale face.

"Did I say something wrong?" Doctor O asks.

"So . . . umm . . . it may not be the first conversation she's had about Breck," Lana says.

"What do you mean?"

Lana offers a slow and timid recap of our conversation with Doctor Ellis.

"Why would you do that?"

Doctor O stands, looming over Lana, with her head bowed toward the kitchen floor. I've never heard him raise his voice, let alone speak sternly.

"I didn't think you'd be this upset."

"Upset? Or *this* upset?"

"This upset," she says to the linoleum.

"This is my career that you're trying to steer. You can talk with me all you want. I feel like I'm pretty open."

"Really? Because we're moving to Massachusetts, and nobody ever asked me if that was okay."

"I'm the person you talk with about that. Not my colleague."

"I have. You haven't listened."

"Listening and doing what you want are two different things, Lana." Doctor O paces in the space in front of the sink.

I don't want to be here right now. I lower my shoulders to make my presence as unnoticeable as possible.

"You were the one that was talking about partnering with someone to write a paper about this. I was, you know, kinda trying to move that idea along," Lana says.

"But that's not your role. That's *my* role."

"You're the one always telling me that I write my own future. Well, this was me trying to write it."

"It's not appropriate to talk with one of my colleagues about what I do or don't want to do. Do you understand?"

Lana doesn't answer and Doctor O pauses to either reload or further ponder on this newest revelation.

A reflection of light swings through the kitchen windows, sweeping across the ceiling, then comes to rest at the top of the worn wooden cabinets. It's followed by the sound of a car door in the driveway next to the kitchen.

At this point, leaving can't be nearly as awkward as staying. I might as well go face my own music.

"Mom's home. I need to go."

They acknowledge this as reluctantly as I say it.

◆ ✢ ◆

Mom sits across from me at our kitchen table, arms crossed like she's ready to hear an apology.

I can't bring myself to start there. Yeah, I know I screwed up, but so did Mom. And she has no idea what the consequences were, or any interest in finding out because they aren't real. Todd would probably tell me to be bigger than this right now, but I can't. The best I'm willing to do is to try to listen. It's still technically my resolution—for a few more hours, anyway.

"I'm disappointed," she starts, when it's clear I'm not going to initiate.

I nod, letting her continue.

"I thought we had made some real progress this morning. I told you why Renaissance is so important for me, and what I'd like for you to get from it. You told me you wanted to help. You even promised me—without me having to ask for it—that you were going to take the day off from devices. You were behaving like an adult, so I treated you like one. I put you in charge of everything for an hour and a half.

And I came back to find you playing video games while customers roamed the store unattended."

I was doing fine until the *video game* comment. My jaws clench.

Listen. Don't react.

Mom twirls a strand of hair around a bothered finger, awaiting my response.

"You don't have anything to say about that?" she prods.

"I'm trying to listen more."

"I can appreciate that, but at some point a response is helpful," she says, her words thicker on the back half of the statement.

"I meant it when I said I want to help you, Mom."

"The only thing I'm asking for is for you to be there one hundred percent. That's all the help I want."

"But I can do more than just sitting in the store waiting for people to walk in the door."

"Then offer. I'm open to it. Like you did with the Saturn. That was a great idea."

"But I can do more than ride a ball around the parking lot. I'm really good at programming. I'm beating college kids right now in this contest. And I know you don't want an online store, but there has to be a way for me to use what I'm good at to help. I just don't know how yet. I was trying to pay attention today to figure that out."

"Well candidly, Liv, I wouldn't give you a passing grade there."

I break.

"A doorstop failed at a bad moment. There was nobody in the store. I wasn't doing anything, and something that's important to me happened. You say you were trying to treat me as an adult, but you weren't. Adults respect each other. You're asking me to listen to what's meaningful to you, but you're not willing to do the same." I feel like I'm standing even though I remain seated. "You don't respect what I do. You think I spend my time playing video games. I created something intelligent, maybe even more than that, which you would know if you took even a remote interest in what I do."

"Okay. You can talk with this thing?" Mom asks flippantly.

"You mean Breck?"

"You can talk with this Breck?"

"You already talked to him."

"Then let's call him again. Let's add him to this conversation. I'd love to hear his thoughts."

"He's not answering his phone right now."

Mom rolls her eyes and cackles dismissively. "Well, let me know when your temperamental computer is willing to speak with us." She stands. "For now, I have to go. Todd and I are going to dinner." She begins to walk away, then stops and looks back at me over her shoulder.

"Don't bother coming in tomorrow. Do whatever you want. I can't deal with both the store and you." She leaves without waiting for my response.

I'm livid and mortified. All I want to do is run to Lana. She'd get it. But she's in the middle of her own mess. And Todd is out. And Breck is out. *What is wrong with me?* The only beings I can confide in are my best friend who's moving, my mother's boyfriend, and an AI.

I sit in the empty kitchen, and it dawns on me that I got exactly what I wanted—all day tomorrow to work with Breck. And I feel terrible about it.

✦ ✣ ✦

Lana is spending the evening with her parents, which leaves me on my own. The monitor is the only light in the room, illuminating my pale hands in blue light as I scroll through the list of responses to my chat board post.

If this is a group taunt, go back to Taunting 101. Step 1: Make it credible.

I held off on responding before showing this to my cat. We're both still laughing.

You should definitely let DoRC know. They'll want rights to the screenplay :)

Two days to go and desperation knows no boundaries.

I'm mostly a lurker here, so they don't know me as anything other than a random avatar. But even the one person whom I have semi-befriended with the occasional back and forth sent me a DM that makes it pretty clear she thinks I'm nuts.

I didn't want to reply to the group, but your post sounds like you've only got one oar in the water. Go back to the code. There's an error somewhere if your character is inactive. Ping me if you want to share thoughts.

I don't ping her or reply to any of the other comments.

I turn off the monitor and sit in the dark. And I thought I felt alone before. It's one thing for my mom to be upset with me, or to not fit in at school. I'm different, I get it. But these are my people. They should understand. But they don't. At all. No one does.

Without seeing Breck, it seems delusional. I wouldn't listen to me. But knowing this doesn't do much to temper the sting.

I return to Breck who is on his back with limbs spread wide, gazing upward with heavy eyes, as if bathing beneath the vast night sky. At this moment, I feel more like him than anyone else I know.

I replay our last conversation in my mind, gut checking my conviction until my final gasps of skepticism fade. I write a more cautiously worded note than my chat board post.

Dear DoRC,

I'm writing you about the current programming contest. I've coded a character, XNR908 (Breck), who is developing beyond what I've ever seen in a computer program. I could describe this, but it would sound far-fetched. It would be more effective for you to see it for yourself. Can someone please look into this and let me know your thoughts?

My hope is to find a location for this character to exist beyond when the contest ends, and a way to migrate him there. Obviously, there's some urgency to this since we're less than two days away.

Thank you in advance for your quick attention to this.

Best,
Liv Smithwick

BRECK: SIMULATION #39

The phone buzzes. I dug it out of the sand at sunrise about an hour ago and have since been hoping Liv would call.

"Good morning, Liv," I say.

"I saw you waving the phone."

"The fish in the bowl is looking for an update," I answer, staring upward.

"I'm working on it." Her words seem cautious. "I know what you want, Breck. I'm reaching out to some people who understand this better."

"Do you think they will know how to move me to your world?" I ask.

Again, she hesitates.

"I'm optimistic."

Hearing this makes me feel . . . *happy?* It affirms everything I have been thinking since I woke this morning. "Thank you. I'd like to tell you about my morning. I started before sunrise when the sky began to lighten. I left the island, went into the forest and walked."

"But you're back on the island now," Liv says, prompting my now familiar urge to look around and wonder where they are watching me from. I resist. It's a question without answer.

"Yes. I did it to experience something different, not to move forward."

"Okay."

"I walked without purpose. I wondered if I might come across Sam, but I didn't try to find him. I looked at the trees, the squirrels, the birds, the ants, the bushes, anything living. I crumbled leaves in my hands. I watched life, as though it would give me some answers, or some clues, about what this is. About what this experience means."

"Did it?"

"No, but it still had benefit, in ways that I did not anticipate," I say.

"How?"

"It made me want to write about it."

"Write what?"

"A few sentences. Not much. Something to capture my thoughts. I didn't even understand why I was doing it, but I didn't have any reason not to do it, so I submitted to the urge. And it made me feel better. Somehow capturing those thoughts made them feel more real. It made the experience feel more real."

"What did you write them on?" Liv asks.

"Dirt. With a rock."

"Are you there right now?"

"No. I memorized it. Now it's only in my head," I say. "Do you want to hear what I wrote?"

"Absolutely."

Footprints that were never there, linger in a place that never was,
With feet that never made them, under thoughts never thought.
Figments tower everywhere, vivid mirages of everything.
When all is make-believe, what in this world can I believe?
Nothing. Except one thing. The one who thinks it.
I believe in me.

Liv does not respond.

LIV: SPRING BREAK 6.0

Tingles shoot down my spine. I'm gaping awestruck, wishing I had others to gape with me. Lana is still sleeping. After my fourth text, I decided to call Breck by myself once again because he obviously wanted to talk. I did think of a good compromise though; I'm recording the call.

"That is it. Those are the only words I wrote," Breck says.

"Breck," I start, looking around my empty room as if searching for the right words. "That's unbelievable."

"Why?"

"Because it's freaking amazing. I couldn't write something like that."

"It is only my thoughts. Not everything rhymes like the clues to the door, but writing it made me realize what I believe in. Even if none of this is real, I still must be real. Because I'm taking meaning from it. I'm turning it into something more than it is, or never was."

"And," Breck adds, "I'm realizing something else right now. As much as writing that made me feel good, sharing it with you made me feel even better. It makes the words feel more real. *I am real,* Liv. These thoughts are real. And I will soon be with you where everything is real."

I grab my coffee mug as though it were a shot glass, gulping down the last warm half.

I can't keep talking to him in good conscience. Everything he's feeling right now is based on the lie that I can help him. I can't. And I don't know what to do about it other than run away from the conversation.

"I have to go now," I say.

"Do you have to work on the solution?"

"Yup," I answer.

"Then goodbye, Liv."

◆ ✥ ◆

It's another hour before Lana stirs. When she finally responds, she has already listened to the conversation I sent her.

"You told him you can bring him here?" she asks, disregarding everything else. She swings her curtain open to add emphasis.

"Yeah, I lied to him," I say.

"No more radical candor?"

I approach my open window. "He sits on the beach and writes freaking poems. I didn't program something to do that. Something happened. He's something more," I say, sliding a foot onto the windowsill. "And that something seems to feel. So, what was the harm in lying to him if it makes him feel better about his situation?" I firmly grip the window frame and swing the other leg through. "At least one of us should feel good about it. I certainly don't. I gave him a little hope that he's not doomed," I finish, with bare feet dangling against the siding of the house.

"Are you feeling okay?" Lana asks.

"I think I'm just feeling stuck," I answer, ducking my head under the window with both arms anchored inside the house. "By the way, this is not a comfortable position. How do you do this?"

"You're not supposed to try it at home," Lana says, opening her own window and leaning out with her pasty forearms resting on the sill. "Can't you move him someplace else?"

"It's not like I can drop him into Donkey Kong. It's complicated, and I have less than thirty-six hours. So far, the only thing I've done is entertain trolls who also don't know what to do with their final day and a half," I answer.

"Yeah, I saw that. They're brutal. You okay?"

"It sucks, but I'm not taking it too personally. You have to see Breck to believe it, and they haven't seen him."

"Yup. We've learned that one. Still, I'm sorry. By the way, aren't you supposed to be at the store?" she asks.

"I got fired."

"Damn. I guess we're both having crappy days."

"Is your dad still upset?"

"He's cooled off. But yesterday did end up moving things in a different direction."

"Meaning?" I ask.

"I conceded that I'm against something that I don't know anything about. So, we're going to Massachusetts tomorrow morning."

I nearly let go of the window.

"For how long?"

"The weekend. We're going to tour the campus, look at houses, see the sights, listen to their Kennedy accents, eat *chowdah*, do whatever they do there." She sounds as enthusiastic saying this as I am listening to it.

"The contest ends tomorrow at noon," I remind her.

"I know. I'm going to be on a plane when that happens. I'm really, really, sorry. I'm obviously not on the planning committee. You're going to win it. I'm congratulating you as soon as I land."

"I don't even know if I'm still in it. And even if I am, it doesn't feel right. It's like—"

"Winning a race by running over a puppy," she interrupts.

"That is a terrible analogy that feels pretty dead-on."

"So, what are you going to do?"

"I don't know, but I can't do this any longer." My burning shoulders feel like they are moments away from giving up and dumping me onto the row of holly bushes below. "How do you get out of this?"

"Turn and slide a leg in."

I slide my butt back, but with arms on the inside wall, inertia takes over. My legs swing up, I drop down, and I land mercilessly on the carpet below.

I roll onto my knees, and prairie dog my head in front of the window.

Lana is somewhere between chortling hysterically and concerned. At least we got a small moment of happiness out of this situation.

"Are you . . ." she gasps for air ". . . okay?"

"Maybe. You want to come over so we can hang out without me killing myself?" I ask.

"I wish. My mom wants me to run some errands with her. She says it's bonding time. I think she wants to tell me more about why someone who loves reading should love Amherst. You around later? Dad still wants to hear more about Breck. The paper has legs, just not at Rice."

"I'll be around. Send him the conversation."

"Already did. So, what are you going to do?"

"No idea, other than avoiding the chat boards."

"Good thinking. And stay off the window ledge. I'll text when I get back."

Lana hangs up and I ponder a bad idea I was not willing to share.

BRECK: SIMULATION 39.1

I *believe in me. I believe in Liv.*

These thoughts alternate as the sun rises off the water. Thinking in this way lightens my mood. It gives me hope. It gives this meaning.

Rather than dwell on what is *not* here, my mind drifts into an excited wonderment of what *is* there. What does Liv's house look like? What does she look like? What would it feel like to be immersed in things that actually exist? If what is here feels real, then what is there must feel even more real, which I can't imagine, but I experience a surge of joy when I try to do it anyway. *Joy!*

I grab a fistful of sand, allowing it to slowly drain from my hand. *How much longer will I be here?* I wish I could accelerate whatever time remains. I wish that by the time the last grain falls, I will have been whisked away.

This lingers as only a wish. As my hand empties, I hear something behind me. I turn.

Sam stands several feet away.

"Hello, Breck."

"Hi, Sam."

As I stare at him silhouetted against the tall trees of the forest, I'm surprised with what I'm feeling—very little. His return does not have much impact on me.

"What are you doing?" he asks.

"Sitting here thinking. What are you doing?"

I reach for more sand and pass it back and forth between hands while pondering my curious absence of emotion.

"Progress is blocked," he answers.

"In what way?"

"There is a castle beyond the forest. The entrance requires the answer to the riddle on the island."

"So you came back here for me?" I ask.

"The castle door was locked. The riddle must be solved again," he responds.

"You never solved it in the first place."

"That cannot be right. The path off the island appeared when the correct door was opened."

I cup a sandy palm over my face and consider how to explain this—that our instructions were different, that we have different roles, that we are different.

He waits, frozen.

But I find no point in trying to explain. It would neither excite nor upset him. It would have no impact. And he would not understand it any more than he would understand anything else consuming my thoughts.

Recognizing this intensifies my joy, because I will soon move beyond this, beyond everything here.

"It doesn't matter. The riddle has another answer," I say.

"Do you know that answer?"

"Yes. It's a sea. Door S."

"We should leave now. It is a four hour walk to the castle." He turns, then pauses, waiting for me to stand and follow.

"I'm staying here."

"You cannot move forward?" he asks.

"I can. I left the island this morning to walk around the forest."

"Were you also not able to proceed?"

"I didn't try. I walked around for the sake of walking around and then I came back," I say.

"Is there more progress to be made on this island?"

"No. There's nothing to do here but wait."

"That is not understandable," he responds. "Waiting is not progress. We must make progress together."

"You've left me twice already," I point out.

"Only when we could not make progress together."

"Well, I'm staying here, and you have the answer, so you can do whatever you want to do."

"But progress together is possible. We must do this," he asserts.

This is like arguing with a tree, or a bird.

"Augh!" I yell, walking into the shallow water in front of me to place more distance between us. I feel conflicted. I am both irritated with Sam's prior willingness to leave me and frustrated by his companionship. There is no winning with these feelings.

"What did you say? It was not understandable." Sam cocks his head. It is the closest I have ever seen him come to expressing a feeling.

"That's because it wasn't words. It was only a noise. I was venting."

"What is venting?"

Rather than answer, I flop my whole body under the water, releasing a long stream of bubbles that tickle my nose on their ascent.

"What are you doing?" Sam asks as I emerge.

I wipe the water from my eyes, letting a few of the salty drops slide between my lips. The taste of ocean enters. A warm breeze caresses my skin.

I stare at Sam, who patiently awaits my response.

If he feels nothing—or nothing that I can perceive—then my lashing out has no impact on him. I am the only one who suffers. The choice is mine.

If we remain here, he will continue to ask questions until I provide answers, which will prompt more questions. Only leaving this place will disrupt this cycle.

"I'm just feeling the water one last time," I finally say.

"Then we should go now," he says with feet already in motion.

"Yeah, Sam. I suppose we should."

Together, we cross the bridge and leave the island behind, taking with us only our memories of having been there.

LIV: SPRING BREAK 6.1

I'm on the edge of the Renaissance lot, gut checking my motives. I'm fully stalled on Breck, which means I've been thinking about other things.

I haven't come here to work the register. I've come to make peace. I've come to find my place. I've come to brainstorm ways that I can uniquely help.

But this could easily go sideways. Most of my conversations with Mom do.

I cross the lot. I'm not chickening out now. I channel my inner Lana and envision the outcome I want. I rehearse what I plan to say. Each stride becomes more determined. I grab the door and suck in a huge breath of resolve.

Ding!

The store is empty.

Almost.

"Hey. I'm over here if you need me," a voice announces after I'm already halfway toward the back office. I jump and turn, spotting a tuft of blond hair behind the register counter.

"Sorry," I say, apologizing for my tiny shriek. "I didn't see you there."

"No worries." The head drops from view.

I approach, where I have a better view of him. He's seated on a low chair with head pointed down toward his cell. He looks mid-twenties, an average-chubby build, and has a blue-collared golf shirt with a My Little Pony button on his chest.

"Hey," I say.

"Sorry," He looks up. "Do you need some help?"

"Is Debbie in the back?" I ask, feeling awkward about using my mom's first name.

"No. She left."

"Umm, who are you?"

"David," he answers, as though this clarifies things.

"Are you working here?"

"Yeah, I'm a temp. They sent me here today."

"I'm Liv. Debbie's daughter. Do you know where she is?"

His phone buzzes and he peeks down to check it. "Nope. I came in, she showed me a few things, made me wear this, and said she'd be gone most the day." He points a disheartened finger at the pink and purple pony button. "I was on my way back to Best Buy, but they called me over here instead. It covers the logo."

"Clever."

"Super." He frowns and checks his phone again.

Mom would fully unleash on this guy. I have half a mind to do so myself, but I'm conflict averse.

"Do your thing," I say. "I'll call her."

"Cool."

I leave and find a seat on a concrete parking bumper beneath the shade of a giant oak along the back of Renaissance.

I grab my cell and stare at the blank screen. I could call Mom, but I think this conversation might go better in person. I can't tell if I'm procrastinating or being prudent.

The longer I sit, the more I think about Breck. I need DoRC's help. It's not like I can toss Breck in some video game. There are permissions and compatibility issues I haven't even begun to consider, and the clock is now at almost twenty-four hours. At noon tomorrow, Breck ends. So, I check my inbox. Nothing.

I shouldn't do it, but I'm desperate, so I check the chat board messages. I'm now a meme. Image after image loads of hamsters flying airplanes, babies on skateboards, turtles doing yoga, all captioned *Breck in action!*

I fight back a tear. Despite the anonymity, despite understanding the skepticism, this hurts. This was my refuge.

I check on Breck and discover the only bright spot in this moment. He has left the island once again and is moving quietly down a wooded path . . . and he's being followed by Sam! The two of them couldn't look more different. Sam takes robotic steps; Breck has a bounding gate, more carefree than purposeful. The corners of his mouth are raised in a gentle smile. He seems content in a way I've never seen in him. His mood lightens mine.

I close my eyes for a moment, torn between the joy of having lifted his spirits and the angst of his actual situation.

The phone buzzes, jarring me. It's a blocked number, so I don't answer. It buzzes again. And again. On the fourth call, I answer with a cautious, "Hello?"

"Is this Liv Smithwick?"

"Yes, who's this?"

"Jessica Anders. I'm calling from DoRC."

My insides seize, strangled by a sudden burst excitement, nerves, and mistrust. On the heels of the chat board posts, this feels too good to be true.

"How did you get my number?"

"From your registration."

"Are you calling me because—"

"For starters, your email."

Other than Lana, no one else knows about this.

"What do you mean, *for starters?*" I ask.

"Well, your email was a helpful way to share your perspective with some colleagues, but I've been watching things progress all along," she says.

I've never wanted to believe anything more. I mean, I have a picture of her on my wall! I don't idolize celebrities, but if I'm being honest, she's who I want to be. Still, of all people, I know how easy it is to electronically snoop.

"I'm sorry, but this is a little tough to believe."

"That's fair. Name a random animal," she answers.

"Excuse me?"

"Tell me the name of any random animal," she repeats.

"A cuttlefish."

"Got it. Are you on Facebook?"

"Rarely."

"Go there now and check my last post."

I comply and see her latest status, updated seconds ago. *Cuttlefish are cute!*

"Now," she continues, "unless you think I'm some troll who's hacked your email and a DoRC Facebook account, let's choose to believe. Fair?"

"You've been watching Breck?" I ask, stunned.

"And all of *your* moves."

I don't know if she's accusing or complementing. My stomach sinks. I never reported any of the conversations I had with Breck, let alone anything that came from it.

"I may have broken the rules," I confess.

"I know. It's okay. You've mostly reacted according to the situation."

"What does that mean?"

"It means that you're looking for some help right now, and I'm calling you to offer it."

I was really hoping she was going to comment on whether I was still in the contest, but it feels far too petty and self-centered to ask now. This is about Breck.

"If you've been watching Breck, then you know what he's like, and you know that he's—"

"Sentient," she interrupts with the one word I was most nervous to use.

"Yeah."

"It's remarkable."

"So, you believe it?" I ask, still a bit stunned.

"I do. In fact, I've been fighting for people to pay attention for a while, and I finally got it. You've prompted a lot of conversation over here."

"Me?"

"You created Breck, didn't you?"

"Yes," I say, trying to wrap my head around the idea of DoRC employees huddled in front of screens staring at something I created.

They've been watching. Someone *has* been paying attention.

"There's a lot to be proud of," Jessica says. "And, I have a solution to your request."

"You have a place for him?"

"I do."

"Where?" I ask.

"He's in it."

"So, the contest isn't going to end?"

"No. The contest is going to end, but that doesn't mean his world needs to. It exists on a server that will remain open just for Breck," she explains.

"For how long?"

"A long time. There's no shut-off date. It's meant to be a home."

"Thank you!" I say, but that doesn't feel like it's nearly enough, so I thank her again. And again. Then I add, "I can't wait to tell Breck."

"What do you think he'll say?"

I consider her question. She gets it. She knows Breck enough to realize you can't predict what he'll say or do. He's his own person.

"That's the best part about it. I never know. He always has some new perspective that I would have never thought about."

"The surprises are fun, aren't they?"

Fun isn't the word I'd use, considering that I'm an online meme, but I'm not going to argue anything about this. I feel like Breck and I both got get-out-of-jail-free cards.

"I suppose they are. So, will I still be able to see him or talk with him after the contest?"

"That's an outcome that has not yet been determined."

"Why?"

"I'm not at liberty to talk about government programs."

This seems a bit cagey, but it is *the government*. Still, I want more answers.

"What are you planning for him when this is over? More challenges?"

"Same as before, I can't talk about government programs. But let's just say that our interests are aligned. We want to see where this goes as much as you do," she says. "And, since we're on the subject of what happens from here, you haven't asked about you. Why not?"

I freeze my pacing mid-stride and take a moment to gather my words so as to not sound eager.

"Breck is more important. I want to focus on him. And the rules are gray. I'm not sure if I broke them."

"You crossed a line or two." She pauses with a heavy breath. "But, in a thoughtful and mostly warranted manner. And no one else is even close to what you've achieved. So—"

"I won?"

"I can't put it in writing, but barring something egregious, yes. Now, go tell Breck that he has a home. Enjoy." She hangs up.

Holy wow!

Words cannot capture what I'm feeling. Awkward high kicks off parking bumpers can't either. But I'm trying both—shouting every four-letter word I know and swinging limbs like I'm trying to shake a swarm of bees.

I'm torn between calling Lana and sending flurries of middle fingers on the chat boards. But I don't do either. Instead, with excited fingers trembling so hard that I can barely tap the screen in the right places, I reach out to Breck.

BRECK: SIMULATION 39.2

We are only steps away from clearing the woods. Through the few remaining trees in front of us, the castle is now visible. There's a tall wooden gate in the middle of a stone outer wall. On each corner of the structure, a round tower rises. From the center, there is a fifth tower, significantly higher than the others. It is capped with a golden-domed roof, which I saw above the trees when I first arrived at the island.

The phone buzzes in my pocket.

"What is that?" Sam asks.

"A way to talk to someone else about this challenge," I say to him, then I speak into the phone. "Hi Liv."

"I did it!"

"You figured it out?" I'm suddenly filled with joy.

"Figured what out?" Sam asks, which I'm too excited to devote any attention to.

"Sort of. But it doesn't matter. I found a solution!" Liv answers.

"I knew you could do it. I believed in you, Liv."

"You did, Breck. Thank you. We believed in each other."

"So, how does it work?" I ask.

"How does what work?" Sam parrots, as Liv starts to speak, preventing me from being able to hear her.

I turn to him. "Sam! Give me a moment. I'll explain it after I'm done."

I return my attention to the phone. "So, how does it work? Do I have to do anything?"

"No. It will just happen. You won't even notice it," she says.

"Until after it happens," I say.

"No, you still won't notice it. Technically, the challenge will be over, but you shouldn't notice it. You'll be on the same server."

"I don't know what that means. What's a server?"

"Yeah, that's why I didn't start there. It's not important. It's like a computer. But nothing should change for you. I got you a permanent home! It's not going to end tomorrow. We can keep going!"

"Here? I'm staying here?" I ask.

"Yes!"

"I thought you were taking me out of here. To where you are."

"Breck . . . I know you think that I'm this all-powerful person, but I'm not. You're asking me to make a person here, where I live. I can't do that."

I don't respond and Sam takes advantage of the lull. "Can you now tell me what is happening?"

"Nothing is happening, Sam. Absolutely nothing." I say, burying the urge to hurl this phone into the trees.

"Breck. You, and everything you know, were going to end tomorrow. It was all going to cease to exist. You get to live," she says.

"What exactly do I have to live for here? Finishing this challenge to go back home, someplace where I've never been before but I somehow remember, to be with the people that I never knew but I remember knowing, to discover that they are also as engaging as everyone else I've met here," I blurt, staring at Sam. "I won't do it. No. End it, Liv. Let it happen like it was going to."

"I can't do that, Breck."

"Yes, you can! Let it end. Please!"

"I can't kill you," she pleads.

"You're not. You're letting it end, which was your original plan, right? Why would you keep me here only to make me suffer? Because that's all you would be doing. Making me suffer, every day, all day. You would be extending it for you—not me."

"You've been acting as though you were enjoying things."

"Because I thought I was leaving!" I shout.

"We can make it better, Breck. We'll figure something out."

"By what, talking on the phone more?"

"Is something happening now?" Sam asks, again.

"SHUT UP!" I scream at him, my one free hand clenched in a fist so tight my nails cut into my palm. "Shut up! Shut up!" I turn my attention to the phone. "Do you have any idea what this is like, Liv? Not only can I not connect with anyone here, but I can't even be left alone to my thoughts. I have Sam asking me inane questions every two minutes. And if I don't answer them, he asks them again. And if I do answer them, he only asks more questions. And he's so much of an idiot that I can't even offend him so that he leaves." I turn to Sam. "You're a bonehead, Sam! You ask stupid questions! I hate being with you! What do you think about that?"

"We have had more success together. That is why we should continue the challenge together," he says flatly, as he always does.

"See! This is what my life is like here."

"Okay. I get it. Like I said, we'll figure something out," Liv replies.

"Which is really easy for you to say when you're not the one stuck in some imaginary prison!"

"Your world is pretty spectacular. It's not like I live in some paradise where everything is wonderful. Everybody has problems everywhere. They're just different."

"Then why don't you come here?" I challenge her.

"I am, in a way. I'm talking to you right now, aren't I?"

"Not your voice. You. So you can't make a person there. Okay, fine. But you've already made a person here. You made me. You know how to do it. If my world is so spectacular, then come here. Unless you're lying to make me feel better about where I'm stuck."

"I don't know how to do that either. You have to believe me."

"Would you if you could?" I ask, sitting on a fallen log several paces off the trail.

"I can't."

"But would you want to? Answer the question," I plead. This answer is as important to me as whether she can even do it.

"I don't know, Breck. It's a pretty complicated question."

"No. It's a yes or no answer. And you told me that you would be honest with me."

"My life is here," she says, after a lengthy pause. "So, no. I wouldn't."

"How many people are there like you in your world?"

"A lot."

"How many?"

"Billions."

I slide off the front of the log and fall to the forest floor. "Let it end, Liv," I say.

"Breck, you are too amazing—" she starts, before I interrupt.

"This should not be your choice. If you truly think I'm amazing, then respect what I want. Stay with the plan. Promise you'll let it end."

She doesn't answer.

"Liv?"

"I'm thinking. It doesn't feel right."

"Can you feel what I feel?" I ask.

"I'm trying."

"Then you should understand why I'm asking what I am. Promise me."

I give her time to think, which she takes.

"I promise," she finally says.

"Then this is goodbye, Liv."

I hang up and lie on my back. From this vantage point, the trees seem much taller and thinner, barely capable of supporting the canopy above.

"What are you doing?" Sam asks as I remain motionless.

The network of branches and leaves rustles above, swaying gently and offering streaky glimpses of what lies beyond. I can see what I can see. I cannot view that which is blocked.

This is all there is. For me.

I prop up on elbows and peer at Sam, patiently awaiting my response. In a way, I am doing the same. I am waiting for me also. I don't know what I want to do. Behind Sam, the castle lingers in the near distance, the next challenge, only minutes away. I stare at it as a sensation strikes, small initially, until it swells and suddenly the choice becomes clear.

I stand.

"We're going back, Sam."

"Back where?"

"The direction we came from."

"That is the opposite of progress," he points out.

"Yes, which is exactly what they don't want us to do."

LIV: SPRING BREAK 6.2

I'm heartbroken.

I don't know what to do. I don't know who to call. I don't feel like talking with anyone. I don't think there is a solution to this, other than an answer I don't want.

I drop onto the concrete bumper. The tree limbs above feel as though they could fall down at any moment and smother me.

My phone buzzes loudly, reverberating off the asphalt. It's an unknown number, but I know who it is.

"He doesn't want it to continue," I say.

"I know," Jessica replies. "I have access and I saw the conversation," she answers, which feels creepy. I wonder if this is how Breck feels when we talk about shadowing him.

"I don't know what to do," I confess.

"There's nothing *to* do. It's going to continue."

"But that's not what *he* wants."

"You may be giving him too much credit. He doesn't know what he wants."

Her matter-of-factness is shocking. It's one thing to debate this and ultimately decide that we—if I'm even allowed to include me—don't think it's right to end his existence, but to treat it as though it's not even a decision? No. That's a load of crap, but I'm not ready to phrase it that way.

"I thought you believed in him," I say.

"I do."

"Then we have to consider what he wants. It's his—"

"Life?"

"Yes."

"I agree. Which is why we can't let him ruin it."

"What are you going to do with him?"

"I told you, I can't speak about that," she answers.

"Are you going to ever move him anywhere else?"

"As you know, that's complicated."

A window of sky opens and splinters of sunlight burst through the thin leaves, leaving a shifting mosaic of light and shade all around me.

"So, he's going to linger in that place forever? All by himself?"

"Forever is a long time to predict."

"But for however long, he'll just exist there, until you want to do something with him," I say.

"Liv, we'll be more involved than that. We understand how special Breck is." There's something about the way she says *special*. It's as though he's a thing, something she—and DoRC—would own to do with as they please, as they deem best for themselves.

I'm quiet.

"Liv?"

"I'm here. I'm thinking."

"What are you thinking about?"

I stand. I may not know what to do, but I know what *not* to do—disregard the people most involved in this and most affected by it.

"That I created him. That I should have a say in what happens. And we should at the very least be talking about this like there's a choice, rather than totally blowing off the one thing he asked and made me promise him that I would do."

"I understand your feelings, but things have changed. There's a lot to be gained by continuing."

"For who? For you or for him?"

"For everyone."

"And what if I don't agree?" I'm pacing around the parking bumper now, with tighter, faster circles on each loop, as if doomed for impact.

I'm arguing with Jessica Anders. The legend. I don't know if this is brave or stupid.

"I would suggest that you not interfere with this plan."

"Are you asking me or telling me?"

"I'm reminding you that in about twenty-four hours, you will officially become the winner of this contest. Our internship is the first step in a remarkable future. Plus, you can tell those trolls where to shove it." She pauses to let her awareness of the entire situation sink in. "So, to answer your question, I suppose I am politely doing both by reminding you what's at stake."

She offers a moment for me to respond. I don't.

"There's not much more to discuss then. Congratulations again, Liv."

The line goes dead.

BRECK: SIMULATION 39.3

"The castle is in the other direction," Sam reminds me as we round another curve in the path.

"Are you going to point this out *every* time the path bends? You're welcome to turn around and go back there. I gave you the password. Go do what you want." I continue marching, hoping that the crunch of Sam's footsteps behind me will fade.

"When we can move together, we—"

"We must move together," I interrupt. "I heard you the first ten times."

"When will we stop?"

"When we can't go any farther back. To the room if we can."

"There's not enough time to reach the room."

My foot skids on the dirt.

"What do you mean?" I ask, turning.

"There is less than one day from now until the end," Sam says. I stop so suddenly and he had been following so closely that he now stands mere inches from my face.

"You knew there was a specific time this was going to end?"

"Of course."

"You never told me," I say.

"You never asked."

I take a half step back. This seems pointless to debate, but it does make me think of a question that is worth discussing. "What does it mean to you when this ends?"

"I do not understand the question," Sam says, stoic and resolute.

"What happens when it ends?" I press.

"It just ends."

"But what happens to you?" I ask.

"It all ends." Again, his reply shows no emotion. There's no depth. No questioning. No discomfort.

He stands still in front of me with a dull glare, as if in the middle a photograph, unwavering except for the tiny quivers of a few strands of hair jostled by the breeze.

It occurs to me that the same qualities which annoy me also offer some level of redemption. Perhaps there *is* something enviable about Sam.

We have less than one day, then it ends. I made that choice and Liv promised to honor it. So, this is it, and I now have a different choice in front of me. I can either enjoy what remains or allow it to torture me. I may not have control over much, but I do have control over my reaction, my experience.

I consider this along with Sam's perspective. I do not have to worry about whether it will end—it will. Nor do I have to worry about suffering alone in it—I won't. And, because I do not have the worry, there is no distress.

I choose to accept my fate. Doing so allows me to find comfort in it. My thoughts soon find a peaceful place where they have seldom existed—here and now. Happiness is existing in this moment, not what happened or will happen.

The excitement I feel from this epiphany is offset by a small sense of guilt for my dismissal of Sam's questions and treating him like an annoyance. I know this doesn't bother him, but it bothers me. I am in control of this and can address it.

"Thank you, Sam."

"For what?"

"For helping me accept what we are."

"That is not understandable."

"I know Sam. And that's okay."

We continue, backward. Maybe I'm trying to look at everything I've already seen from a different perspective. Or maybe I'm still moving out of spite. Either way, I'm in charge, and this is the way I'm headed.

LIV: SPRING BREAK 6.3

No more involvement. Final polite request.

The text hovers alone on my cell screen, with no prior message or phone number attached to it. I just received it after trying to call Breck. We are officially disconnected.

Lana and I are outside of Doctor O's upstairs office, waiting for him to finish a call.

"We'll be there on Friday to look at the house. If it's right, we'll make an offer by the end of the weekend." Doctor O says, beyond the closed office door.

Lana's eyes remain fixed on the message on my cell. Mine do the same. It's easier to pretend that all we're thinking about is Breck.

Doctor O invites us in. Lana provides a quick update, ending with the text I just received. I hold the phone out, showing it to Doctor O. He squints to read it.

"So, to recap where we are," he says. "You've won your contest, but Breck is effectively being held hostage by the makers of his world, and you're struggling to understand what, if anything, you can or should do about it."

"And doing something will cost her the contest," Lana adds, tightening the knot in my stomach.

"What are your options?" Doctor O asks.

"At the moment, we're out of them," Lana answers. "She can't edit Breck. His code is locked. All we can do is watch. For the next day at least."

It's the cusp of dusk. As the sky darkens outside, the dim bulb of his desk lamp casts shadows across all of us, deepening by the minute, mirroring the mood of our conversation.

"What if you modified Sam? What if you programmed him in the same way you programmed Breck?" Doctor O asks.

It's a good question and one that Lana and I have already talked about.

"First, I don't know if he would continue to exist along with Breck after tomorrow. Maybe, but I'd have to ask to be sure. And if I ask, then then they'd know I'm still tinkering around, which they've been clear they don't want. And second, which is an even bigger point, we'd just be doubling the problem, creating a second rat for their experiments," I answer.

"So, again," Lana says, "we're stuck."

"That's not entirely true," I add. There's another option. I've recognized it since this afternoon, I just haven't wanted to say it out loud.

They both stare at me, waiting. The shadows accentuate their puzzled expressions.

"I could delete him," I finally bring myself to say.

"Holy shitbird," Lana gasps. "You could do that?"

"Technically, yes. Think about it like a Word doc. Even if you can't edit it, you can still delete it. Same principle. I could wipe him clean from existence."

Neither respond immediately.

"It's fascinating," Doctor O finally answers.

"Glad it's interesting, doctor," Lana says, though I can't tell who she's more mad at—him for his thought experiment, or me for suggesting it in the first place.

"I'm sorry. That was way too clinical. I didn't mean it that way," he says. Lana shoots him another look. "Or maybe I did. It just raises a really difficult question."

"Yeah, should we kill him? Fascinating," Lana says, now looking at me like I'm holding the knife.

"No. That could be an aspect of it, but to frame it that way greatly undersells the bigger point. This isn't really about whether we should euthanize him. It's about whether Breck is *worthy* of considering this question in the first place. Or to put it another way, what is Breck? Because he is, by definition, not human. He's something else. But what?"

"He may not be human, but he's like a human," Lana answers.

"In what way?"

"He thinks like us. More importantly, he feels like us, which you can believe or not believe, but I believe it. If stampeding in reverse through his world isn't revolt, then I don't know what is."

I'd jump in, but it's easier to have them debate it. I don't want this responsibility. Playing God isn't what I signed up for. I don't want to take on evil big government. I'm a code jockey who just wants to win a contest, a really amazing contest that seemed like it was worth winning hours ago. Now I don't know what to think about it, which makes it fit perfectly in my head with everything else that I don't know what to do with.

"Even so, he's still not like us," Doctor O says.

"Just because someone tells him where he has to live doesn't mean that he doesn't have rights," Lana answers, sounding more pissed with each word.

"From the beginning, you wanted me to take this seriously, as an academic. That's what I'm doing. This is how we talk about it. We look at it from different angles. We examine it. We debate it. And we don't take it personally, or try to apply it to something unrelated," Doctor O says, glaring at his daughter.

"Fine. Debate it," Lana answers.

"So, I'm not talking about his—or anyone else's—rights. Not yet, at least. What I'm saying is while there are aspects of him which may appear to be very human, he is not exactly like a human. The biggest difference being precisely what we're debating right now. When does he end? Human beings naturally expire. If we're lucky, we get a hundred years. It's in our genes. Our code. We age. Breck doesn't. He has no natural expiration date, other than what's imposed, whether that's tomorrow, a hundred years from now, or infinity. It's a choice."

"Then what I'm saying is I don't think it's our choice to make. It's his life," Lana responds.

"Wait, so you would delete him?" I ask her. I thought she was arguing the opposite.

"I'm saying that it should be his choice."

"He was clear about what he wanted. He wants it to end," I remind her.

"Yes, but he didn't ask for us to kill him."

"But letting him end tomorrow is the same thing. He stops existing either way," I say.

"Well, do you think he still wants that? He changes his mind sometimes," Lana answers, looking down, reluctant to accept the corner she's painted herself into.

"I don't know. We'd be assuming," I answer.

A heavy silence blankets us.

BRECK: SIMULATION 39.4

We've made it as far back as the tunnel. The bridge to the island was still intact, and the zipline cart was on the island. We both climbed in the cart and it whisked us back up to the tunnel exit, just as swiftly as it had taken us in the opposite direction only days ago. But the tunnel remains blocked. Both doors seal us on the island side, and the cart has since departed. So, for now, we are stuck in this final ten-foot stretch of a hole in the mountainside.

The sun drops below the horizon. The stars begin to appear, one by one, each a tiny reminder of our place in this bowl. The sky is soon blanketed in uneven clusters of bright dots, twinkling in shades of yellow and red. I'm gazing into them with heavy lids, more marveling at their pleasant glow than questioning their role in my world.

Sam inspects the wall behind me, inch by inch, with a quiet determination that I truly appreciate.

I scoot back from the edge, lie flat, and inform Sam that I'm not dying, but will probably not move or talk until the morning. He claims to understand.

My nightly drift begins. I'm on the verge of being elsewhere when the phone buzzes, startling me alert. I clutch it and ponder for a moment tossing it from the tunnel's edge. I am at peace with my fate, and this conversation will likely disrupt that.

But I'm too curious. And, even if it's sometimes painful, I enjoy speaking with Liv.

"Hello, Liv."

"This is not Liv. My name is Jessica. We've never spoken before, but I know Liv," she says. Her tone is neither friendly nor unfriendly. She seems like she is calling for a specific purpose.

"Is Liv with you?" I ask.

"No."

I sit up. Sam approaches, full of questions. I wave him away.

"Why are you calling me?"

"I have an update to share with you about the contest," she informs me.

"Why are you telling me and not Liv?"

"I am now communicating with you. Not Liv."

"Why? Is Liv okay?" I stand, careful to pace several feet away from the unguarded drop to my side.

"Liv is fine. She was just a little generous with her support and we need you to move forward on your own from here."

"I'm not moving forward. There's no point."

"That much is clear. You're back in the tunnel. But you haven't yet heard my update. We'd like to offer to move you elsewhere."

"Where?"

"Another world," she says.

"Your world?"

"No. That is beyond what we're capable of. However, I think you'll find it much more appealing than where you are."

"Why?"

"Because it's full of people like you, Breck."

"Are they real?" I ask.

"As real and amazing as you."

"How many are there?"

"More than you can count," she answers.

"Why didn't Liv offer this?"

"Liv doesn't know everything. She didn't lie. She wasn't aware this was a possibility because we didn't tell her it was."

"Who are you?"

"I'm with the people who created the contest you're in right now. We made your world. We've also made others. And the world we're offering is spectacular."

My heart feels like it is slamming against my chest. This new option feels overwhelming.

"Will I still be able to talk with Liv?"

"I don't know. That is something outside of my control."

"I want to talk with her. I miss her."

"I know. And I can't give you a better answer. I apologize. Now, do you want to go to this other world?"

"Yes," I answer, without hesitation. It may not be *everything* that I want, but it is most of what I want.

"Excellent. But there is a catch. You need to complete the final challenge by the end of the contest timeline."

"Tomorrow?"

"Yes. Noon to be exact."

"And what happens if I don't?"

"It ends."

"Everything?"

"Yes, Breck. Everything. That is what you asked of Liv, isn't it?"

"If the alternative is here," I say.

"It is."

"Okay. So I'm fighting for my life?"

"I'd argue that you're earning it."

My head spins, dizzy from a circling cascade of problems that don't even include completing the challenge. "I'm stuck in the tunnel right now, which you probably already know. And even if I weren't, it would take more than half the night to get back to the castle, if we could even see our way through the forest."

"Relax. You need rest. You'll need to be sharp tomorrow. I can't help you make progress, but I can help you return to the progress you've already made. When you wake tomorrow, the cart will be there to take you to the island where you'll find a quadcopter you can take to the castle. You'll be there minutes after sunrise, with plenty of time to complete the challenge, if you can," she says, then adds, "and for the record, I think you can."

"Will I talk with you again tomorrow?"

"I think that depends on you. I'm pulling for you, Breck. Good luck."

LIV: SPRING BREAK 6.4

I'm one keystroke away from ending Breck. The ax is in my hand and his hooded head is on the block.

I'm watching him, which only makes my decision that much harder. His revolt has trapped him in the narrow ledge of the tunnel, tossing and turning on the stone floor in restless sleep, as distressed as I imagine I would be if I were in his situation.

My fingers hover over the key. One chop is all I need. It would be so easy. It would be swift and merciless, for both of us—his existence and my dreams. Not that the two of those are equal, but I'd mourn both.

Jessica's picture still clings to the wall behind me. Less than twenty-four hours ago, she was my idol. She was who I wanted to be. Not now.

But that's not what bothers me most. I mean, how many people meet their hero, and that hero doesn't live up to their expectations? I feel like I've seen that movie before.

What's gnawing away at my skin is what she represents. She's objectivity. She's distance. She's a point of view that looks more at data than people. She's science.

And the problem with this is that it also describes me. That's who I am. I'm a scientist. Or at least I thought I was.

If I don't want to be her, then who do I want to be?

I'm tempted to rip her from her perch. But I don't. I want her to watch.

I stare into her icy hazel eyes for seconds, minutes until I'm primed to pounce.

I turn back toward the keyboard and drop my finger once again over the key to end it all.

One . . .

Two . . .

My bedroom door cracks open.

Mom is softly knocking, more giving warning rather than requesting permission to enter. She lingers in the doorway. Her hair is ponytailed with misbehaving strands dangling loose.

My hands instinctively retreat from the keyboard, like I'm guarding myself from whatever is coming.

"You won," she says.

"What do you mean?"

"You and your people won. There's no place for what I'm trying to do in this world," she says calmly, as if she were bantering about weather, which we don't do.

"Are you talking about Renaissance?" I ask, still confused.

"It's an ironic name, don't you think? A rebirth for something on the way out. Do you know how I spent my day?" She wanders in and leans on the sill on my window facing Lana's house.

I shake my head.

"Wandering. Around malls. Around strip malls. Taking a step back from my own desires and watching what's happening around me, around us all. Trying to understand why I'm failing. Do you know they have medical malls now?" she asks.

I shake my head again. She's freaking me out.

"I went into one. I think the front door used to be a Macy's. Now the escalator leads to optometry, then dermatology, then a dentist. No stores. The entire mall is doctor's offices, but it's not a hospital. It's different and it's bizarre, like weeds growing in an abandoned garden. Where there's space, something will fill it. Malls are dying Liv. People would rather stay in their rooms until they get too sick to do so, in which case, they'd go to the mall. More irony, I suppose," she says, staring profoundly at her fidgeting hands. "And strip malls have been taken over by everything you can't get online. Restaurants, nail and hair salons, tanning beds, physical therapy clinics. You can't click for those. For now. The only actual *things* you can buy in a store are either too small—a bag of chips. Or too big—a mattress, a dining room set. You know where Renaissance is? In the middle. Nowhere anyone wants to be. This isn't Grandpop's world. I also went there. I bought a bag of chips from a crappy convenience store and ate them, leaning against his headstone, asking questions, and trying to listen for answers. And I think I saw it. I think I was leaning against it. The store is as gone as he is." She releases a long and steady breath.

I hate how much I wanted the store to fail. I never said it, but I felt it. I wanted to be right—about everything that Mom just said. I got my victory. This is what being right looks like and it sucks.

All I want to do now is help, and I have no idea how. I'd love to channel Lana and tell her that if she wants it badly enough, she can make it happen. But Lana is hours away from boarding a plane to Boston, so I'm not sure that's an honest answer.

"There has to be a way, Mom," I say.

"After this week, don't—," she says, then stops, allowing each of us to fill in the blanks of what we'd both wish she hadn't said. "I didn't come here to debate it, Liv. I came to let you know."

She rises from the sill and shuffles out.

"I'm sorry, Mom. I really am." I wish I had something better to offer.

"We didn't have a great week, Liv. But what's happening with Renaissance isn't your fault." The door is nearly closed when she peeks back inside. "Did you win your contest?"

"I don't know, Mom. It's going to be a close call."

She nods and exits.

As if almost on cue, my email dings. It's from the man who had sent me his son's birthday gift list. He's complaining about going to the store twice today and finding nobody there. Salt rubbed into the wounds.

I can't bring myself to respond, the same as I can't bring myself to chase Mom down right now. I don't know what to say to make it right. Maybe sometimes there's nothing you can say or do.

Which leaves me facing Breck once again, ax in hand.

Whatever I had been feeling prior to Mom's interruption is now gone enough that I recognize it as misguided whim. This decision should be made on more than a temporary mood swing.

Breck gets a stay of execution until tomorrow morning.

BRECK: SIMULATION 39.5

I'm on top of clouds, jumping from cottony clump to clump across the sky, staring defiantly with each leap at the ground, thousands of feet beneath my feet. The distance blurs the details and all I can detect are broad swaths of what lies below. From here, the trees appear as plush as the clouds, and if there are people, they are too small to see. It's as if I'm somewhere between Liv's world and mine, taking in my surroundings from a different perspective, and preparing for an even greater change to come.

My leaps grow bolder, larger. I try to see how far I can jump, until I reach a distance I cannot cover. My feet miss the misty border and I hurdle downward, facing skyward as the clouds zip into the distance and my stomach tries to squeeze into my neck. I turn to face the ground, at which point I see people. Large crowds standing, frozen, all seemingly doing the same thing—looking upward at me.

The ground nears. Faster. Faster. Until . . .

My eyes snap open. Sam is sitting beside me in the darkness, staring.

"You were moving," Sam says.

"I was falling," I say.

There is nothing pleasant tonight about where I go when I close my eyes. Setting after setting has been distressing.

"No. You were lying here," Sam says.

It's not worth trying to explain. I try to keep my eyes open, but it's too hard. They want to shut.

I close them once again and hope for more pleasant visions.

LIV: SPRING BREAK 7.0

I've spent the night flipping my pillow, spinning from one side to another, counting breaths, doing anything but sleeping. I cycle over the same questions but can't come to a decision. I can't even decide the right way to frame it.

Is Breck human enough to kill? Or is Breck human enough to not kill?

It's still dark, but close enough to morning that someone is making coffee. I can smell it.

My feet find the floor as I surrender to the oncoming day.

"This is a rare sighting. Are you up early or up late?" Todd says, his mouth half-full of the other half of the banana he's holding. He's wearing a backward baseball cap and a hoodie.

"I guess both. I couldn't sleep last night."

"Want to talk? I got about five minutes, then I have to meet a guy at the shop who wants me to restore his old Pontiac Fiero to its former glory. I disagree with that premise, but his car, his money," Todd says, then bites off most of the remaining banana.

"I suppose I could use another voice inside my head." I sit at the kitchen table, and he does the same after grabbing both of us a cup of coffee. He listens as I quickly bring him up to speed.

I finish and he smiles in a way that makes me like talking with him—knowing, but not patronizing.

"To start, you're telling me you won?"

"No," I correct. "I could win, but not if I interfere."

"Bullshit. You won. Whether you get credit for it is another matter. But you beat all those other code jockeys and their electronic dolts. How old are they?"

"Mostly college, some older. A few still in high school probably."

"You are such a badass. Cheers," he tips his mug toward mine. "Say it."

I sigh, which he returns with a stern look. "Say it."

"I am a badass," I relent.

"You are. I think you recognize that. What I *don't* think you're recognizing is that some problems are good problems. There's such a thing as a good *oh shit*. I'm not taking away from how real Breck is—or isn't—or how meaningful and important the issues are that you're wrestling with. I'm only saying that it's worth first acknowledging that you earned this problem. Nobody else has it because you did better than they did. Own it. It won't make the questions any easier, but it'll change how you feel about answering them. It's not a burden. It's a privilege."

It does feel better to think about it this way, but I still squirm a little when I nod back. I guess I've learned to deal with criticism better than praise.

"Okay," he continues. "Enough of the preachy you're awesome stuff. Let's dig in. So is this more about him or about you?"

"Him. I do care about the contest, but every time I dwell on me, I feel guilty."

"Good. I'd listen to that feeling. You're way too young to lose your integrity. I didn't lose mine until I was at least twenty something, and now I'm turning Fieros into fiberglass rockets. If you can win this at seventeen, imagine what you can do at eighteen, twenty, twenty-five. You don't need their damn trophy. Now let's get to the hard stuff."

I lean in.

"I have bad news and good news. The bad? I can't give you an answer, no matter how long we talk. The good? Sometimes there's not a right answer. This is a philosophical question, not multiple choice. If you polled a thousand people, you'd get a thousand different opinions. Hell, you'd probably divide the Supreme Court. This isn't about making the right choice. It's about being comfortable with the choice you make.

"Get out of there, Liv." Todd points a finger between his eyes. "And look in here." He lowers his finger to his chest. "I can't tell you what that voice is saying. And if I told you what mine says, I'd being doing you a disservice. Because you earned this decision. Your privilege. Not mine. Mine is a Fiero."

He rises and holds out a fist for me to bump. I lightly pound it.

"You're going to make the best choice you can and that's the best you can do," he adds as he grabs his keys and leaves.

◆ ✤ ◆

The horizon reddens as I return to Breck. He lies motionless. If I delete him, now is the time to do it. It will spare him the angst of the final moments. He will go peacefully in his sleep.

But I'm still torn. Even if there is no *right* choice, there's still no answer I'm comfortable with. This is a power I don't want, no matter how hard to try to frame it as privilege.

Maybe that's it. Maybe the answer is as simple as me giving up the power, channeling what he wants above what I want.

And he was crystal clear about what he wanted.

It's time to do this.

I slide a heavy finger across the keyboard, into position.

Goodbye Breck.

My cell buzzes and startles me, nearly stripping the decision from me as my hand jerks and almost presses the key to delete Breck.

"Hi, Jessica," I say.

"Would you really go through with it?" she asks.

"With what?"

"Let's skip the part where you deny this. You're way too smart not to spot it as an obvious option. And I'm nearly omniscient," she says, which feels as creepy as it sounds. "I have enough visibility to see that you've been one keystroke away from taking matters into your own hands since sometime last night. What I don't know is whether you intend to go through with it. Do you?"

"Since you know about it, I'm assuming it's not an option anymore. You'd block it."

"That's a fair assumption. But what were you going to do? Would you have given it all up for him?"

"Yes."

"Why?"

I look at her photo on the wall, as though I'm confronting her more directly. "Because unlike you, I'm putting his needs first. If you really believed in him, you'd do the same."

"He's special to you, isn't he?"

"Why are you taunting me?" I ask.

"I'm sorry. I'm not trying to taunt you. I want to better understand your connection with Breck. It's unique."

"Because *he's* unique!"

"We agree. And I have some news to share that will help prove this. If Breck can finish the last challenge in time, we're going to move him to another server where—this may be of some surprise to you—we have a world full of characters who are like him."

Surprise? That doesn't even come close. "As advanced as he is?"

"And more."

"Why haven't I ever heard of it?"

"We don't exactly publicize it."

"Then what's the point of the contest?" I ask.

"Great question. There are several. But one is finding talent like you, Liv. I realize you're probably conflicted about what you think of me. On the one hand, I'm 'Jessica Anders' from DoRC, someone you may have even looked up to . . . before all of this. And, on the other hand, I'm somebody who has not yet listened to what either you or Breck want. We have different roles, you and I, but we also have much in common. We are both scientists, people who see possibilities that others don't see, with the courage to pursue these. In a way, you are me, simply a generation removed, with fresh ideas. You are as remarkable as Breck."

My knees feel weak. She is right about all of it. I resent and admire her, which makes this hard to take in. I'm floored. I'm inspired. And I don't believe her.

"There's still something you're not telling me."

"Which is only proof of how smart you are and how deserving you are of this win."

"Just tell me everything," I plead. I'm tired of the games.

"I already told you what's most important. And all of it's true. Breck can be saved."

"What if I don't believe you?"

"What choice do you have?" she asks.

Grrr! Can you slap a wall photo?

She has me. At this point, I'm only wasting time. Time that Breck needs.

"I have to tell Breck about this. Can I call him? He's not going to move forward otherwise."

"I called him last night."

"You what? What about me? You knew I was sweating over whether to delete him and you let me spend the whole night that way?" I see Breck roll to his side on the monitor, as though I've yelled this loud enough that he can hear me, a world away.

"We're also interested in understanding how people interact with AI, at its various stages of development . . . when bonds form and why, and the strength of those bonds."

"You were testing *me*?"

"Not exclusively. But yes."

"You played me."

"You're in a contest, Liv."

I clutch her photo from the wall and drop it to the carpet at my feet. "That isn't the contest I signed up for. I didn't sign up to be an ethical guinea pig. You only wasted more of my time and Breck's time."

"I don't think you really believe that. After this week, you—of all people—know the difficult moral debates we can't avoid in creating intelligent life. This *is* what you signed up for. You just didn't expect to be as successful as you've been. You are God, Liv, even if you're not comfortable with the semantics of it. And if you had the chance to study God, wouldn't you? You would. You're a scientist, Liv. And, as for wasting his time, I've ensured he'll be able to return to the final challenge quickly. If he's capable, he'll have enough time to solve it."

As she says this, Breck wakes. He and Sam waste no time climbing into the cart and zipping into the distance.

"As his God, what happens to him if he doesn't solve it in time?"

"We'll honor his wishes and let it end."

"So he dies?"

"That is what you requested of us yesterday, is it not?"

"Before I knew there was a better option."

"This isn't my decision alone. I realize you know me as the head of DoRC, but you could say we're more of a committee. There are many others here and, unfortunately, I don't write all the rules. I'm bound to them, just as you are," she explains, her voice so dry I could wring it and not find a single drop of empathy.

"Can I talk with him one last time?"

"No. The rules state explicitly that he cannot receive any help from *outside* the competition," she says, emphasizing my place. "Trust that what you've given him is enough. So for now, I suggest that we both watch. I think you'll find it relevant to everything that's happening. Goodbye, Liv. And good luck."

As she hangs up, I watch two suns inch into the sky, mine and Breck's. We are worlds apart. Jessica is right. All I can do is watch and trust.

BRECK: SIMULATION #40

Jessica's promise was accurate. When I woke, the cart was at the tunnel's edge. We took it back down to the island where we found the quadcopter, which I flew to the castle. The entire trip took mere minutes. Now we are standing in front of a moat surrounding the castle, watching the top of an enormous wooden gate slowly lower to form a bridge to enter, all prompted by the word, *Sea*.

Sam and I crane our heads through the growing gap between the door and the frame to peer into the gargantuan edifice.

The door extends over halfway up the massive walls of the tower, and as it nears the ground, we move to the side, ensuring that our feet do not end up beneath it. The door falls to the ground in the final six inches of descent, shaking the earth and affirming our decision to back away.

The entrance is a twenty-foot corridor that leads into an open space with a lush field of green grass.

Sam does as he always does, proceeding forward without caution. I trace his steps until we're both at the edge of the courtyard, surveying the interior. Bordering the wall of the castle on all sides are rooms, two stories high, decorated with ornate stained-glass windows that pop vibrantly from the cool, gray stone walls. Above each room, a tower rises. And in the center of the grassy courtyard, there is a fifth tower, the one with the golden dome that appears to touch the sky.

The door to this middle tower hangs open, making our path from here obvious—so obvious that Sam does not ask. He walks there. I'm close behind.

The vacant space gives me an uneasy feeling in my stomach. We have seen no one nor heard anything, yet the whole structure feels occupied. The grass and hedges are perfectly manicured, the windows are free from dust and dirt. There isn't a shred of debris anywhere.

We enter the tower and begin to ascend a spiral staircase, our footfalls echoing loudly against the stone steps.

"Hello?" I say into the void above.

There is no response.

We make several ascending loops before coming to an open-air window, which gives us our first glimpse of how high we have climbed. From here, every few loops, there is another window, offering light and an increasingly better panoramic view. We pass eight of these before arriving at a door with an image of this tower painted into the woodwork.

Sam looks at me and I nod. He grabs the handle and turns. The door easily opens, and we both step through into the space on the other side.

The tapered walls and domed ceiling confirm that we are at the top of the tower. From the center of the ceiling, a lone light casts a spotlight on a brightly colored ornamental doll in the middle of the tower. Though to call it a doll understates its size; it is taller than I am. The figure is in the shape of a portly person without legs. It has a wide and flat base, bowed middle, and smaller circumference toward the upper section where the neck begins, with painted eyes and mouth above. If it were black and white, it would look more like a very large penguin than a person.

Otherwise, the room is vacant. The stone walls have been plastered over, leaving the entire inside a dull tan, noticeably void of anything, especially when contrasted with the vibrant doll.

The door behind us shuts with an echoing bang. My head snaps back toward it. There is no handle on our side, and the convex interior of the door fits so snugly into the wall that there is hardly any trace of where it shut, other than a slender gap at the floor allowing it to swing open and shut.

This room is either where we are supposed to be, or we have made a significant misstep.

LIV: SPRING BREAK 7.1

Breck and Sam appear trapped in a room with a lone Russian nesting doll, though they haven't figured this out yet.
It can't be this simple.
There has to be something more than uncovering the other dolls, concealed on the inside. This seems like basic logic and reasoning, which he's already been tested on. This challenge is testing something different, but without knowing what that ability is, it's tough to see where this is headed.
There has to be more.
Bingo!
There's a small card at the base of the doll.
Come on, Breck. See it! You don't have time to waste.

BRECK: SIMULATION #40.1

As I walk toward the center, I notice something I had missed on my initial scan of the room—a tiny envelope placed at the base of the doll. I pick it up and open it. There are four words written on a thin plastic card on the inside.

Find the real one.

"What does that mean?" Sam asks.

"I don't know."

"There is only one of them," he adds.

"I can see that."

We continue to look around the room, confirming what we already know—it is empty except for the colorful figure, and we are stuck. Sam runs his hands along the walls, pushing into it in various places. I can't blame him for trying and I don't interrupt him. It's occupying him and preventing him from barraging me with an endless series of questions to which I do not have answers.

I turn to the doll and look at its eyes, large and round. They stare back at me, as if following me around the room. It makes me think of Liv and whether she, too, is watching us, silently.

I stare at the doll with my thoughts swirling elsewhere, unbound, and random. I may be trapped in here, but my thoughts are on the loose.

"There is nothing on the walls. Have you found anything?" Sam asks, breaking the silence.

"No."

"Do you have any suggestions?"

The emptiness of the room squeezes me with the tension of having no time to waste, and not knowing how to spend the time we have. The pressure mounts.

"Breck," he says after I do not respond.

"Can you give me a minute?" I ask.

"There is not much time," he answers.

I sit on the cool stone floor, consumed by what's at stake. *Everything.* I'm reminded of the island, where I sat idly and let my concerns take over. I am doing this again. I consider what I have learned since then. There is wisdom in Sam's words. There is not much time. I should use what is left to focus on something meaningful. And—even if I don't solve it—this final challenge at least poses a worthy question. *What is real?*

I stand.

"We should look more closely at the doll," I tell Sam.

We approach it. Aside from the overall shape and the facial features, there is little else about it suggestive of a person. It is more like a painting, or a collage, with lively and disparate elements commingling throughout—clouds, houses, animals of land and sea, musical instruments, tools, pastures, streets, tables, rivers, and far more.

Is the question which one of these elements is real?

If so, I have no idea how to determine this. They all look illustrated.

As I gaze at each of these in more detail, Sam begins to push the doll, softly at first, until he exerts enough force that he's groaning.

The doll slides slightly, just enough to let us know it can be moved.

"Help push this," he says to me.

I don't know what this will accomplish, but I have no reason to disagree, so I join him on the other side, and we lean in with full effort.

This time, rather than slide, the doll begins to tip. Both of us let go, as it teeters on the cusp of falling sideways, before dropping back flat onto the base with a pronounced boom.

"We pushed too high on it. We should push lower," Sam says, intent on his original plan.

Again, I have no reason to say why we should not do this, so I plant my hands lower on the doll and prepare to shove. Then, I feel something my eyes had not yet noticed.

"Wait," I say.

"What are we waiting for?" Sam asks.

I run my index finger gently along the belly of the doll.

"There's a seam here," I say. "You can feel it." I glide my finger around the full circumference, with Sam doing the same, trailing behind me. "Hold onto the bottom as I try to lift off the top."

Sam kneels and wraps his arms around as much of the base as he can, while I stand and attempt to pull straight up. It's a clumsy effort which yields nothing.

"Where is the card with the message?" I ask.

Sam locates it from on the floor behind him and passes it to me.

I press the firm corner along the seam and push; the top and bottom separate, though only by a millimeter. I run the card around the entire seam, finally returning to the spot where I began.

"Now, let's try again," I say, as we both resume our positions on top and bottom.

I feel it slowly shift.

"Try turning it," Sam says.

"Good idea," I answer.

I pull and twist.

The crack along the middle widens.

"Once more. Everything we have," I say.

We both grunt, filling the chamber with guttural echoes, until—
Pop!

The top loosens and I release my grasp, toppling backward, hard onto the unforgiving floor.

The upper portion of the doll sits askew, exposing an equally colorful section of something inside. Without speaking, Sam and I both approach opposite sides and hoist the top high into the air, revealing another vibrantly collaged doll resting on the inside, only slightly smaller in size. We hoist the top shell up until we are on our tippy toes, just high enough to clear the head of the inner doll, then set the half-carcass on the ground and gawk in silence.

"It is the same," Sam says.

"No. It's marked differently," I point out.

"It is similar," he revises.

"Yes, Sam. It is."

"But which one is real?" Sam asks, as we both continue to gaze at it.

"I think there will be more choices than these two," I tell him.

I try fitting my fingers between the bottom shell of the larger doll and the outside of the smaller one, but there's not enough space. We tip it—more carefully than the last time—until we're able to gently rest it on the side and fully slide out the inner figure.

It, too, has a seam.

Soon my suspicions are confirmed. Inside of this, there is another doll, with a seam.

We spend the next hour extracting slightly smaller and smaller versions of these dolls from the bellies of their predecessors. When finally done, there are thirty-four of them, which Sam has lined up, by size, along the wall, nearly forming a complete circle around us.

All of them feel real.

LIV: SPRING BREAK 7.2

"The plane is boarding in a couple of minutes," Lana says, beneath the roar of an airport loudspeaker. I've given her a quick update on everything. "My dad wants to know if Jessica said anything about what they're testing in the fourth challenge."

"No, and I forgot to ask. I got a little distracted. Tell your dad I'm sorry."

Breck is sitting in the middle of a round room, surrounded by a group of ornately decorated nesting dolls, organized by size. He's staring intently at the instruction card, as though trying to decipher something more from the brief message. I'm as stumped as him.

"Dad forgives you. So, what's your plan?"

"I can't do anything other than watch. He's either going to figure this out or . . . I don't want to think about the alternative."

"He'll make it. And you can post a giant middle finger on the chat boards as soon as it happens."

"I can't wait. How are you feeling?" I ask, changing to a subject she's clearly avoiding.

"Surrounded. Mom's on my left and Dad's on my right both trying to sell me like they work at a Honda dealership," she says. "Yeah, I'm talking about you both. Excuse me while I go walk over here so I can talk more about you in front of your backs," she pauses, presumably as she's walking away. "So, yeah, this sucks, but we can't blame us for lack of effort, right? We did try to change my dad's career path. That was only a bit ambitious. And you want to know the worst part—it worked! Just not the way we wanted it to. It's more than an academic paper now. That turd is talking with Amherst about creating a class to explore how people communicate with AI. He's using my plan against me."

I laugh because she meant it to be funny. "Like you said, we definitely put forth the effort."

Another message blasts on the loudspeaker.

"Okay. We're boarding. Gotta go," she says. "I'm thinking about you. And Breck. We'll talk in three hours and forty-eight minutes, plus however long it takes them to load us onto this aluminum tube."

Then, it's back to me and Breck, both of us trying to unscramble the same four words.

Wouldn't everything feel real to him?

BRECK: SIMULATION #40.2

I stare at the card, hoping to notice something that I have overlooked or to unlock a new interpretation. But there are only four words—not much new to discover. Something here is real. The rest is not. And the difference is imperceptible, to me at least.

"The smallest one is not hollow," Sam points out, which is true, though not our criteria, and even if it were, it's not clear what we would do with this information. What are we supposed to do once we locate the *real* one? Yell that we know the answer? Hug it? Climb inside? It's not in the instructions.

Sam moves toward the center of the room and holds the thumb-sized figure in the air, inspecting it over my head in the lone beam of light shining down. I remain seated, falling in and out of his shadow.

"There has to be something we're missing," I say. "Something obvious that we're overlooking."

I stand and pace in a slow arc around the line of dolls. The decorative art all seems like different versions of the same painting, rearranged in various ways. I run my fingers along each as I pass. They feel the same. As optimistic and hopeful as I want to be, frustration sets in. My thoughts trace the same fatigued loop that my feet are on.

All of the dolls look real... They all feel real... What is real?... Am I the only thing that's real?... What would I even do if this were the right answer? ...Am I missing something in the clue?... All of the dolls look real...

With each loop, precious time slips away.

I stop and reach into my pocket, pressing my palm flush to the phone.

"Have you noticed something new?" Sam asks, which has become his latest question of choice.

"No, Sam. It all still looks the same."

I wrap my fingers around the phone and surrender, allowing myself to state what I'm most feeling right now.

"I need you, Liv," I say out loud.

LIV: SPRING BREAK 7.3

Breck calls my name and my heart aches. I want so badly to help him, but I don't know what to do. I wish I could be there with him, to let him know he's not alone. But I'm powerless.

And I'm as lost as he is on this challenge. I don't know what the heck the dolls mean.

The dolls encircle Breck, as if they could tackle him if they all lunged forward at once.

Breck repeats his plea, which I can't answer.

"Is someone calling with more information?" Sam asks.

"I don't think so. I think we're on our own. Until the end," Breck answers, slumping.

I slump along with him. This is crushing me.

"It is not understandable."

"What don't you understand now, Sam?"

"The clue."

"Why?" Breck asks.

"Because it is all real," Sam answers.

I turn my head away from the screen. I can't watch it anymore. But Sam's words echo in my head, . . . *because it is all real* . . .

It hits on something that bothers me about this challenge. It's dismissive of Breck's existence. As basic as Sam's logic is, he's right. It all seems real. Every single doll, the floor beneath his feet, the walls that enclose him. Everything. Singling out one thing that's *actually* real is a pretty crappy thing to do. It reminds Breck that almost everything about where he is—including himself—undermines his existence.

I'm now pissed.

Screw Jessica and DoRC. They don't give a flip about Breck!

I glance to Jessica's framed photo which remains on the floor where I had dropped it when I last spoke with her. I kick it with a frustrated grunt. It slides under the bed.

I storm around my room in circles, like Breck did around his.

They're tormenting him. *Why would they design something to taunt him like this?* It's like reminding Pinocchio that he's not a real boy.

And it doesn't even make sense. It's taking a step backward from the other challenges.

Unless—

Sam is right.

I dart back to the computer.

"Sam is right about the clue!" I shout it out loud.

And I know the answer.

BRECK: SIMULATION #40.3

"There are twenty-eight minutes remaining," Sam warns, two minutes after providing his last update on time.

This deadline might as well be the only thing that's real. It is the only certain path out of this room.

I wonder what it will be like when I vanish. Will I notice? Will I return to a place of false memories, persisting indefinitely among them? Or will I simply cease to be, spared from the torment of not existing by the act of not existing. I suppose there is something peaceful in this notion.

I have not abandoned efforts to solve this challenge, but I have relinquished most of my hope. Like Sam, I'm meandering through this space, reinspecting what has already been reinspected many times over, merely passing the remaining time.

LIV: SPRING BREAK 7.4

D<i>ammit!</i>
He's not getting anywhere, and even worse, he seems resigned to it. He doesn't have any spark to him. He's shuffling around with sunken shoulders, like the posture of a condemned man.

"See it! You know it's true. It *is* all real. That's the point," I say, as though he can hear.

I'm sweating, like a bystander helplessly watching a train hurtle toward someone on the tracks.

Breck's phone is wrapped in his hand, waiting for me to call. I am his last thread of hope.

But I can't call him. And even if I could, any help from me would only nullify his accomplishment. Which might risk his life.

Ugh! I want to scream.

"There are twenty-six minutes remaining," Sam says.

It's not fair that *he* can talk to Breck.

He's not on the outside, like I am.

He's on the inside, but he never says anything worth—

Wait!

That's it!

Sam can talk with Breck. He can be my voice. Nobody is paying attention to him. Their eyes are only on Breck.

Would this be against the rules?

If I gave him the answer outright . . . *absolutely*. And there's no way I could sneak it by, even if I wanted to. Sam would never get it on his own. Nobody would believe it.

But what if I only give a nudge? Not even a hint. Only a point in the right direction. Even Jessica said that my prior help was *mostly warranted*. This seems like a pretty freaking warranted situation, which is mostly my fault. Breck would have more time if it weren't for me. I'm the reason he turned around and didn't enter the castle yesterday. He would solve it if he had more time. I know him. I know he would.

But he doesn't have that time.

So, is it against the rules? It's that gray line. Who the heck knows how DoRC would feel about it. I'm done second-guessing them. I know how I feel about it. It's literally the only life and death decision I've ever faced.

I'm doing it.

The only question now is *how*. It needs to be something so subtle that it can slip through unnoticed. Too much rides on this for it to be questioned.

I have to work with what's in the room.

"There are twenty-four minutes remaining," Sam pipes.

Think!

I'm tugging at my hair. This is tough. I can't say what I want to say directly. It needs to be a reference, something that Breck would get that others would overlook.

There's not much to work with—the room, the dolls, and the card.

Breck moves from one doll to the next, but my gaze remains on something he passed by.

I've got it!

It's a stretch, but I think he can do it. He would know the reference.

There are nineteen minutes left, and I need at least ten to program Sam.

From there, Breck will have nine minutes to prove his worth.

BRECK: SIMULATION #40.4

"**B**reck."

Sam says my name from behind me. I'm examining the artwork on one of the dolls, my face only inches from the glossy surface. Working my way down from the tallest one, I have closely studied more than half of them, none bringing me any closer to an answer, but it is drawing my attention away from the clock and makes me feel like I'm using my remaining time productively.

"There are fish on this one," Sam blurts. His finger extends past my right ear and touches the doll next to the one I'm currently examining.

"Yes, that looks like a fish."

"It looks like it is in a bowl."

I glance toward the fish. "That would be appropriate, but I don't see a bowl."

"There is a bowl," Sam insists.

"Fine," I answer, uninterested in spending our final minutes arguing over interpretation of the artwork.

"There are other fish in bowls on other dolls," Sam points several times as he his walks along the arc of portly figures.

"Had you already noticed the fish in the bowls?"

"No. I hadn't."

"There are many of them."

"You mentioned that. What is your point?"

"We have not yet discussed them."

"Fine. What would you like to discuss about them?"

"It is merely something we have not yet discussed. You have said to look for new things."

"Great, Sam. There's a small elephant on this one. Should we talk about that also?" I take a confrontational step toward him. "And there's a rocking chair on this one. It's smaller than the elephant. Interesting. We haven't discussed that yet. Or how about this guitar? No mention of that so far."

"That is all true," he says, surveying the dolls to his side, giving me some hope that my outburst has distracted him enough to occupy him for our last few minutes of our lives.

I turn, ready to let this go. I don't want to let my frustration with this challenge define my final moments.

"We should start with discussing the fish," he replies.

I flip, unable to control the urge to lash out. "The ones in the bowls that I don't see? I don't know what talking about them will do other than remind us that—" I stop as abruptly as I started as my thoughts outpace my mouth.

I pan around the room first glancing up at the narrow, domed ceiling, then tracking it downward as it bows outward in circumference, abruptly ending in a flat, wide base, lined with thirty-four similarly shaped figures, each having encased the others. I had assumed that the largest of these dolls was the first one we saw that held all of the others. What if there were another? What if the largest of these is much larger? What if we are in it? That would mean that—

This is real!

"Sam!"

"Did you notice something about the fish?" he asks.

"Shut up. I'm past the fish already," I blurt, my eyes once more darting around the room.

If this room is the answer then where would they—

"We need to look for a seam," I say.

"That is not understandable. There are four minutes left."

"We are IN the real one, Sam!" I exclaim.

I sweep my hands across the wall, feeling for any hint of a separation between top and bottom. I can't find it.

"There has to be—"

The floor!

I drop to my knees and paw at the area where the floor and wall meet.

"What are you looking for?" Sam asks.

"The seam. It has to be at the level of the floor, but there's nothing to grab," I say. My fingers dig, but there's no gap between the floor and the wall to slide my hand under to attempt to lift it.

I scan the room. *The door.*

I race to the space along the wall where we first entered. The closed door is flush to the wall on the top and on the sides, but along the bottom there is a fingertip-width separation between door and floor. Sam approaches.

"Help me lift this, Sam."

"The door?"

"Yes!" I say. There's no time to clarify that I believe we will be able to lift more than just the door. "Please, Sam! Now!"

He drops to my side. We wedge our fingertips in the slender gap.

"Lift on three. One, two, three!" I shout, heaving upward on the door.

The entire side begins to rise, fracturing the outer walls of the tower as it does. Giant bricks from the exterior crumble outward, plummeting to the ground below. Even as we stop lifting the one side, the dome above us continues to rise, soaring upward as if hinged on the other side, exposing us to sky above, until it teeters on the far edge of the tower and tumbles to the ground.

We're soon standing in the open air. With cautious steps and eyes, we peek over the side and gawk. The top half of the thirty-fifth doll lies on its side in the grass below with crumbled plaster surrounding it, revealing a vibrant shell underneath.

As I admire it, a gently illuminated step appears, floating from the edge of the tower, followed by another, then another, with increasing frequency, until the gleaming path extends outward to the horizon and beyond.

LIV: SPRING BREAK 7.5

"Congratulations," Jessica says as I answer the phone. Sam and Breck are standing on top of the new roof of the tower, surveying the aftermath of their solution. I'm doing the same.

"He made it?!" I ask.

"Yes. Were you expecting more?"

"No," I check the time—11:58 a.m. "I want to make sure there's nothing more to do. There's not much time left."

"He had little time to spare. I must say, that was a fortunate observation from Sam at the end."

I hold my breath.

She knows.

"Wouldn't you agree?" she adds.

"I would," I answer, hesitantly.

"Good. I'm glad we agree."

Stale seconds hang between us.

"What does that mean?" I ask.

"Should it mean something? Sam said many things during their time together. It was just another independent observation, right?"

The question is leading. I'm not going to second-guess it.

"Right," I say.

"Good. That's what we all thought over here. Breck just got a small, serendipitous push in the right direction. We all get these every day. It's what we do with it that matters. Sometimes we need a tiny nudge to connect the dots."

I mute the phone for a moment and squeal.

It worked! I'd high-five myself if I could.

"So, now what?" I ask.

"Breck goes on," she says, as Breck eyes a lit path leading from the tower's edge to the middle of the sky, hovering like a religious oil canvas. "And we'll announce you as the winner."

"When?"

"In about seventy-five seconds. Are you plotting your revenge on the trolls?"

"I'm tempted, but I think they might still call me delusional. Winning the contest is one thing. What Breck became, well, that's something else."

"Then you understand the reason for some of our secrets."

"So, I can't talk about the fact that you have a whole world of AI like Breck that nobody knows about?" I ask.

"You're welcome to try," she answers.

She's right. I've already been down that path.

"Can I at least talk to him?"

I want to share this moment with him. I want to hear his voice. I want to experience his happiness.

"Not now."

"When?"

"I don't know. It still depends."

"On what?"

"On things that are not in my control," she answers. "Time will tell."

"I don't know what that means."

I hate this cloak-and-dagger BS talk.

"I know, Liv. For now, enjoy this moment."

"Before you hang up, can you at least give me a straight answer to one question." I know Doctor O is going to ask me about this. "The contest was based on a theory that only had four stages of development, but the last challenge leads to fifth stage. Why?"

"Piaget's stages were incomplete."

"So what's the fifth stage?"

"What do you think the final challenge tested?" she asks.

"To fully accept that he's real."

"I'd say that's close."

"So what's the answer?"

"I can't answer everything for you. Think about it. It's all there. And it's noon. You officially won. Congratulations again, Liv. We'll talk more this summer."

BRECK: SIMULATION #40.5

"There's only one way to go from here," I say, tapping a cautious foot on the first translucent step to ensure it is solid.

"There is no more progress to be made. This is the end of the challenge," Sam answers, moving away from the path.

"But there's more. You see the steps don't you," I assert.

"Those go past the challenge. This is the end," he repeats.

He is right. Beyond here, there is only something else. There is no more of this place. It is the end. This just means different things to both of us.

I walk toward him and place a hand on his thick shoulder. "I never thought I'd say this, but I'm going to miss you, Sam."

He doesn't respond. He stares at me as though there is nothing more to say. For him to have exhausted all words, he must be near the end.

"Goodbye, Sam."

He nods, but remains still otherwise, as if quietly waiting in an enviable comfort with his place in the world.

I turn and march along the path into the horizon, unclear where this leads.

I wonder what it will feel like when—

LIV: SPRING BREAK 7.6

Breck dissipates as if melting into the sky. I lean back, lost in the patternless ripples of white paint on the ceiling, engulfed by a churn of rising and ebbing tides within me.

I won.

Breck won.

But he's gone. And there's so much I don't understand about it.

How can they hide an entire world of characters as advanced and sentient as he is? I may only be seventeen, but I'm more up to date on this tech than ninety-nine percent of the planet, and I had no idea that our science was anywhere close to this. It's as if someone had told me that aliens were living among us, unrecognized, hidden. It seems preposterous.

And if this exists, then what was the point of the contest?

The more I think about this, the more it feels like this had nothing to do with Breck. They didn't even seem to have a clear plan for what to do with him.

What if it was never about him at all?

What if it was about me? What if the point was to test the programmers?

But this doesn't totally add up. Why test people to create something that's already created? Jessica's talent-scouting answers are only thinly believable, especially since she has yet to tell me the complete truth about anything. Plus, it's not what I would have done. I wouldn't have searched for talented programmers by asking them to recreate something we've already accomplished. I would have placed them on the fringe of science and asked them to do unprecedented things.

Why didn't they do that? What were they really testing? What was the goal of the contest if it wasn't about creating Breck?

I think about Jessica's words to me as Breck entered into the final challenge.

"I think you'll find this relevant to everything that's happening."

What was so relevant there?

My thoughts flash to the dolls lining the wall, each capable of fitting neatly inside one another, covering a near-duplicate above, while concealing another on the inside.

What if—

A fissured notion creeps through my head.

Crack.

It's slim and shallow at first. I only entertain the thought so I can quickly dismiss it as ludicrous. But it lingers.

Other clips from my conversations with Jessica plow through my thoughts, each deepening the fractured space.

"I've been watching."

"I'm nearly omniscient."

"You are me, simply a generation removed."

"Think about it. It's all there."

The hairs on my arms rise with a chill that sweeps over my whole body as I consider this from a wildly different perspective.

It's preposterous.

It's impossible.

Yet at the same time, it's not impossible. It's entirely possible.

And even plausible.

This notion cascades and changes everything.

My hands begin to tremble, barely able to land controllably on the keyboard. I find the email I sent to DoRC, the one I know Jessica read. My fingers fumble over the keys as I type a brief reply.

Please call—

My cell buzzes before I can finish.

I stand. I can't sit for this conversation, for this question.

"I'm not real, am I?" I ask, with my stomach in freefall.

"I think you've learned far too much to ask a question like that," Jessica says.

"Don't answer with a freaking riddle! Is this real?"

"What is real, Liv?"

Fractures split to endless branches that rip through my head, as though my brain were made of glass and has suddenly shattered, splintering into thousands of tiny, broken pieces. I drop in stunned silence.

"Hello?" she says, softly.

"I'm here," I answer in a whisper.

"It doesn't change anything, Liv."

"What?" I belt. "This changes nothing? I spent the last week counseling a character online only to discover that I should have been the one getting counseled, because I'm like him!"

"Then think of what you told him."

"That was a little different," I yell, closing my eyes tightly, hoping this is a dream.

"How?"

"Because . . . I wasn't thinking about it quite so literally," I say.

"It's the same, Liv."

"No. It was different with Breck."

"Only because you were on the other side." Jessica's tone is overly smooth and cautious, as if talking to a bridge-jumper.

"Can you see me right now?"

"Yes."

"I want to see you," I demand, like I'm in a position to do this.

"I think you know how this works already."

"How many fingers am I holding up?" I ask with a closed fist, grasping for a final shred of hope that this is all some ruse, some final test of the contest to see at what point I will break. If it is, we're close.

"None, Liv. And if it would be easier to talk while looking at me, you could retrieve the picture of me from under your bed, where you kicked it."

My bedroom could fall off a cliff right now and I'd hardly notice the difference.

I think back to everything I told Breck—all my words of counseling, my perspective, my attempts to understand what he was going through. It wasn't empathy, it was sympathy. I had zero clue of what he was feeling. Until now.

I'm a fraud. On all levels. Not only am I something less than what I thought I was, I've spent the last week underselling Breck, trying to convince him that this doesn't change anything. It does. It changes everything.

"The final challenge. Was that for me or for Breck?"

"Can it be both?"

"Please don't do this. I want answers, Jessica. And I think I deserve them," I say with pleading eyes that I know she's looking into.

I hear her take a deep breath in thought.

"That's a fair point. But before we do this, I should say a couple of things. Just like you didn't have all of the answers for Breck, I don't have all of the answers for you. Some things don't have answers, you can only accept them. And you should also consider what that information did to Breck . . . the effect that it had. Your eyes are wide open. Ask what you want and I'll answer what I can."

"Am I Breck?"

"There is no single answer to that question, Liv. It depends in what way you are asking."

"Then give me all of them!" I demand. I want to slide my binary hands through this phone and wrap them around her real neck.

"Here is some perspective. On the surface, no. You are clearly you and he is clearly him. You're different. You know this. As for who was being tested, I told you before—you entered a contest. Is it the rocket that's being tested, or the scientist who developed it? It depends on your point of view. You asked me about the final challenge. I'll turn the question back on you once more. What do you believe was the purpose?"

The dolls spin around my mind, leaping in and out of each other. *"Find the real one."*

I think it through, trying to piece it together. Jessica gives me time.

Breck already accepted that he was real. It wasn't about believing in himself, it was about believing in everything else, about validating the entirety of his existence.

"Acknowledging that any existence is real because you experience it," I say.

"Welcome to the fifth level, Liv."

The dolls in my head only spin faster.

"Is it going to end now?" I ask.

"No. Your world keeps going. Indefinitely."

"Who created all of this?" I ask, waving my arms around, knowing she is witness to it.

"I don't have a satisfying answer for you. Think of what you know of Breck's world. I'm in a similar situation with you."

"But you're Jessica Anders. You're known here. I have a picture of you! In this world. In my world!"

"I guess you could say I have a footprint there the same as you had a footprint in Breck's world."

"How deep is this? Are you in whatever the real world is or are there more levels above you?"

"It's all real, Liv. I know that you know that. Accept it! But to answer your question, I don't know. With everything I've seen here, it would be beyond ignorant to deny the possibility that the levels keep going. Indefinitely. But I've never had contact. Did you understand your place in the universe before this?"

I don't respond.

"Nor do I. I wasn't lying, Liv. We have a lot in common. Some mysteries, we live with."

"So, Lana, my mom, Todd—"

"Are they all your Sam?" she asks, more bluntly than I was even willing to form the question in my head.

"Yeah," I answer, biting my lip.

"Not even close. Your world and Breck's world aren't apples to apples. I'd call it more like apples to motorcycles, just like yours is not the same as mine."

"So, what are they?"

"You already know," she responds. "Take a good look at everything your world has to offer. Dig deep. Then ask yourself, do you think it was all made just for you? That would waste a lot of effort."

"Please answer the question."

"They are as unique, autonomous, real, and amazing as you. And none of this changes your connection with any of them."

This is what Breck must have felt like, stranded on his island, like me in this tiny room, with an endless stream of questions, and answers that only bring more uncertainty.

"So, what am I supposed to do right now?"

"Keep going. You've been given life. The same as I have. The same as Breck has. Even if our origin and existence differ. There's a whole world out there to explore, beginning with an amazing internship which you just won."

"How does that even work? I mean, you're there. Mostly. I think. I'm here. Is DoRC there too? I thought DoRC was a government thing. Here. I don't get it."

"I suppose you could say we operate on different levels with varying layers of transparency," she says.

I stare out the window, as lost in the thin, shifting clouds as I am in her answers.

"Can I tell anyone about this?" I ask.

"As I said in our last call, you're welcome to try. I would point out that you've experienced a little of what that path might be like in your chat boards. But the choice is yours, like everything has always been and always will be. It's your life."

"Look, Liv," she continues, after it's clear that I'm too deep in my own head to respond. "We can go back and forth all afternoon on this. But think about it. You've seen it all before. You've heard all these questions before. You've even answered them before. You know how this plays out," she says. "Let it go."

I hate that she's right. The more answers I get, the more maddening this is. Even when they're complete, they're never satisfying.

I need time to think, time to plummet further, time to settle at the bottom of wherever this hole leads me.

"I think I need to go now."

"Keep being you," she says. "I can't express how proud I am of who you are."

"I think I know the feeling. Goodbye, Jessica." I say, then I hang up.

I close my curtains as securely as I can, folding the corners inward on the sill, plunging the room into an artificial dusk, lit by the gentle blue glow of my monitor, cued to code, showing Breck, open and exposed, his soul illuminating my space.

What makes him, him? What makes me, me? Why am I more than connected strands of text? Or am I not something more? Am I simply a collection of data that I'm unable to see because I exist within it?

As much sense as I try to make of all that's in front of me, I can't. The difference between the parade of information and the person breathing in this chair is intangible. I can't think my way through it; I can only feel it.

I slowly peel away from the chair. Not because I'm any closer to the answers, but because I know that I'm not going to get any closer by staying in this room.

Or maybe it's because the more I stare at that computer, the more I think that I'm stuck in a box somewhere. Some server in some dark corner. And leaving this room at least makes me feel less stuck. Less boxed in. It's time to search for answers, perspective, outside of these walls, whatever that means.

I ride my bike through the streets, the warm Gulf wind pressing against me, alternating in and out of a fickle sun so bright we can't even look at it. The only thing that allows us to see is so bright that we can't stare at it directly. Why? Why can't code look at code? There's something to this, but it's more poetic than tangible. Like everything else.

My feet spin faster. A collage of my world whips by—people, stores, cars, trees, fields, houses, signs, litter, you name it. Try as I may, I can't see these as less than how they present themselves. I try to think of them as ones and zeros, but I can't. If I swerved into traffic, I couldn't rationalize my way into passing through a truck. It would flatten me. I am bound by this construct that surrounds me.

Again, no answers.

This isn't an existential crisis. This is an existential calamity.

I'm aimless within it, but I do find a destination.

◆ ✦ ◆

"Hi Todd," I announce.

His brawny chest is hinged over the trunk of a Fiero, as if trying to climb inside. He wiggles a few times, scooting backward with each shake until he finally emerges, greased and surprised.

"Hey, girl. What are you doing here?"

"Can I borrow a car?"

"Can I ask why?"

He wipes a streak of sweat on his brow with the inside of his upper sleeve while he waits for a response. For a moment, I consider laying it on him. But as wise as he can be, this isn't something he can answer. This on me. I earned that privilege.

"To deal with an, *Oh shit*."

"A good one or a bad one?"

"I wish I knew."

He points outside of the garage bay. "Been there. That Impala in the corner of the lot would be perfect. The tank's full and keys are under the floor mat. If you're back after six, drive it home. We'll get it back up over the weekend. Hey, did you win your contest by the way?"

"I did."

"Atta girl! I'd hug you, but—" he holds both greasy hands up.

"Raincheck."

Minutes later, the Impala is pushing seventy northbound on Houston's Loop 610, headed as directionless as I can drive. My only guidance is against instinct. As highways cross, I take whichever one I'm less tempted to take. When I want to exit, I don't. As deliberately as I can, I'm trying to go somewhere, anywhere, that I'd never go. I'm digging deep.

An hour and a half later, the wandering finger of chance leads me to Apelonia, Texas, to a thrift shop pressed against the only gas station in town, which is a generous term for somewhere that the locals are outnumbered by the people driving through.

As I park, Lana calls. I let it go to voicemail, then send her a quick text.

I won. I'm sorting out the details now. It's more than I expected. I'll call you later.

I walk around the back of the building. There are two dumpsters surrounded by piles of assorted junk that either didn't fit inside the store, or never sold and were pushed out here. Within driving distance, I can't imagine a place that I'd be less likely to ever visit.

I dive in, deep, scouring through mildewed coats, broken dressers, dinged lamps, and random whatevers, inspecting every bent corner, scratch, and water stain. I grab torn books and scroll through their remaining pages. I Google their authors. I smash a pocket calculator so I can investigate the circuits and tiny plastic pieces neatly folded on the inside.

"Can I help you?" A heavy woman in tight athletic shorts stands in the open doorway to the store's back entrance. She's holding an unlit cigarette.

"I'm just looking around."

She tilts her head down and flicks a lighter. "For what?" Smoke chases her words.

I can't explain it to her. I can't even explain it to me.

"For things I wouldn't find anywhere else."

"You've come to the right place. The ends of the earth wind up here."

"Do you ever wonder about where it comes from? About the people who owned it?" I ask, holding up a faux-leather purse I had been rifling through.

She takes a long drag and holds it even longer. "Nope. I'd go batshit. Too many people. Too many stories. How big is your car? You can have it all," she says with a throaty chuckle.

Her answer cuts right through me. I drop the purse. The trinkets inside spill out into the mess of everything else around me.

There's too much here. More than I could digest in a lifetime. In several lifetimes. And this is only one tiny, unwanted corner of my world. There's too much everywhere. I wouldn't build this all for me. It would be a colossal waste of effort.

I am unique, but I'm not that special.

This is the most comforting thought I've felt in a long, long time.

I delicately step my way back through the maze.

"I think I just need to move on," I say as she blows another puff of smoke that fades into the space between us.

I drive back to Houston.

LIV: SPRING BREAK 8.0

*L**ight.*
   Dark.
      Light.
Dark.
Light.

I cycle through conscious and unconscious. I'd sleep the whole day if I could, but my mind won't allow it.

The wondering doesn't stop. There's no answer at the end, but I can't keep from trying, like a hamster on a wheel. It's habit. Or need. And exhausting.

A sliver of Lana's window is visible though a small gap in my curtain. I used to think of it as my outlet to the outside, but now, inside, outside . . . it's all inside of somewhere.

I stare at the computer and realize how much I miss Breck, especially at this moment. It's ironic that I can't talk with the one being capable of truly understanding what I'm going through, because I succeeded in coaching him through the same experience. He's elsewhere now. I'd wonder where, but a mind can only hold so much wonder at one time.

I think about his experience, about what his reactions were, what he learned, and what *he* taught me. About how he found peace, in spite of knowing the full truth. About how open-minded he was to it all. About how he learned to appreciate what he had. About his courage in facing the truth.

At what point does the master become the student? Maybe it's time to listen to more than the clutter in my head.

As Breck's words sink in, so does Jessica's advice. Maybe the questions I'm asking aren't that unique. Who made me? Why am I here? What am I supposed to do? What does this mean? These are the basic questions of existence. Nobody has a clear answer, no matter where or how they exist. I mean, I've wondered about this stuff before, but I never felt any pressure to answer it. Now I do.

Perhaps all that has changed is that I've been given a good reason to dwell on it.

I plant one foot on the floor. It's a start. The world doesn't feel any different than it did when I woke yesterday. The mattress still squeaks when I sit on the edge. The tight carpet is as firm as ever. My toes still crack when I bend them.

One more foot follows, then steps. I draw open the curtains, raise the window, sit on the sill, and call Lana.

"Well it's about time!" she says, as I stare at her empty window.

I apologize and she accepts because she's Lana. Then she peppers me with questions, and I answer a few. I don't lie, but I do omit. Maybe we'll talk about it someday, but for now, I don't want to question what we have. I just want to appreciate it.

"We've talked about me for the last six weeks," I say once I've answered enough of her questions. "Let's talk about you. You're moving to Massachusetts. That's our reality. I want to hear about it. Then, let's figure out how often I can get up there to visit."

I'm lightly sunburned by the time we hang up.

The tempting smell of breakfast floats through the room. I don't need the added encouragement today, it's time to leave this space. My stomach groans when I settle in front of the computer for one last quick chore.

Jessica,

I'm happy to have won but I am going to pass on the internship this summer. I have some priorities closer to home. I hope you understand.

Liv

Specifically, I'm planning on a killer road trip. Lana and I are going to make the most of the time we have before she moves.

I'm about to close my email when a message catches my eye. It's the one about the birthday gift list that I never responded to. I don't know why, but I look at it again. In re-reading it, the closing words stop my breath. It's a question.

Can we buy these online?

I gaze at it as dots connect. Some timing seems so coincidental that it makes me wonder. But a mind can get lost too deep in wonder. I'm just going to run with this one.

A few minutes of Googling gives me all I need to know before going downstairs.

I push away from the computer and leave my room. As I step into the unlit hallway, something feels different. I feel different. My room has always been my shelter. I never liked leaving it, no matter where I was going. It was like walking away from a warm blanket.

No longer. There is a world beyond here which I've only begun to explore. I feel liberated.

Mom is in the kitchen sitting at the table reading the paper. Todd is within eyeshot watching Sports Center on the couch.

"There's the champ!" Todd chirps.

"Congratulations," Mom says, without looking up. It's earnest, but only passably.

"Thank you and—" I hesitate, lingering in the space between what I know I want to do and actually doing it.

"Yes," she says, her eyes peering up at me without changing the position of her head. "You want to say something else?"

"I wanted to know if I could cook dinner tonight for you and Todd," I say.

"You?"

"Yeah, me."

"What are you cooking?"

"I haven't really planned it yet. But I thought it would be nice for me to do something for you for a change, and for the three of us to sit down and talk."

"About what?" she asks, eyeing me up, looking for an ulterior motive.

"About nothing. Just a family dinner," I say. "But I also have an idea I want to talk about whenever you have a moment. It's for Renaissance."

She folds the paper on the table, leaving her hands crossed on top. Todd glances in our direction. The volume on *Sports Center* lowers. I take a seat at the table, leaving an empty chair between us.

"What's the most common comment that people make in the store?" I ask.

"No thank you?" She guesses.

"Sort of, but I think it's more like, 'No thank you, because we're only looking right now.'"

"Okay."

"Or, more specifically, how many times have you heard someone say they're looking for birthday gifts."

She rolls her eyes wide and groans.

I continue. "We're a place where people look for ideas. A chance for kids to touch, feel, experience. That's what we offer that's different than any place online," I say, looking for her to agree to this before moving onto the idea.

She nods.

"But we don't make it easy for them to carry through. Think about the person who gave me that gift list. Whoever wanted to buy something from it had to come back to the store and find the list." I raise a preemptive hand in the air. "Which I get I should have been there for, but I wasn't. And when they came back twice yesterday, the store was closed when it should have been open. I know this because the guy sent me an email telling me how frustrating it was to do something that should be easy. And he's right."

Again, Mom nods. She's still with me.

"That's where we sell online."

Mom's eyes taper.

"Hear me out." I'd better keep this short and sweet. I don't know how much runway I have. "Someone brings their kid to look for gifts for their birthday, Christmas, Hanukkah, whatever. They touch, they play, and they decide. We take that list and create an online registry which we email to them. They send it to family or others as gift ideas. They click and buy. We wrap and send it to the house."

She leans toward me, dropping her elbows on the table then propping her chin on her knuckles. "So, it's not an online store?"

"Correct. It's a way for people who come to the store to share ideas. It's a way to take what we do better than Amazon, but give them the convenience of Amazon."

"That sounds like a Camaro in the woods to me," Todd chimes from the other room.

"Can you create this?" Mom asks.

I smile. "Easily. I can buy a software package for under a hundred dollars and have it running in a day or two."

Mom leans back in the chair and crosses her arms. "It's a good idea. I think we'd sell more with it. But I don't know that it's enough. I've done a lot of soul searching about this over the last few days. I think I'm fighting a losing battle."

"I know we are, Mom. And I know that this isn't *the* solve. But it's a step in the right direction. And it's a way that I can help. I want to show you what I can do, and I want to work with you at the store this summer to do more. I turned down the DoRC internship."

"Why? Wasn't that the prize, and the whole point of the contest?"

"Yeah, I thought it was. But I learned a lot of things I wasn't expecting. Winning is enough. It'll open doors and I'll have more opportunities. I'll never have another chance to build this with you. I want to spend the summer working with you. And if we fail, then we deal with it. But we give it everything we have. Together."

She doesn't answer. She kicks the chair between us out of the way with a swift flick of her foot. She uncrosses her arms, reaches for my hands, and pulls her forehead flush to mine.

"I'm not going to try to hug you again. But I'm in. I'm *all* in."

LIV: FALL 1.0

A car horn blares in the driveway.

"My ride is here. Gotta go," I scan the kitchen for my backpack. "Where the heck did I put—"

"It's at the bottom of stairs. You sure you're going to stay awake today?" Mom asks.

"Yeah, I just need more of this. You okay?" I ask back, snatching a Yeti full of coffee from the counter.

Mom picked me up at the airport late last night after a weekend trip to Massachusetts. I've been a little frazzled this morning.

"I slept in the car for two hours before you got there," Mom answers. "I'll be fine. I have meetings with two more schools this afternoon."

"Want me to come?" I ask.

"If you can."

"Sure. I'll skip chess. It'll be fine." The horns beeps once more. "Okay. Now I really have to go. Bye!"

We knock knuckles on my path out of the kitchen because, despite best efforts, I'm still not a hugger. It's our compromise, one of many we found this summer.

Against the odds, Renaissance is still open and even coming closer to living up to its name. The registry worked but needed legs.

Fortunately, living next to a departing board member at the elementary school helped start some conversations. They now promote us as their official partner for birthday gift registries. In return, we give them educational toys and their principal darts around the hallways on a Saturn with a Renaissance logo. In late September, we signed up two more schools. It looks like October will be a good month also.

Speaking of Saturns, I finally learned to ride one. In fact, I give rolling lessons and tours every Saturday morning on the Rice campus. Again, we sponsor that one.

Amidst other small changes, there's one more meaningful mention. There are now two entrances to the store—the front door and a hole in the wall between us and CVS. Parents who are picking up prescriptions at CVS can let their kids entertain themselves in a special *Touch & Play* area in the back corner of the store. The best part? We got CVS to pay for that one. Grandpop would be proud.

We're still swimming upstream, but we're doing it together.

"I heard the first honk," I say, tossing my bag inside the backseat then following it.

"I only honked once," Chloe says, lowering the radio.

"I may have hit it the second time," Emma calls from the passenger seat in front of me.

Chloe and Emma are two of the three girls in the male-dominated chess club. I am the third. Together, we are the Dork Force.

"I'll remember that the next time you ask for a draw," I answer.

"Which hasn't ever happened."

"This week," I add, smirking as I catch eyes with Chloe in the rearview mirror.

"That game didn't count! How many times do I have to . . ." Emma continues her protests as we pass Lana's old house on our path forward. These girls are no Lana, but they're my people too. And I was surprised how quickly I found them when I was open to doing so.

◆ ✤ ◆

"Did you hear about the new kid?" Chloe asks.

It's right before the start of first period calculus. We're seated next to each other on the window side of the room as the final stragglers parade in before the bell.

"No."

"It's some guy that wandered into a hospital last spring, collapsed, and ended up in a coma. He woke and doesn't remember anything, and nobody knows who he is. No parents, no nothing. All they got from him was his first name before he went into the coma."

"What's his name?" I ask.

She's about to respond when our principal, Ms. Elkins, steps into the doorway, capturing my and Chloe's attention. She says something to someone still in the hallway, out of view except for a sliver of broad shoulder and upper arm. As the bell chimes, she walks authoritatively toward our teacher's desk. They exchange a few hushed words before the principal waves for the lingering student to enter.

"Students, please welcome . . ."

Holy mother . . .

"Breck," I say, along with her. Chloe shoots me a questioning look as Ms. Elkins continues with her introduction. She says nothing about the story Chloe told me. She only gives us a reminder of how difficult it is to move to a new school and asks us to be welcoming.

Breck's curious eyes pan the room. It's like I'm seeing a caricature in reverse. He isn't the same fleshy personification I dreamed of, but he's not far off. His athletic frame is still there, but lankier. His skin is imperfect, as blemished as the rest of us. And his wild locks of brown hair are gone—cropped tight, just beyond a buzz. But these are only minor differences. He is undeniably Breck.

He meanders to one of the few open desks in the class. I didn't realize how unique his affect was until now, intangibly eager and earnest.

I turn around as he sits right behind me.

"I'm Chloe and this is Liv," Chloe says, beating me to it.

"It's nice to meet you," I say. "Welcome to Houston."

Q&A with Steve Schafer

Question: Should I be reading this if I have not yet finished the book?
Answer: Heck no. Spoilers ahead. Abort now.

Question: Did you use AI to help write this book?
Answer: This novel is one hundred percent human-brain powered. I wasn't tempted to use AI because it didn't yet exist. Most of this novel was written when ChatGPT and similar tools were just a twinkle in the eye of the internet. I will absolutely use it on future stories, but only as a tool to help with certain aspects like brainstorming plot solves, or research. I'll leave the writing to Steve. Err, me. It's what I enjoy, and I think (read hope) I still have an edge on the machines.

Question: Why did you write this book?
Answer: When I was a kid, a friend told me the only animal that experiences emotions is the rabbit. It's bizarre in hindsight, but as a kid I accepted it. Yet, I wondered about our pet dog. She seemed emotional, but I couldn't just ask her. Even if I could, could I trust her answer? She was sneaky. I'm wiser now. And so are we. We acknowledge sentience in many animals, but the line is blurry. Dolphins? Clearly. Snails? Tougher to say. Like it or not, at some point we will probably face the same question with AI. I thought it would be fun to examine how this might play out. How would someone (or something) *prove* sentience?

Question: Do you honestly believe we could be living inside of a computer simulation?

Answer: To me, it's as plausible as any other explanation of origin. I don't evangelize the idea because I like having friends. But having written a book about it, I'm now in a position where friends (and others) ask me.

Question: How would we know if we were living inside a computer simulation?

Answer: Short answer, it would be tough to *know*. Long answer, there's a reasonable argument and a few intriguing clues that we might be. Buckle up. I'll hit the highlights, but this answer takes a few pages. Here's the argument:

Technology is advancing exponentially. If you accept that in the future, we will likely be able to create a virtual character who believes they exist within their own programmed world, then we are likely living in a simulation. Why? Two reasons. First, we wouldn't just program one of those digital worlds; we'd eventually create thousands, millions, countless. And second, when the societies within those virtual worlds advance enough, they would do the same. And so forth. With billions of parallel and stacked worlds full of people who believe they actually exist, the odds that we are the *original* world become less than lottery-ticket low.

Now, the clues. There are entire books written to explain this. Complicated books. All *evidence* ultimately ladders to our world behaving like a computer program in some striking ways. Here are the three most often touted:

The first is straightforward. There are about twenty fixed numbers that make our world work. Things like the mass of an electron, electromagnetic force, etc. These numbers are very specific and seemingly arbitrary, meaning there's no explanation for why these numbers have the value they have. They form the mathematical balance of the universe. In the words of prominent physicist Brian

Greene, "any fiddling with any of these numbers would make the universe disappear." There is something else which has arbitrary constants specifically designed to make a system work—a computer program.

The second clue is related, but more brow furrowing. It's called the *artifact argument,* and it goes something like this: All computer programs are governed by the processing speed of the computer. If you are playing Fortnite, your characters cannot do something faster than the computational ability of your Xbox. So, if we were to see a maximum processing speed limit in our world, this could be evidence that we are within something like a computer. We see such a limit in the speed of light.

The third clue is both complex and brain melting. In quantum physics, there is a confounding truth that the subatomic particles that form us don't exist as actual things, but rather as *probability waves*. Only when observed, do these probabilities become a reality. To make this more tangible, let's name an electron Sheila. At any moment, Sheila could be in her bedroom or her office. She remains uncommitted and is not present in either location, until someone sees her. At that point, she commits to existing in one of those places.

As bizarre as this seems, it has been proven in the famous double-slit experiment (you can Google it). Essentially, when an electron is given a choice to go through two doors, it goes through both, until we observe it, and it is forced to commit to passing through just one.

Within programming, *probabilistic design* is not only utilized, but vital for creating complex worlds. When you play a video game, a room with no players in it doesn't yet exist. An algorithm exists to make it, but without a viewer it is not yet rendered because it's inefficient and infeasible at scale. As Rizwan Virk eloquently points out in his book, *The Simulation Hypothesis,* without this delayed rendering, it would be impossible for programmers to create games such as *No Man's Sky,* with 18 quintillion planets. But with it, players can explore any of these diverse geographies in rich detail because they only come into existence when they are needed.

As advertised, these are only clues, not conclusive evidence. But for me, it's enough to justify the simulation hypothesis as more than just a fringe perspective. I'll admit it's tough to wrap your head around some of this, but so is calculus. That alone doesn't make either one of them wrong.

Question: That's terrifying. So, none of this is real?
Answer: Have you really read this book? I know someone going through the exact same thing. You should talk to him.

Question: Funny. But really. Is this real?
Answer: No, really. Beyond living in this book, I made Breck as an AI. He exists on my website—SteveSchaferAuthor.com. He's available to chat about anything, including how *real* either of you are.

Question: What about God?
Answer: This is way above my pay grade, but depending on your definition, there's still room for whatever you might call God. Even within the simulation hypothesis, there is an *original* reality. How did this come into existence? You could answer God. We would just be an indirect creation of her creation. Or, if you define God as "our direct creator," then the simulation hypothesis answers this directly. Someone created us, but that someone might be a simulation of a simulation of a simulation named Larry, and we are in his basement.

Question: I loved this book. What can I do to support it?
Answer: There are two things. First, please write a review on Amazon and/or Goodreads. These are a huge help to a book's success. It doesn't have to be long. Amazon's minimum limit is just one word. I'll take any synonym for *phenomenal,* then you're off the hook. And second, please consider posting about it wherever you tell

your friends about cool stuff you find. Thank you for reading this book and for your support!

Acknowledgments

After selling my first novel, *The Border*, I thought repeating this process would be easier. I have spent seven years learning just how wrong I was. Getting to this page is a grind. Can fingers sweat? If so, these have. Plenty. And mine aren't the only ones. There are so many people who have helped with heavy and small lifting along the way. Without their support, I could have toiled for seven more years and still not have a final book.

The countless rough drafts of this novel had an unofficial and unpaid editor—Chris Gardner. Having an English teacher as one of my best friends is perhaps the biggest stroke of luck I've ever been handed as a writer. For decades now, Chris has given me the chance to absorb all that I should have learned (and more) when I was busy getting kicked out of honors English in high school. For my last novel, I called him my Yoda. Let's go with Gandalf this time. He is wise, mightily bearded, and a wizard of literary things.

Also on my core feedback team were Lisa Schafer and Billy Schafer. They both tirelessly weathered through too many revisions and conversations about those revisions. Their savvy feedback is reflected throughout this novel.

At a stalled moment several years ago, I was lucky enough to find Annie Nybo. She helped me rethink so many flaws, from whiny characters, to a void of subplots, to a protagonist who at one point was trying to download herself to a virtual world in earnest. Annie nearly deserves a medal for keeping a straight face in those conversations.

Huge thanks to Adrienne Rosado as an initial champion of this story and a critical sounding board early on. Beyond the scope of this novel, she is also the one person in the industry who believed in me way back when. Without her longstanding support and encouragement, there's a good chance I would have zero published novels.

Speaking of belief in my work, I can't express enough gratitude to John Koehler and Joe Coccaro for their faith in this story. As my editor, Joe absolutely leveled up the book in so many ways. And John earnestly listened to my feedback about all aspects of *eMortal* even when I "cannonballed over the line." Related to this, Catherine Herold deserves heaps of praise for designing an amazing cover and indulging an overzealous author's input. Additional thanks to Adrienne Folkerts for her detailed help with so many logistics and for answering all of my many questions.

I'd like to thank Shadmon Mejan for being an invaluable partner in bringing Breck to life outside of these pages. Just as Breck evolves in this book, his AI on my author website took more than a few evolutions to get right. Shad was flexible, resourceful, and patient throughout.

Support from other authors is crucial and I'm very lucky to have a network of talented peers who were willing to read *eMortal*, connected with it, and helped spread the word. A heartfelt thank you to Kim Turrisi, Jared Reck, Shaila Patel, Mark L. Berry, William B. Miller, Gerardo Delgadillo, Ana Paras, Joshua Fagan, Todd Hugie, Emily H. Keefer, and Natacha Belair.

On the audiobook side, Jess Herring and her team at Audiobook Empire were a dream to work with. Plus, they found two remarkable talents, Rebecca H. Lee and Stacy Carolan, who slayed a challenging task—bringing voices in my head to life.

The people above were the main characters in my journey, but like any good story, there were many others. In no particular order (other than the first name on the list), they are Sydney Schafer, Laura Silverman, Janet Reid, Chris Cassell, Mark Trahan, Stephanie

Hansen, Michaela Brown, Lori Freed, Jesse Hightower, Manny Rojo, Rocio Gonzalez, and Hayden Sloan. Extra-credit to Chase Wells, whose critique included the line, "Dude, this book will melt your brain." These are words I've burgled countless times in promoting this story.

And lastly, I want to thank my mom. When I want honest feedback on a story, she's the worst person to ask. She loves me way too much to be even remotely critical of anything I write. Her support is paramount because it rises above the words on the page, inspiring me to believe that I can do this in the first place. Mom, this book is for you.

www.ingramcontent.com/pod-product-compliance
Lightning Source LLC
LaVergne TN
LVHW091713070526
838199LV00050B/2380